Walk Until

SUNRISE

J.J. Maze

PAGE PUBLISHING, INC.
New York, NY

First originally published by Page Publishing, Inc. 2017

ISBN 978-1-64082-297-9 (Paperback)
ISBN 978-1-64082-298-6 (Digital)

Printed in the United States of America

I want to thank Evan, Kristin, Holly, and Kelly for their support and encouragement. I want to also thank the Victims of Violence Program in Cambridge, Massachusetts, and Dr. Kathryn Tecza for introducing me to EMDR (Eye Movement Desensitization and Reprocessing) therapy.

This book is dedicated to people who look and actually see.

Contents

CHAPTER 1

Surrender

I broke down in Las Cruces, New Mexico.

Making one last feeble attempt to join in, to partake of, to affiliate myself with civilization, I politely responded in the affirmative to a young bohemian-looking photographer leaning against his green VW van. He wanted to take pictures of me down by the Rio Grande River. I was highly amused at my ability to actually be *flattered* by this invitation in spite of . . . and how willingly and instantaneously I reverted to my overdramatic level of angst-ridden teenage vanity and self-consciousness. Oh my *gawd*! My hair wasn't done, and the faded yellow T-shirt with the peeling parrot decal looked tacky! I must be okay . . . sane . . . perfectly fine if I was able to care about these things.

Not so. The one shot he snapped sent me into a state of frenzied panic. I ran off. I didn't understand my very specific fear of a man with a camera. I ran off and locked myself in a gas station bathroom. The attendant knocked.

"You okay? You seem scared. My trailer is behind the station. Stay there until you think it's safe . . . if you want."

He sounded less than concerned, as if frightened-looking, almost-grown girls routinely locked themselves in his gas station john.

Growing bold at the sound of his fading steps, I came out and spotted the dirt-layered ten-foot aluminum can of a trailer. In five lunging steps I reached its front door and locked myself inside with a nervous hand. I spent the next hour watching the attendant through the parted blinds of the window. As he worked, his clear-colored eyes were filled with a look of concentration as strong as the contrast they played against his high cheekbones, aquiline nose, and sun-beaten bronzed skin. My childlike approval of his Native American looks (he had straight black hair too, though he wore it short) helped me rationalize letting my guard down. I figured he would be working long enough for me to relax, and I promptly fell into that hard, deep sleep that hurts.

Hands all over me and an angry one halfway home—that's what woke me up. His translucent eyes now full of ice-hot determination and my soul, already so beaten yet unable to die . . . He wasn't going to take *no* for an answer; I couldn't afford to be defiled yet again. We fought. And I got away.

I ran and ran. This was not the run of fear where you don't feel your body, just your heart pounding and a sense of heat or cold. No, this was the run of the living dead. My skin was so dry on my face I thought it would split. My stomach was tied up in constipated knots. My feet felt like bricks. All I knew for certain was that I was as tired as a person can possibly be, and I'm not talking about physical fatigue.

I was really sick and tired—tired of needing food, air, sleep, and, most of all, people. I ran back toward the desert, back toward isolation, back toward that nagging, implacable loneliness. And the closer I got to it, the more tired I became.

It made no sense to me. Why did I feel lonely? Why did I need people? People were bad. People could only be trusted to use you for their twisted perversions and anger. People were guaranteed to hurt you and push you down. Why did I need this? Just the thought of smiling at someone—even the nice ones—made me ill. They would use your body and soul while commenting on the weather. A smile was their gun, a warm caress was their fist in your face, and a *thank you* was their "f——k you."

I wasn't even angry anymore. I was simply too tired to participate. Count me out of the game. Pictures by the Rio Grande . . . what had I been *thinking*? I slowed to a reticent walk.

Yes, I noticed the quaint charm of Las Cruces as I retreated. I couldn't miss it even in my semi-catatonic state. I noticed the immaculate backdrop of white adobe, red clay, and brilliant blooms, but . . .

There was no point in walking any further since I had no destination, no point in eating since I wasn't going to use my body. Sleep sounded good since I hoped it would last forever. I wasn't suicidal. I had just given up. I had no worries anymore because I wasn't trying to do anything. In my mind, it was all over.

My last goal was simply to find a resting place and rest in peace. Even this seemed too much of an effort.

I walked on a little further, feeling every step was wrongly placed. Why was I going somewhere? A great sense of relief washed over me as I spotted my final destination: a plain wooden bench just off the left side of the road. Perfection lay in that bench facing away from town so I wouldn't have to look at anything except the sky, desert, and a few trees. That bench placed just far enough off the road so that people would have to go out of their way to talk to me, yet close enough so my sitting there wouldn't seem strange or suspicious.

I sat down, my goal in life, to sit on that bench until I was no more. Serenity took over as I sat and thought of nothing. My soul was still for the first time ever. A couple hours went by. Nothing happened. Nothing was almost mine.

I was aware of the sun changing position and the wind fluctuating. Soon, I wasn't even aware of that. I only saw a gray tunnel with murky yellow-green light at the end. No thought went through my mind. No feeling went through my body. I'm not sure how long I sat like that.

As in a dream, when a repetitive sound is there and you awake and realize it's the alarm clock, that is how I was forced back to the present. The click of a camera shutter was the offending noise. Its unnatural presence in my tunnel of gray made me lethargically aware. Something simply was wrong, and I could no longer disappear.

It felt as if it took me two hours to turn my head in response to the sound. My eyes focused in on a wiry, energetic man with one foot up on the bench, *my* bench, bending down and aiming at me through a camera. He was in his midforties with a salt-and-pepper beard, plaid shirt, jeans, cowboy boots, and Foster Grant shades hanging out of his shirt pocket. He put the camera aside and was now talking to me. But I couldn't hear him. My eyes tuned in to his voice, taking special note of his uneasy smiles.

"I work for several magazines, and you look so aboriginal staring off into the distance like that. I thought I could use these shots for several different things. You don't mind, do you?"

I couldn't hear my own voice, but I formed and hopefully spoke the word "yes."

"Oh, okay. I'm really sorry. You just look so interesting sitting here. If you don't mind my asking, what are you doing? You've been sitting here for quite a while. I noticed you over an hour ago."

"I'm resting and I don't want to be bothered. You are bothering me. Please, go away. Leave me alone."

"Just one more question. By the way, my name is Paul—Paul Sutner. How long are you going to sit here and rest?"

"Forever. I'm not getting up again and I'm not saying anything else."

I could hear my voice now—edgy but hollow sounding, angry yet apathetic—finally fearless.

He left. He had truly disturbed my peace. I was now aware of all noises, the little chill in the air, and the fact that I felt weak. This imposition named Paul Sutner had ruined everything. His being there was almost the last straw. But not quite.

The sun had shifted, and it was beating on the back of my neck. This seemed to make everything all right. My body was almost numb again, so I wasn't uncomfortable. Hours went by without anyone coming near, allowing my frantic watchfulness to merge with subtlety back into calm. My little wooden bench regained its worthiness and reclaimed its right to be my final destination. It would just be a few more hours before I reached the point of nothingness.

I don't want anyone to think something is wrong with me. I must keep my clothes clean and smile so no one will know that I am on the streets . . .

CHAPTER 2

The American Dream

Though I was born in Minneapolis, I consider myself to be from California. We moved there when I was five and my sister, six. It was just the three of us: Ma, Sis, and I.

Up until that point, we'd had a lot of money. Our early days were spent living in Robbinsdale, Minnesota, as an upper-middle-class suburban family with two Chihuahuas, a parakeet, three cars, and a white picket fence. Time and money flowed in excess enough for us to raise Himalayan show cats and host weekly barbecues (steak, not hamburger). The man of the house was Ralph Jacobs, a retired police detective turned restaurateur/chef. Sounds pretty good, eh? There were, however, a couple of glitches that left this picture wanting.

First of all, it just didn't make sense. My mother, born Mary Jane Rawley, was a twenty-five-year-old voluptuous, Marilyn Monroe type with auburn hair and perfectly classical features topping her sensual body. An almost ideal specimen of her Irish-German lineage, at five foot nine, her only flaw was the fact that she was tall for the beauty of that time. One of seven children born to Hester and Tracy Rawley (a railroad Rawley no less), she had a winning smile and a colorful yet sweet personality—an upstanding Catholic housewife blessed with beauty and grace.

She was married to Ralph, a sixty-year-old Jewish man with a balding head and a weight problem. His harsh demeanor helped him carry his size with distinction, and he always wore a suit. He was not attractive. He wasn't nice. All I ever heard him talk about was food, money, and how he was going to blow my mom's head off one day.

He'd take the gun out of the nightstand drawer while Sis and I sat on his lap. With each of us propped gingerly on either knee, the gun swinging precariously in his right hand, and his already menacing face erupting into violence, he'd say, "See this, kids? I'm going to use it to blow your mother's head off someday. She's going to drive me to it."

He'd laugh. We'd cry.

My sister and I looked a lot alike. She was slightly lighter in complexion than I was. Her soft curls had hints of blonde and honey brown. My coarse, tight curls were a solid seal brown. I mention the skin tone and hair texture because both were noticeably different than either my mother's or Ralph's. We were definitely black. I didn't understand that at the time or even realize we were a different color for that matter. Nobody said anything about it, and it didn't occur to me to wonder.

So there you have it: our slice of American pie.

Every now and then, Ma felt compelled to sit us girls down at the round wrought iron glass-topped dining room table to tell us the story of how she and Ralph got together. She'd explain how she didn't love Ralph at all. With a coy little smile playing across her lips, she would boastfully tell of how he had asked her to marry him every day for a year until she finally said yes, how he'd been fascinated by her beauty, and how she was going to *work* that fact to the max.

"You'll understand when you get older, girls. Women have to be smart, not in love."

They had a business deal. He had the money. She was the arm piece. This justified their not sleeping together after the first few months of marriage. Yes, they argued a lot, but she didn't care. Ma had lots of secrets dancing in her eyes. I liked seeing her eyes sparkle so. I just wish it were more wholesome things that made her shine.

So, we did all the normal things that little ones do. We played cops and robbers, had best friends and worst enemies. I was afraid of Danny Lang, the neighborhood bully, until I showed up on his front doorstep at my mother's order, shaking and tearful, with shovel in hand, and threatened to beat his ass if he didn't stop scaring me. I'll never forget how good my reward hot-fudge sundae tasted when I did actually beat his ass instead of running and crying. Forever gone was my fear of him and his jarred "killer bees"; he couldn't make me pull up any more flowers or split any more pumpkins. We loved Kimi, the white fluffy dog down the alley to the right and hated Bruno, the guard dog down the alley to the left that almost jumped the fence in his ferocity every time we walked by. I got my mouth washed out for saying *goddamn*, and Sis and I had stare-downs on a regular basis. Sis could talk me into cleaning her room for a glass of water any day of the week, and, as all girls do, we played dress-up. I wanted to be pretty like Nancy who lived down the street. I always cried when the older kids ditched me. Yes, everything was normal if you could just ignore the constant yelling, the slamming doors, the dramatic exits, the silent and tense dinners, and the waving gun.

Ralph stopped coming home. I don't remember it as an event; I merely noticed that he wasn't around anymore. What a relief! The tension I felt from my guilt for being so happy that he was gone was not nearly as bad as the anxiety I had experienced when he was actually there. We soon learned that he had taken a hotel suite downtown. Ma, Sis, and I packed up and moved to Colfax Avenue in Minneapolis.

Forty-one fourteen Colfax Avenue was in a family neighborhood, our house being one of the few split up into rental units. This was a very happy time for me. I embraced the new environment wholeheartedly. Apparently, I was not even remotely attached to our recent past. I experienced no sentimental woe and felt no need to reminisce. Good riddance! The change of scenery and the people that went with it was refreshing and sparked my curiosity.

Mr. Alexander lived two houses down. It became part of my daily routine to walk over to his house and eat breakfast with him. He was Army all the way with a blue tattoo on his shoulder, buzz haircut, and white T-shirt. I loved having this burly man show me how to dip my toast in the soft yolk of an over-easy egg. I didn't mind his cigarette smoke or his gruff voice at all. He kept his loaded shotgun by the table and would occasionally shoot skyward out the back door to scare off stray dogs from his yard.

Maria was the lady that would come and take care of us. She wasn't a "Spanish Maria" as you may assume. All I see when I think of her is a horsey face surrounded by graying chestnut curls, glasses covering dark bright eyes, and always the same brown dress with a little white flower print.

If not Maria, then Mrs. Kovle would appear in all her Jewish "grandmotherdom." She was bent with age, but that didn't stop her from marching Sis and me through the neighborhood picking wild mushrooms. She knew how to differentiate between the poisonous ones and the ones you could eat. I loved her very much until bath time. She would scrub us raw. "Can't get too clean. Have to be thorough," she'd say as she pushed the little wooden hand brush back and forth across our bodies over and over again with tireless resolve.

I loved and hated nine-year-old Kelly Green next door and always tried to find an excuse to go visit the middle-aged couple across the alley. Their house had stacks of old newspapers in it heaped higher than my head. It was creepy and fun to walk through the piles of press. Why did they save all those papers? All of us neighborhood kids would dare each other to knock and see if they would let us in.

The only frighteningly bad memories I have from this part of childhood are when Ma renounced her religion (Sis and I were so relieved when she didn't spontaneously combust on her first church-less Sunday—she actually had sat us down and said her goodbyes) and one of the few nights Elaine babysat.

Elaine was the Alexanders' oldest daughter. She had long black hair like Cher hanging in her white freckly sixteen-year-old face. She only babysat now and then, and most of her time with us was spent on the phone. We got to eat lots of popsicles as long as we didn't interrupt her.

I was quite content with this arrangement until the particular evening I am recalling occurred. On that night, Elaine let a boy in the house as soon as Ma left. They sat in the living room drinking, smoking pot, and making out. "Don't come in here, guys, and don't make any noise," said a sleepy-sounding Elaine, her voice intermingling with the pulsating rock music.

The situation seemed very grown-up and interesting to me. I was much too curious to stay away. I'd keep peeking around the corner. Afraid of getting caught, I was only able to perceive blurry images of their private party in my hurry to hide. This gave the reality around the corner a dreamlike quality more intoxicating to my imagination than if I had allowed myself a longer glimpse. Chuckling, they'd shoo me away with a little less verve each time until, pretty soon, they ceased shooing me altogether.

"Come here."

I went in and sat with them on the afghan-draped couch. They asked me questions and giggled at my every answer.

"Have you ever been high? Do you know what high is?"

I had no idea. They were paying attention to me. That's all that mattered. I was elated.

"Here. Drink this."

Whatever it was, it tasted just like Kool-Aid. They watched in eager anticipation as I gulped down the bright red beverage. They watched. Nothing happened. They stared. Nothing happened. After another five minutes passed, they sent me off to watch TV with Sis, unable to wait for me to walk around the corner before they resumed groping and doping.

Everything was fine until it wasn't. Without warning, ticks by the thousands started crawling up over the back of the TV until the screen was completely obliterated by them. Yes, *ticks!* My fear was paralyzing. They began to blacken Sis's body, nestling down into her hair. Only then could I take action. I tried to scrape them off her, screaming as my hands came in contact with their hard, vibrating bodies. I clawed to no avail. Now they were digging in her eyes and up her nose. Amazingly, she didn't seem bothered by them. She kept pushing me away as I tried to help her.

A door slammed somewhere in the distance. Sis was afraid and ran into the bathroom locking herself in. I looked down. The ticks had covered my legs. My heart seemed to stop. I couldn't move. I fell to the floor and became a scream. I couldn't tell how long I lay there.

Forever describes what it seemed if not reality. Blinded by this horrific trip, I felt, rather than saw, hands on me and heard Ma's voice asking, "What's wrong? Where's Elaine?"

Panic suffocated my voice, and I could barely wheeze out, "Ticks! Help!"

I was scratching myself, my ears ringing unnaturally loud. I could hear myself panting as I gouged at my arms and face. Ma carried me to the bathroom.

"Open the door!"

Into the tub she set me. She and Sis poured big cups of water over me continuously.

"Everything's okay. See? I'm washing off the ticks. We're washing off the ticks."

I wasn't convinced they were all gone until seven thirty the next morning. We were all so tired and traumatized. I couldn't focus enough to get the story out, and Ma didn't have the energy to press me.

We didn't have to go to school that day. I lay on the couch "cozying" and breathing my way back to safety and calm. Ma stormed out of the house around nine after a short rest. I was pleased to be protected but felt very sorry for Elaine.

Ma's wrath was no joking matter. It hadn't come my way full force yet, but I'd seen her in action. She was the kind of woman that could instill fear with one withering glare. Mix that with motherly protection, righteousness, and unleashed rage—it was all over. She truly saw red and snapped. Ma was capable of anything from scathingly filthy language to a solid right to the jaw or a full force kick in the groin. I don't know what she did to Elaine that day, but we never talked to her again and my morning breakfasts with Mr. Alexander were forever over.

Life went on. I actually enjoyed visiting Ralph at the downtown hotel. Dinners were always sumptuous. I relished the smell of some kind of candied vegetable or other mixed in with that aromatic cigar smoke of his. The low lighting and clinking glasses made each visit a special event. All the fancy people dressed in black and silver, the hushed tones of talk and laughter . . . I loved it! Ma and Ralph were ironing out the details of their divorce. I didn't mind at all because they were so very pleasant to each other—lots of smiles and lots of drinks clinking at our very own table.

And Ma was becoming more beautiful with each passing day. She wore colorful clothing and fussed about her hair and makeup. I was in love with her at this point. She was so pretty and had such a big, bright smile.

She started leaving us for one, two, even three weeks at a time. Maria explained that she was a performer and had to go far away for her work. I didn't understand. All I knew was that my pretty fun Ma was gone. I would cry and cry, and then forget all about it when she came back with stuffed toy in hand.

Life was taking on a certain, albeit strange, rhythm (fancy dinners with Ralph, exciting reunions with Ma, stupid kid stuff). Then it all changed almost overnight.

Ralph died of a heart attack. I really didn't feel emotional regarding this fact. It seemed to affect me about as much as a light bulb burning out—perhaps less if the light bulb was in a hard-to-reach spot.

I watched Ma closely, looking for some kind of cue as to how to act. Her behavior was guarded. I couldn't tell what she was thinking or feeling. I didn't know what was going on with Sis either. No one seemed sad; of that I was certain. Ma sat us down at the round wrought iron glass-topped dining room table once again—time to talk.

"Girls, I need to explain something to you. It's okay if you don't feel any great loss because Ralph is gone. He's not your father. Your father is a black man named Jesse—Jesse Hayes. He was a friend of Ralph's, a good man. He's dead now, but I just wanted you to know about him. That's all."

I wanted to jump for joy. Again, what a relief! Ralph was not my father. Now I could admit to myself that I despised him, and I was so glad I wasn't related to him in any way, shape, or form. I had never liked him or felt love for him and was so glad to know I didn't have to.

"Your father was a black man."

17

The black thing escaped me. I didn't know what she meant by that. Who cared? I was happy. Ralph was not my father. My father was a man named Jesse Hayes. He was a good man. And I liked that idea a whole lot.

My face is falling. It can't be saved. No longer can I play this game. I've got to keep moving or it's all over . . .

CHAPTER 3

───※───

I Hate You

It all changed almost overnight. All chances of routine, security, comfort, and confidence were lost at this sharp juncture in life's road. The house in Robbinsdale sold. Between that and the money Ralph left her, Ma suddenly had a big wad of dough. She decided it would be nice to live on a farm and bought a hundred-and-fifty-acre ranch in Syracuse, New York. Off we went. Just like that. She didn't hire help or have a game plan. All at once, poof! We were living on a huge ranch in upstate New York in a rickety, drafty old farmhouse with wood-framed beds. As large as the house was, it wasn't big enough, because Clifton came along.

Clifton was my mother's new boyfriend. Simply put, I hated him. An extremely well-spoken black man with an *enormous* chip on his shoulder, he reveled in negativity and cynicism. Clifton hated white people but was dating my mother and another white woman she knew named Pat. As a matter of fact, Ma and Pat looked a lot alike. It was now 1970. Long hair teased high was the fad, as well as black cat suits and severely tailored pantsuits. Their tearful lunches together—sometimes united, sometimes opposed in their love for this asshole—sickened me. I was dragged everywhere with them and party to all the sordid details of their depressing conversations.

Harshly critical and exceedingly uptight are the adjectives Clifton personified. I don't recall him talking to us kids directly—only on rare occasion. But he never, ever missed an opportunity to

19

put down Ma in his arrogant, berating, phony-baloney, ivory-tower tone. He was constantly on her case.

He beat her almost nightly in that ramshackle old house. Sis and I would go upstairs to bed, and as soon as we were out of sight, he'd start lecturing, haranguing, harassing, and patronizing Ma, getting louder and louder, breaking some object for emphasis, and then laying into her full force. We'd creep halfway down the stairs to hear, whispering in the darkness, our comfy flannel nightgowns in stark contrast to the events below—the scent of dusty old wood permeating the air. I never felt worry. I never felt fear. I just could not understand why my mother would let him do this to her. It was so illogical to me.

He was yelling at her about the Himalayan cats now. We had brought two with us: Leroy and Chickybits who was pregnant. Louder, longer, nastier, and even louder . . . throwing Chicky against the wall for emphasis.

"These cats are another symbol of the white way of life. It's so frivolous. A sign of status . . ."

Let the games begin. Whatever.

It was now time to enroll in school. The stingy landscape of leafless trees poking out of the thin layer of dirty snow was metaphoric; new friends did not await me here. As I awoke on the morning of the first and last day of classes, I tried to shrug off my instinctive dread. It correctly prevailed as I almost clinically observed my physical manifestation of fear: the quick dry breaths, the cold clammy face, the ice-cold extremities, and the ringing blue aura around my eyes and ears.

The icy paved path leading toward the campus entrance felt precarious beneath my feet. Empty hallways signified that Sis and I were entering our respective classrooms late. I'm sure the teacher greeted me in some manner, but I was too consumed by my fear to hear her. She walked me over to an empty seat and sat me down. Everyone was drinking milk. I was afraid to look at the children, so I relied on my peripheral vision to inform me. The black kids were civil enough to the white kids and vice versa; however, neither race appeared happy with my mixed presence. A thick hatred tactilely filled the air. What I exuded toward Clifton back at the ranch seemed like love compared to this.

Unnerved, I decided it was best to concentrate on the little red-and-white carton of milk in front of me. This posed a great challenge. I couldn't figure out how to put the straw into the carton. No way was I going to ask anyone for help, and if I didn't do it myself, they would all think I was dumb. So, I took the straw out of the plastic wrap with shaky hands and tried to inconspicuously stick it in the milk carton. I opened one flap and then the other, very conscious of the fact that my carton was all messed up while everyone else's flaps were sealed in nice neat little triangles. I jabbed the straw at the carton harder and harder until it partially punctured the waxed cardboard. With one final, mighty jab, the carton crumpled. Milk sprayed all over the table. The classroom broke into one huge roar of laughter.

"Stupid little nigger! Albino nigger! Yellow dummy!"

The teacher shushed everyone, walked over to me, and actually gave me a little smack as she told me to go stand in the corner for making such a mess. I was crestfallen but determined not to cry. My level of concentration was so high that I could not think or hear until more laughter and snickers cut through.

"How many times do I have to tell you to go back to your seat?"

I suddenly forgot how to walk and stood there, afraid to look up. The teacher wasn't shouting. She sounded annoyed and loudly nonchalant. The teacher's aide gently pushed me to my chair. All I could do was stare at the table and pray the bell would ring soon—it did.

The name-calling resumed once we were in the hall. I saw my sister experiencing the same thing a few classrooms down. I ran to her. We held on to each other and walked down the stairs.

"Don't look up, Hedy. Just keep walking."

We held each other tight and walked toward the school bus.

"We don't want no yeller niggers here! Don't come back or we'll beat your ass!"

"Yah, we'll kill you!"

"Yah! Yah! Yah!"

I felt a rock hit the back of my head. A clot of dirt broke on my sister's forehead. We broke into a run. So did everyone else. I thought we would be safe on the school bus. Not so. Yelling, laughing, pushing, threats—my head was pounding.

This is the first time I remember my sister clearly. We held on to each other, heads together so no one could see us cry. Luckily, we didn't have far to ride. The bus door opened, and we were pushed, poked, and spit out onto the sidewalk.

"I don't want to see you on my bus again!"

That was the bus driver's parting sentiment as she slammed the door and drove off.

My first taste of racism. Even the bus driver had told us not to come back. I didn't get it. I thought something was terribly wrong with my sister and me. I truly did not understand that we were a different color. I just figured we must be really weird or deformed, and that all this time, no one had let us know. I felt naked, foolish, alienated, clumsy, weak . . . ashamed of myself and how stupid I was not to know how gross I appeared to others. All this time I had held my head high when people must've been laughing behind my back. I was completely mortified.

The argument lead-up that night: "You have to explain race to these children. They are black and have to know the pressure, responsibility, and burden of this in a white man's world."

My mother refused to accept this.

"No. I want them to feel like people, not like a burden."

She took an extra hard beating that night.

Now that we didn't have to go to school, we got to hear Clifton's constant onslaught without pause. What a strange way to go through the days! It got to the point where I couldn't even hear the words, just a highly charged monotone pervading the air at all times—static, stupidity. I really thought they both were dumb and felt a deep sense of disappointment in my mother. She was not the person I thought she was, the person I had fallen in love with. I accepted it readily enough. I wasn't down or sad—indifferent and arrogantly tolerant is a better description.

One day, Clifton got mad at me while my mother was out. It was very nasty having all his criticism and condescension coming my way. He grabbed a spatula and said, "You know I have to punish you."

He bent me over his knees, pulled my pants down, and started spanking my bare ass. Ma came home in the middle of all this.

"These are *not* your kids to punish!"

He got distracted, I crawled off, and he started beating on her. This was the first time I actually witnessed it. What a bizarre exchange it was. A possessive, righteous, disgusted vibe exuded from his every pore. Each blow was delivered as punishment. Ma did not ward him off, fight back, or make any noise. She took it as if she deserved it. If he hit her to the floor, she merely lay exactly where she fell until he hit or kicked her into a new position.

I was furious, not with him, but with her! Why did she accept this? What was wrong with her? Clifton finished and stood over her in smug silence for a moment, then left, slamming the door to punctuate his grand exit.

"Hedy." That was my nickname. "Go put your clothes in a bag, and you and your sister pick out some toys. We're going on a trip tonight."

This scene is etched in my mind: My mother looking like a broken rag doll leaned up against the wall, talking to me in a voice more suitable for inquiring about the weather, and me feeling absolutely no pity for her, thinking her to be a complete idiot. Why did she let Clifton treat her this way without protest? She didn't make sense.

I started feeling the unconscious beginnings of self-preservation taking root. The first bricks of the wall soon to be between us had been laid. At least we were going on a trip. I liked trips.

Clifton came back around eight that night, drunk. Another first. I'd never seen him intoxicated. He didn't drink. He looked so watery, weak, and bitter in this state. It inspired violent thoughts. I wanted to push him down and kick him repeatedly in the head in all my contemptuous rage and loathing. He stumbled off to bed.

My mother quietly packed a suitcase and told us to go to sleep, that she would wake us when it was time to leave. I couldn't sleep.

My subconscious agitation mingled with my gleeful anticipation of the trip juxtaposed on my childish curiosity and excitement created the perfect cocktail for sleeplessness. My eyes would not shut. Hours later, I heard a car drive up and a soft tap on the door.

A few moments passed, and Ma came in whispering, "Hey, kids, come on. We're going on a trip."

At last the moment had arrived. I bolted out of bed, leading my groggy sister down the stairs. We got in the back seat of a big black car. I could hear Ma putting things in the trunk. She kept shoving stuff in our laps, more clothes, the cats, two rabbits in a cage, blankets . . .

A man's voice said, "All set, Mary Jane? Is that everything?"

"All set."

"Okay. We're off."

The man got in the driver's seat and started the car, marking the end of our two weeks of ranch life.

Just keep me distracted so I don't have to see what is happening—so I don't realize that I'm young, stupid, and out of my league with nowhere to go and no one to trust . . .

CHAPTER 4

Through Rose-Colored Glasses

"Kids, this is Jerry Row. Don't worry. He's a nice man. Guess what? He's driving us to California!"

Wow! We were going to California! I was more than excited. I'd always wanted to go there. Being stuffed in the back seat with pillows, blankets, animals, and my sister wasn't so bad. Actually, I rather enjoyed it. It was so unusual leaving in the middle of the night like this. We must be on some kind of grand adventure. I could hardly contain myself!

Jerry had a low, soothing voice, which I very much liked the sound of. The voice, so mild and sane in tone, made it easy to forgive his rather gawky appearance. He was a tall skinny white guy with big bushy sideburns and an even bigger Adam's apple. I couldn't see much else in the darkness. All I knew for certain was that Jerry was very tall, very skinny, and he seemed to make Ma very happy, so everything was cool with me. She was almost pretty and fun again.

Morning light came quickly. I could see Jerry had big blue droopy eyes as I watched him through the rearview mirror. His gaunt frame was topped off by golden hair cut in a Lancelot bob that didn't match the rest of him. Every now and then, he'd throw one arm over the back of the seat, and his hand would casually dangle. I had never seen such a big hand with finger joints protruding almost as strongly as its gargantuan knuckles. I found it truly fascinating. Its size alone made me relax. The combination of the low friendly voice and the big masculine hand made me feel safe and completely at ease.

Details of our journey escape me for the most part. I was more impressed with its ambience, which was golden like Jerry's hair.

We kept the radio on all the way to California. Three tunes dominated the airwaves. Each time we crossed a state line, there would be a moment of static prompting us to adjust the radio, but still, the same three songs: *I've got a brand-new pair of roller skates. You've got a brand-new key*, and *It's the last song I'll ever write for you. It's the last song to show you just how much I really care*, and *Bye-bye, Miss American pie. Drove my Chevy to the levy, but the levy was dry. And good ol' boys drinking whiskey and rye singing this'll be the day that I die. This'll be the day that I di-ha-hay.* Yep, the same songs again and again and again *and* again. That in itself was a lulling comfort.

By adult standards, the trip was pretty uneventful; from a child's perspective, it was exhilarating. So what if it was the middle of winter? Each hour was filled with something new—a kind of tree, the gas attendant's accent. It was so exciting stopping down some random country lane to let the cats out for a stretch and clean the rabbit cage. Even the stupid, crappy little arguments with Sis were fun.

One night, we stayed in a youth hostel. I remember being amused by the fact that Jerry slept on top of his guitar as if it were a pillow; he was worried that someone might steal it. All these average little hiccups along the way read as new angles on life to me—a broadening of my horizon, if you will. I approved.

The further we drove, the warmer the temperature became. We were literally driving into the sunshine. True, the car was becoming pungent with the smell of human sweat and rabbit droppings, but I didn't care. As far as I was concerned, this was the life. That is, until Jerry left. Things felt a bit scary after we said goodbye to him.

We'd gotten as far as Denver. The time was 11:00 p.m. I knew things were about to change because Jerry was driving slowly and looking at street numbers as if he were trying to find a specific address. He slowed to a stop and parked. Guess we'd found the place. The street was dark except for the dirt-covered neon sign of a bar. The sound of a live band thudded through its walls. Jerry got out of the car and grabbed his duffel bag from the trunk. Ma scooted over to the driver's seat and rolled down the window. Jerry leaned in, whispered something in her ear, and kissed her on the cheek.

"Goodbye and good luck, girls. I'm going into this jam session here. I'll play the first song as a prayer for you kids." One more kiss for Ma, and then, with guitar slung over shoulder, he disappeared into the bar. Goodbye, Mr. Sunshine.

The cold came as soon as Jerry left. We were heading up into the Rocky Mountains. Ma had a detached retina and couldn't see things correctly unless they were at a forty-five-degree angle left of straight ahead. No doubt, this made for interesting driving as she refused to wear her glasses. I wasn't too worried even though it was pitch-dark and the roads were minimally marked. Logically speaking, as long as we were climbing uphill, she couldn't build enough speed to be dangerous. My sister and I took turns riding in the front seat. It was spookily fun being in the middle of nowhere winding up, up, up among the night and trees.

Downhill was a different story; no more front seat for me. Ma let the car gather speed with each turn. With no guardrails and no lights, it looked like certain death. I tried to will myself to sleep but had no such luck. We had a momentary respite when we hit the Mecca of Salt Lake City. There, the warm glow of the cabins and salt deposits around the lake charmed a little color back into my cheeks. Not for long. Ma said we couldn't stay overnight. So back on our dark erratic rollercoaster ride we went. Thank God nights end.

Things were less stressful by day. It wasn't slow and sane as it had been with Jerry, but I'd been used to this vibe with Ma for years; I could handle it. When Jerry had been around, he had been the grown-up and we were the kids. With Ma, we were all kids, and she was the most wayward child.

We made one last stop for a short glimpse of the Grand Canyon by which, surprisingly enough, I was not impressed or excited. Being in that environment felt as subconsciously innate to me as breathing. The still air, dry heat, warm golden earth, and endless blue of the sky felt wholly natural. The canyon awoke in me a sense of wisdom and strength beyond my years, overriding the impact of its stern beauty and expressing the essence of my existence to perfection. Its barren, fossilized beauty validated and completed me as if it were my one true love. I took note.

We were now heading into the final stretch of our cross-country trek, and it wasn't long before we rolled into California. Now *this* was impressive. *This* was thrilling! The coy glimpses and brief rendezvous I had with the ocean amazed me the most. I was enamored with this unrestrained body of water and the fine warm white sand surrounding and cupping it in love. The strong misty breeze equaled sinful delight as it blew against my uninitiated face. I had great reverence for the strength of this world wonder as I resisted the undertow and was ruthlessly pummeled about by waves only to be unceremoniously deposited ashore gasping in glee and basking in sunshine. So magnetized was I by this magnificence called *ocean* that my mother had to constantly yank me out of it lest I drowned. I would've gladly surrendered my life as an offering to *this* that made me so exhausted with pure joy.

Oh, yes, indeed, our first two weeks in California were sheer heaven. Every night we stayed in four-star hotels that hugged the coastline, eating and drinking whatever our hearts desired. We even had live lobsters in the fridge and all the desserts we could want; I was hooked on Oreo cookies at the time. We went to game rooms, plays, and movies. The rabbits stayed on the balcony. The cats were properly groomed. Chicky lost her babies (thanks, Clifton!), but was otherwise okay. Needless to say, I was happy, happy, happy. Ma looked great. She was back to her colorful, beautiful self. This was a fairytale time—a fantastical whirlwind of entertainment and luxury.

Our surreal game of make-believe continued as we took an odd detour to the Gulf of Mexico. This involved packing a small suitcase and getting on an airplane with the animals, while leaving the rest of our things in the California hotel. There was no prep time. One minute we were swimming and building sand castles on a beach somewhere in California, the next, Ma was calling us in telling us to towel off and hurry because we had to be at the airport in an hour. Upon landing in Houston, we rented a VW bug, drove down to Galveston, stopped at a mall, and went on a *huge* shopping spree before checking into yet another luxury hotel right on the beach. A fantastical whirlwind . . . We snuck the animals into the room in some of the shopping bags but left everything we bought and the suitcase in the car in the parking lot.

In retrospect I realize Ma must've met a man who promised her the world. I can vaguely see in my mind's eye a red-faced man in a cowboy hat and a gray business suit chomping on a cigar, handing out twenties to me and Sis, telling us to go check out the hotel and have fun while he talked to Ma. He was some kind of famous car dealer. I had seen his face in TV commercials before. Whatever.

Money! And no supervision! Sis and I continued our splurge, buying bathing suits, stuffing our faces, and laughing, laughing, laughing . . . By day we explored the new Texas seaside, catching blue crabs with big sticks and storing them in a trash can filled with sea-water out on the balcony near the rabbits. Crabs on the balcony, lobsters in the fridge, cookies in the cupboards, twenties in our hands, and now flowers upon flowers from the red-faced wooer filling our room—the red-faced wooer who came to talk to Ma an awful lot.

In the evening, we'd tiptoe back into the hotel room hearing muffled laughter and voices behind the closed bedroom door. We'd feel so special when we saw the room service metal-lid-covered plates waiting for us; we'd giggle with surprise and delight every time as we removed the covers to dig into our food with relish. Then we'd pull out the hideaway bed in the couch and flop on our distended stomachs to watch TV through all hours of the night. I'd hear the brief sharp sound of the bedroom doorknob as it turned in the earliest part of morning. Red Face would come out fully clothed with his cowboy hat in place. I'd catch blurry views of his silhouette as the light from the TV glanced off his hat and shoulders. He didn't tiptoe or creep but walked straight-backed with full authority. Funny how those cowboy boots never made a sound at that early hour—almost like magic. They definitely clicked during the day.

It didn't last. Within a week we were buying new suitcases to pack up all the fluff we'd bought in the hotel stores and were headed back to California. We missed our flight because we couldn't find the VW bug in the parking lot. Someone had stolen the car with all the stuff in it from our initial shopping spree when we'd parked there a week ago. So, we taxied it, animals and all, to the airport. We were back in our California comfort zone in a matter of hours. The big black car was still in the airport parking lot. Our stuff was still in the hotel room. Red Face showed up once or twice and made a few pleas over the phone, but it was official—we were once again a trio of playmates. No men, no women, just three little girls on a constant sleepover. *Wheeeee!*

On one of our nights of decadence when we were out to dinner, Ma appeared unusually thoughtful . . .

"Kids, get whatever you want tonight and really enjoy it because after tonight, we're going to be living the simple life. We really needed this fun, but I don't have any more money, so I have to get serious again. Don't worry. We'll be all right. Just enjoy tonight and we'll deal with tomorrow when it comes."

"Okay, Ma."

Any excuse to indulge—I only translated the "go for it, kid" into child language and did not hear nor heed the warning.

Yet again, things were about to shift significantly. I now knew all the signs. Whenever there was a complete break in pattern, I knew that it meant a total change was going to take place in how our day, week, or month went. We received a wake-up call at five the next morning. We never got wake-up calls. Something was afoot. Lots of packing and getting the animals ready . . . Perhaps another plane ride? Instead of using the elevator, we went down the fire stairs. Now I was frightened. This was an extreme measure. Ma wanted us to be quiet so badly. She glared murderously at us whenever we uttered a single peep, startling us into silence. What was the big deal? We loaded up the car in a silent panic and took off fast.

Yah, we were on the road again, but something didn't feel right. Ma's answers were vague when we asked questions about our destination. Now that we were in California, she couldn't just blurt out "We're going to California" anymore. We needed the name of a town, or place, or . . . something. Clearly hard-pressed when it came to specifics, Ma snapped defensively until we hushed. It felt like we weren't going anywhere.

We drove to San Francisco and rode up and down the hills all day long looking, pointing, and *enjoying* . . . Yet, I still had a sense of great foreboding. At dusk we drove over the Golden Gate Bridge. Ah, there was the ocean again. Okay, things weren't all that bad. We went back over it again into San Francisco and then took the Bay Bridge into Oakland.

I couldn't ignore the fact that Oakland was not so nice, at least the part we were in. It looked poor and felt ugly. Ma kept driving up and down every street aimlessly. It was getting late. Even I could no longer find the fun in our everlasting Sunday drive. Ma was emanating waves of stress. No one spoke. She took a left turn into a dead-end alley and turned off the engine.

"Okay, kids. Get comfy. This is our campsite for tonight."

She lay across the front seat with a pillow and blanket and closed her eyes. Fun! We were sleeping in the car! Sis and I pet the kitties and tried to sleep, but it was, as usual, too exciting for me. Finally, I fell asleep as night hinted at morning.

We got up around ten. I took a closer look at our "campsite"—a shallow dead-end alley with dumpsters at the back, a partially demolished building to the right, and rusted old car parts to the left. I'm not sure if it's a child's power of rationalization, or the change of pace, or an overdeveloped sense of looking on the bright side, but, believe it or not, I thought this was all really cool. Ma opened the car doors, and we let the animals out to play. They stayed near as they stretched. We locked them back in the car, cracked the windows a bit, and went walking . . .

Walking, walking into the night, through the night, into the day—through the day, into the night . . . night . . . day . . . night . . . day . . . dark . . . light . . . dark . . . light . . .

CHAPTER 5

Going Nowhere Fast

We spent about three weeks living in the car. It was cozy in a let's-play-house manner with towels hanging over the windows acting as curtains and flashlights on the dashboard at night. We ate our meals on top of the occupied rabbit cage and read or played cards while listening to the radio, humming along with the popular music.

Our routine was simple, just as Ma had said it would be. Most of our daylight hours were spent hanging out at the Cactus Café, a dingy little diner on Telegraph Avenue. It was run by a middle-aged man with a round leathery, grill-cooked face whose slanted eyes defied his predominantly Irish features. Ma yakked at him incessantly while Sis and I sat swiveling round and round on the seat-buffed counter stools, occupying ourselves with nothing for hours on end. The sunlight shone through the yellowing blinds, never quite able to touch the faded pink walls in that dusty humble corner of the world. We would walk out of the quiet, almost-rural atmosphere of the diner into the slick, quick, agitated city streets, and meander our way back to the "car-house," stopping first at Vern's Market for one of their yummy sweet potato pies (still the best I've ever had).

Once "home," we'd let the animals out to play; they never wandered any farther than they would have in a fenced-in backyard. Chickybits and Leroy stepped gingerly among the rusted car parts and empty bottles. This was all *so* beneath them. The last bit of daylight would be filled with the omnipresent strains of hit tunes. If we felt really ambitious, we would drive over the Bay Bridge to San Francisco and head up to the "Cross"—the white neon cross where people went to kiss or pray. The view of the city from said cross was a steep eerie silhouette mysteriously covered with a layer of fog, which hung just below the subtle sparkle of lights dipping in and out of the hills. Eventually, we would make our way back to the dead-end alley and fall into cramped, furry, smelly sleep.

The way I saw it, life was good. I was too young to be embarrassed by the circumstances or feel the hardship. This was a great adventure to me—yet another extension of our ongoing game of make-believe. I'm not sure how Sis felt about it. She didn't look too thrilled. Her silence conveyed nothing.

After those initial three weeks in the "car-house," we moved into Louis's apartment. Louis was a good-looking, young, thirtyish, fiery, wiry "nigga" that Ma had taken up with. When I say "nigga," I mean it in the street sense of the word. We were on the street, and Louis was a fast-talking, good-looking strutter—a quick-thinking survivalist who could act any part in the blink of an eye to stay alive and well; he was a "nigga." In his world, this was the ultimate compliment.

Life with Louis consisted of greasy breakfasts, games of tag, and me always asking "What?" because he talked so fast that I couldn't understand him. Moving in with him was the beginning of a series of unstable and stimulating environments.

We moved into our first apartment alone a couple of months later. We moved to a lot of places. Ma went through a lot of jobs and a lot of men. Most of the apartments were just there. Most of the jobs were mindless. And most of the men were big and black.

My favorite was a dapper, tall, strong, beautiful black man named Jim Kent. I was only five, and even I knew he was incredibly sexy. I loved strong, fearless male energy, and, boy, did he ever have it! It made me relax and laugh from the belly. He'd do dumb, silly stuff like cross a big busy avenue, saying, "Watch this," and stick his leg right out in front of a car, bringing rush hour traffic to a screeching, angry halt. My terror was so fun because as long as his strong arm was wrapped around me and I could feel the muscle of his leg flexing against my cheek from me being pulled so close to him as we crossed the street, I knew that no real harm could come to me. God, what an incredible feeling! In those moments I was truly a child—trusting, dependent, safe, and happy. And he cooked great breakfasts to boot. We'd laugh and eat ourselves into a state of paralysis overstuffed with food and joy.

Everyone else was substandard at best. Each relationship reeked of sex, drama, and violence. The joy was missing, and Ma became expert at saying goodbye. Louis got dumped because he blew up the big black car with a bomb in a political rally. Lots of others came and went. My least favorite is a toss-up between two guys: eighteen-year-old nappy-headed Eugene who sat on our front porch in a pitiful puddle of tears every day for a week straight when Ma dumped him; and Bill, the funny, smelly, crunchy *granola* white guy who fancied himself to be a philosopher.

So, the Bay Area was our home for the next five years as we moved from place to place. Each apartment became associated with certain incidents in my life.

Apartment one—the second floor of a white house with yellow trim just down the street from our old "campsite"—was our first place alone after moving out of Louis's. This is where we added doves and a snapping turtle to our pet collection. I played with matches here and found an old forty-five of *Spooky*, which I listened to over and over again.

Ma became part of a hippie commune down the block. All the people there had given themselves new and colorful first names, such as Prospector, Roots, Empty Sky, and Kookie—that was interesting. They were very free. Prospector was tall and willowy with a beard— kind of Jesus-like; Anya, his wife, who always wore overalls, was a short cute buxom freckle-faced woman with wavy strawberry-blonde hair. They believed in giving their children LSD and teaching them to swear. Hey, they were free. My incredulous gulp never lessened no matter how many times I heard four-year-old Blake say "F——k it all" with great conviction, his two-year-old brother Morgan trying hard to follow suit.

Reefer smoke filled the neighborhood air. I was fearfully mesmerized by Sonja the albino black girl who lived two houses down.

I couldn't come to terms with her blonde kinky hair, her white freckled skin, and her eyes—one blue and the other a kind of pink. She looked otherworldly to me as she sat on her front porch in her Catholic schoolgirl uniform slinging a pink yoyo.

Sis and I spent hours alone. I used that time to satisfy my curiosity about everything that went on in the neighborhood. I liked walking around talking to people and seeing so many blacks mixed in with everyone else. After all, up until this point, I'd been raised in white-bread America. This integrated panorama was quite a treat.

Unfortunately, I learned more than I ever wanted to when the eighteen-year-old boy next door took my virginity at knifepoint on the garage floor. *Cold, hurt, dirty sex—warm, slimy gunk running from my crotch in between my cold, gritty butt cheeks making me feel humiliated and guilty like you do when you're too old to wet the bed and it happens anyway.* Waiting for the right moment to run back in the house so my sister wouldn't see, I, at five and a half, had my first big secret to keep.

Move number two—a small house with dark wooden shingles, directly across the street from the school we would attend—the school where I got routinely beat up by gangs of second- and third-grade girls that called me chicken because I wouldn't help them beat up other people. Cedric used to chase me into the girls' bathroom and hit me because he liked me. Velda was the freak in the school because she stood five foot one in first grade. The vicious guard dogs on chains in front of many houses I passed on the way to school intensified my already heightened fear of dogs.

Ma couldn't afford rent on our place. We kept the front of the house dark and only lived in the kitchen and one room in the back so the landlord couldn't confront us. Every other day we'd hear a knock on the door and the landlord David's exasperated voice, "Mary Jane, I know you're in there. I need the rent."

We would turn out all the lights and sit still until he would go away. I could see his tolerant profile through the missing shutter slat. His slightly tinted glasses couldn't hide the conflict—landlord versus humanitarian—in his eyes. He would wait for a response, one hand nervously running through the hair flip and down the sideburn. This routine went on for a couple months.

One night, instead of knocking and talking, we heard a picking at the door. My handsome Irish six-foot straight-looking, very gay cousin Scooter, who was visiting at the time, became very upset.

"Mary Jane, you have to face him. I'm sure you can work something out."

She shushed him, and they argued in whispers for a minute.

"Enough is enough! I'm letting him in."

Scooter walked over to the door, opened it with great flourish, and exhaled, "All right, David."

He found himself face-to-face with a nervous-looking little black man hunched over the lock with crowbar in hand. They stared at each other, frozen for a moment. The would-be thief ran off into the night with the most bewildered look on his face. We laughed about it for hours, recalling the moment again and again with more mirth each time.

"What if his name actually *was* David? Wouldn't that be funny? Ha, ha!"

It wasn't long after that when we snuck away to another house in the middle of the night, not, however, before we lost the rabbits to insecticide-covered leaves.

The next three moves were insignificant, merely variations on the same theme. But apartment number six . . . apartment number six deserves a whole chapter.

Reality versus the moment—the big picture versus this microcosm in time. Which one distorted my sense of self and confused my thoughts? What time is it, and how old am I again? Am I the lion or the lamb?

Home Sweet Home, Part One

Move number six—Howe Street, the middle of the block—an eight-step cement stairway sandwiched by large patches of ivy heading up to a three-flat with peeling dove gray paint—the eyesore of the block.

We moved into the second-floor apartment. The first floor was divided into two apartments occupied by our immediate neighbors, ninety-year-old Mrs. Frickholm and sixty-five-year-old Agnes Graham who'd smoked so much over her many years there that her dinner plates were stained yellow and gave the food an acrid, ashy flavor.

Our city block appeared to be on the verge of being run-down. A walk around it starting left brought one to a lone crabapple tree looking sickly and out of place on corner one. There was a beautiful well-tended rose garden on corner two with some of the biggest roses I've ever seen. The third corner boasted a long expanse of browning lawn. And two vicious unchained, unfenced German shepherds stared hungrily while keeping their post on corner number four.

The Catholic school across the street stood as an architectural beacon of light amid the fading two flats and the partial view of a tacky red-and-white gas station peeking through from Piedmont Avenue. A few long blocks south brought one to Kaiser Hospital and the Mayfair Market. Mosswood Park brushed up against all of that. Walking in the opposite direction led one to a huge cemetery immediately followed by a long row of rustling eucalyptus trees. The aromatic trees melted into the mini mall located behind the College of Arts, which took you straight into College Avenue, the gateway to Berkeley, California—the infamous land of intellectuals, freaks, and philosophers.

Up the eight cement stairs, to the six wooden stairs, through the door that opened to the dozen-plus once-carpeted stairs, to the second-floor flat one would go. Once the stairs were traversed and you collapsed on the landing, you would find yourself faced with two doors. The one on the right opened into the front room, now turned into Ma's bedroom, and the one on the left opened into the kitchen. The kitchen led into a hallway with a small, narrow bathroom. My and Sis's bedrooms were off to the left next to the back door. Heading right through the hallway brought you to a small room, which functioned as the living room. That room had French doors, which led into Ma's bedroom where there was a small balcony. The place was set up in an oval of sorts.

Mr. Albertini, our landlord, was a quick-moving little Italian man with fresh, faithless eyes. He and my mother instantly fell into a volatile, love-hate banter. He'd be screaming at her, half in English, half in Italian, that she had lied about the number of pets, children, blah, blah, blah. All the while, his eyes never left her breasts unless they were locked firmly on her crotch. She, in turn, would display the perfect blend of disgust and lust while delivering blatantly empty and therefore punishable apologies. In retrospect, I felt I was privy to some type of perverted fetish and really should not have been in the room while they carried on in this manner.

So here we were in our first home—home because we actually lived life in these rooms for what must've been two years, maybe even three; home because we knew the people in the neighborhood and became familiar with certain smells and patterns; home because this was the most routine my life had been thus far.

Ma went through lots of changes here. She literally crashed. I don't know how else to describe it. Everything seemed such an effort for her. There was so much weight and stifled sorrow in her voice. She looked swollen or beat up. Her solution for everything was sleep. She wouldn't, or perhaps, couldn't get off the couch for days on end.

We'd pull her, pinch her, yank her, but . . . nothing. No more lovely smiles . . . just a mild frown or a weak moan. When she was awake, her brow was always furrowed so I could study well the unusual, solitary vertical crease that would form between her eyes. She didn't talk much. Sometimes she'd disappear altogether for days on end. This upset us at first, but she'd always return, and we soon became impervious to her unexpected absences. The initial feelings of fear and worry due to her being gone were quickly replaced with the distractions of noise, TV, lights, reading, candy, and eventually a rationalized relief.

I liked Ma this way. I was now seven, about to turn eight. The last couple of years had been so tumultuous; I had already written her off. It was the only way I was able to embrace her fragmented way of living. Tired of surprises and sudden change, her sleeping for days on end or disappearing altogether seemed a blessing to me. Now that she was depressed, I could get on with life.

And we compensated very well for Ma's inaction. We learned how to make scrambled eggs, homemade pancakes, biscuits, and *Cream of Wheat*. I recall most fondly the two or three months I had Kraft macaroni and cheese and hamburger for dinner every night. I never got sick of the synthetic cheese taste and the hamburger drenched in Heinz or Del Monte ketchup. The first bite was the highlight of my day. It never let me down. Sis became the bread and pie baker, and I specialized in cakes. We had a good time eating too much and sleeping with the lights on.

Every now and again Ma would snap out of it and we'd have great fun together. She was a gloriously creative soul. All our activities revolved around music and art. Dancing, singing, drawing, paper-mache—fun! And it was always glamorous with Ma. We didn't draw flowers and stick figures. We drew ladies with three shades of eye shadow, mascara, contemporary hairstyles with flips covering one eye, luscious, lipstick-covered mouths, and designer clothes. Nothing was cute. It was all beautiful and precise.

Ma was lenient, too, as long as it was done in the name of art. I recall that strange paint job I did in my room one weekend afternoon while she was gone. I found some aqua paint in the garage and expressed myself on the walls. I thought my three-foot-wide aqua stripe on each wall was beautiful. So did Ma!

Once in a while Ma would "come to" with more fire and try to make us jump through her ridiculous, paranoid hoops. Sadly enough, I'm not exaggerating. She really was paranoid. She always thought someone was trying to brainwash her, or kill her, or something. It wasn't unusual and actually was quite routine for her to wake us at three or four in the morning demanding that we sit in a circle with her in the living room wearing copper bracelets and chanting to ward off evil. Or she would insist that we hide in a closet because some bad guy was in the house trying to find her. She'd come stomping into our room shaking us awake with adrenaline-pumped hands.

"Shh! Get up! Come on. *Now!*" she'd hiss.

No bad guy or boogeyman was ever there. I don't know if I can convey to you how highly unnerving it is to witness someone experiencing so much fright and torment when there is clearly nothing wrong and no danger in sight.

Again, the only way I could process her behavior was to detach—to write her off. Sis seemed to be using the same method. Our response to Ma's overactive imagination was unsophisticated, cold, and completely in the moment. We thought she was weird, and, at least for the first few times, almost hoped there *was* someone or something lurking in the shadows to offset the bizarreness of the scene. Eventually over time, it took a lot to get us kids to worry about *her*, let alone *them*. We just wanted to have a good time, and she was ruining it. I would roll my eyes behind her back and make the crazy sign to Sis or pretend that I didn't hear her to avoid the issue entirely. Back then I didn't know words like "schizophrenic" or "delusional." If only she would calm down and get the crayons out.

It got to the point where I was certain that something was terribly wrong with her. No longer could I humor her imagined emergencies even with my condescending attitude firmly in place. The instinct to protect myself from her delusions, so intense and panicky, became overwhelming. You know how when a mosquito is humming and buzzing right by your ear, how after a while you snap and start swatting at it in a hysterically violent manner? That hyper-frustration is what Ma inspired in me. The only reason I couldn't snap is because she was bigger than me. All I could do was wish her gone after one of her episodes and be ever so thankful when she finally did disappear for a few days.

My limit was finally reached, and I became fed up enough to draw the line out loud one day. "You're not a real mom," I told her in my childish voice. "You don't think right. You can tell me to do whatever you want, but I won't do it unless I think it makes sense." I looked her right in the eye as I said this. My statement was unprovoked, which gave it more weight. That particular morning she was sitting at her vanity applying mascara as I lay watching sprawled across her sheepskin-covered bed. She didn't argue with me as our eyes locked. Time just stopped, and those few seconds froze like minutes punctuated with icicles for exclamation points; then, she went back to her makeup. Subtle as it was, that is the only time she ever acknowledged her illness.

This is also the exact point and time where my sister and I lost all chance of forming a real bond. I knew Sis wanted, needed things to be normal. She needed Ma to be a parent you could listen to, and this made her a prisoner to my mother's insanity. She *did* do what she was told; Sis *did* jump through Ma's farcical hoops, and she had a lot more pain in her life as a result.

Home because we had most of our family pets here. Our place was a virtual zoo. Ma loved animals so.

There was a large balcony through Sis's room. That's where we kept the cats that Ma kept bringing home. The cat adoptions started because Leroy had been stolen and Chicky had run off. But Ma's efforts went beyond replacement. She kept bringing these kittens home. They'd get big and have babies; before you knew it, we had twenty-one cats. Chicky miraculously found her way home three months later, but the pattern had been irreversibly set.

A visit to the Japanese Botanical Gardens in Golden Gate Park gave Ma a yen for carp. Of course, the only logical thing to do was to fill a child's wading pool full of carp and stick it out on the balcony with the twenty-one cats. Those poor fish. None died, but all incurred battle wounds from the many attempts on their lives.

On Easter, we added a baby duck to the compound. Once big enough to hold his own, he, too, went out on the balcony. It was only natural, having never seen another duck since birth, that he thought he was a cat. I found it highly amusing to observe him slinking in the house to lie under the bed or sit on my lap while I watched TV. He would show his affection by maniacally biting ones toes. No one got as frenzied a toe attack as I—true love!

The real cats didn't like another kind of love he was trying to offer them, so, without further ado, Ma got Ducky a girl duck to solve the problem. They honeymooned in the garage for two nights. I can still hear Mr. Albertini's ranting . . .

And you can imagine, with twenty-one cats and a couple of ducks all sharing the same porch, a hygiene problem soon developed. One had to watch one's step, there being no litter box. Every Sunday we'd get out some laundry soap, a janitor's broom, and a hose, and we'd get down to business, scrubbing and spraying away. That meant poor Mrs. Frickholm was subjected to watching globs of cat crap slide and dribble down her lovely sun porch windows on all three sides. At ninety, standing just under five feet tall, it's safe to say her protest was feeble at best.

We can't complete the food chain without dogs. Sidney, a short-haired collie, was our first. He got mauled by the shepherds on corner four and got hit by a car twice (the first hit made him blind in one eye) before he died. Casey, dog number two, was a German shepherd. She only had to get hit once to die a particularly dramatic death in the front yard with Ma pushing the blood out of her body to hasten the end of her misery. Dog number three, Doggie, was a little sheltie we rescued from the dog pound. He was hit by a car as well. We think he died. We saw him get hit, but there was no corpse to speak of. Sis and I were convinced that he was a ghost or a magic dog, because he seemed to have disappeared into thin air.

We didn't have money for food, and it was becoming a real problem. Yes, we got the government-issue cheese and peanut butter. Yes, we were on the list of human guinea pigs for new cereals, but it just wasn't cutting it. So . . . we got chickens.

Ma had interesting logic. There was, indeed, a method to her madness. The practicality of her farm training paired with her creativity formed a curiously efficient result. She was trying to stretch what little money we had as far as it would go. So, because chicken feed was cheaper than human food, she bought two chickens, and we ate their eggs (protein problem solved!). I don't know if it was gratitude or compassion that sensitized Ma to the hens' quality of life, or maybe she thought it would make them lay more eggs. But she was concerned about the chickens' sex life or lack thereof; hence, in walked Roosty.

Ma forgot about the fact that cocks crow. Now we were getting lots of questions from the sleep-deprived neighbors. Roosty, his leghorn majesty, was definitely disturbing the peace every sunrise. Eventually we hit upon the simple yet effective solution of putting him in a dark kitchen drawer at night and not letting him out until around eleven the following morning.

Let me state the obvious. The apartment was getting excessively crowded; it was virtually overrun with animals. Consequently, we needed to expand beyond the front door. This is when our bigger projects, born of necessity, began. Ma wanted all these animals, which, by volume, was defeating the purpose of stretching the food money. This being a reality impossible to ignore, she now had her sights set on a garden. Without Albertini's permission, she had me and Sis pull up all the ivy on either side of the eight cement steps in the front—not just a little patch, but *all* of the ivy. We planted corn, Swiss chard, tomatoes, carrots, etc. Once that was accomplished, we moved into the backyard to build a chicken coop—accommodations for our ever-growing hen farm (some of those eggs had hatched). Ma came home with supplies: wire, wood, nails, and a hammer. Sis and I threw something or the other together. After the coop, it was a fence she wanted us to build. We made a monstrosity of a contraption four feet high and twenty feet long that was impossible for us to pick up and put in place. Ma came out to help us and, with one mighty heave, tore all the muscles on the right side of her torso. She was bedridden for a month. The fence just lay there in the middle of everything, inconveniencing everyone. A mysterious someone put it in place after several weeks.

Meanwhile, the animal theme continued spanning beyond our own pets and food providers. Sis and I surrendered to the call somewhere along the line and became a superhero team of sorts. We successfully carried out several rescue missions throughout the neighborhood.

We discovered our first victims while building that sorry excuse of a chicken coop in the backyard. Rumor had it that our neighbors in the house directly behind us raised and killed rabbits for money. To our horror, this rumor was confirmed as a fact by the anemic-looking fourteen-year-old girl who lived there. She told us in great detail how she helped her dad skin and boil the little innocents three times a week! We occasionally heard the poor babies' shrieks of terror as they left the world. Something had to be done.

Hopping the fence, Sis and I raided the pen and put as many bunnies as we could fit into a cardboard box. We walked them up to the cemetery to their freedom. So proud of ourselves were we! Every time I saw a bunny scurrying among the tombstones, I was sure it was one of our rescues or their babies.

Our next victim was found on top of a garage roof while we were building a fort with the leftover wood from the chicken coop. He was old, dirty, decrepit, and his days were undeniably numbered. This foul-smelling, weak, wobbly legged white tomcat immediately won our hearts. Even though he was so close to death and winced with each step taken, he seemed to be in remarkably good spirits and was always genuinely pleased to see us. Our expectations were realistic enough. We just wanted to offer him a little comfort in his last days. An old pillow served as his bed, and we fed him scrambled eggs until he was no more; however, this kindness backfired on us. His disease was contagious and knocked off many of our own cats. May you rest in peace, dear Jason, Sweetmeat, et al.!

One more rescue needed to be made. I had given my friend Luba a mouse for her birthday. Mice and those black-and-white tame rats were very popular pets in the seventies right around the time the movie *Ben* came out. Shortly after the birthday party, I went to Luba's house to play and went up to her room only to find her twirling the poor rodent round and round in a wrapped-up curtain. Shocked and appalled, I snatched the mouse from her in an indignant huff and took him home to the zoo.

Mousy was so forlorn, he looked like a prisoner in his yellow and orange Habitrail. His front claws were almost constantly pressed against the yellow plastic walls in a wistful, pleading manner. I built him a large cage, planted grass on the bottom of it, and moved him out on the front balcony in Ma's room. I prayed the fresh outdoor air and the natural grass would brighten his spirits. Still, Mousy moped miserably. I asked Ma if I could set him free in the house.

"Sure."

Now Mousy was happy! We hardly ever saw him. I knew he was there though. Every morning I'd check the little clay dish I had made at school that was on the kitchen floor by the sink to see if the small glob of government-issue peanut butter had been eaten. It was gone every time. Mousy showed up in a plant pot every now and then, or once in a blue moon I'd feel him run across my toes at night. Startling and heartwarming it was.

Though we enjoyed snippets of the animal experience, it wasn't without a lot of annoyance. Ma made me sigh and shake my head a lot. We whined about taking care of the fifty-plus animals, tending the garden, and building the chicken coop and the many other contraptions too numerous to mention. The whining was brought on by the fact that, other than the rescues, all of these animals were Ma's idea. She wanted them, but we took care of them. I, for one, was not happy with all the mess and responsibility. One or two pets sounded good, but more than fifty and a huge garden too? And besides, we were typical kids in that respect. Yuck, chores!

The animals were with us for the entire two or three years we were there. We lost one chicken to a stray dog, and, as stated, many cats to disease, and all the dogs to cars, but other than that, they were a constant presence. Ma's depression, absence, and paranoia were also constant, which is a grand testament to her resilience . . .

Please, I just need a moment to catch my breath. Just one moment . . .

CHAPTER 6

Home Sweet Home, Part Two

Now, don't let me mislead you. Home was not just animal farm and omelets. Ma was down, but she wasn't dead. We had a very sexy mother, and she had no qualms about flaunting this undeniable truth. Ma loved attention and got plenty of it. In fact, our house oozed sex from just about every corner.

Ma was the kind of lady that wore silver go-go boots and plunging necklines. She'd dye her hair to whatever color was *in* that week, and I must say I've never seen a woman work her walk better. I have witnessed men on two separate occasions walk directly (*bam!*) into a telephone pole because they were staring at her so hard. I liked looking at her, too, and loved having such a colorful mother. My silent Sis's face registered enough distaste for me to realize she did not approve; however, this did not keep either of us out of Ma's closet.

We loved all the exciting clothes Ma had. We'd dive into her closet and dress up in the boots and fringe vests and have an absolute ball. It was so fun going to *Bizarre Bizarre*, the vintage clothing store that Ma frequented almost daily. We'd try on all the thirties-style heels while Ma did her shopping. She'd *ooh* and *aah* over the jewelry with the store clerk as Sis and I ran our fingers over all the different materials appreciating the sensory delight the various textures afforded—satin, suede, wool, silk . . .

But back to the merciless aura of my mother's sexuality—it wielded an awful lot of power. One grand example is when she persuaded the entire construction crew from around the corner to drop everything they were doing in order to move an old piano for her that she'd found by someone's garbage can. They heaved, huffed, and flexed that heavy old upright all the way up those three sets of stairs. It got wedged at the turn to the landing on the final flight. But fear not! Those macho men toiled and sweated for eight hours to get that thing through the door. All of this for some spaghetti, a few beers, and the opportunity to bask in the glow of Ma's flirty smile, firm breasts, and endlessly long legs.

I don't think she was ever a prostitute. I'll never know, but she didn't seem the type to tolerate that. She needed too much control. That may seem a rather extreme idea to ponder, but not really when you take into account the neighborhood we lived in and the dialogue we heard.

She definitely was a go-go dancer. She used to take us with her to rehearsals. We'd sit reading on the floor, while Ma and company coordinated their jiggles, bumps, and grinds on the tabletops. They all looked so lovely and "Hollywood" to me as they batted their false eyelashes and tossed their fake hair.

Even though Ma accented her physical femininity, she's one of those ladies that could not look tacky, no matter what she wore. She was woman. Not a woman, but "woman." Not cute, adorable, soft, or pretty, but "woman"—the beautiful epitome of female.

My disapproval of her didn't kick in until the men started coming home. I saw red and raged just like Ma when that happened. I didn't understand exactly why I was so upset, but I could not control my anger. When the living room door closed and locked, I would lose it completely and start banging, kicking, crying, and screaming, "Get out! Get out! Ma! *Pleeease!* Make him leave!"

No threats from them could stop me. I would tantrum relentlessly until the "he" of the day would leave or I fell asleep with my fist to the door. On days I could bear it, I would go to the front room door to Ma's room and put my eye to the hole where the doorknob was missing (that was her way of locking the door). I'd watch, cry, beg, and shout. It wasn't jealousy. I think I was upset that my innocence was being infringed upon, and, also, horrified with my own morbid curiosity. Or perhaps it was some kind of territorialism. Maybe I was simply grossed out and disgusted by the live pornography show taking place in the front room. I didn't want to know about these things, or hear these sounds, or see these actions. I wanted to shame them into stopping. All I knew for certain was that my anger ran deep. My rage raged.

I was so happy when Ma didn't come home for days on end during this stage. Things got stranger every time she returned. I couldn't relax for even a moment in her presence. The culmination of circumstances, daily events, underlying sexual tension, and the general chaos was making life feel like a frayed tight rope. Everything set me on edge.

And things were making Ma edgy, as well. She couldn't stand the sound of the telephone ringing anymore. The *brrrng* sound truly sent her into a sort of mental discord, triggering a kind of writhing response in her body. Her melodramatic reactions to the phone made me defensive because they seemed embarrassingly abnormal. I didn't want to participate in what I thought were theatrics. She always wanted me to lie to the callers for her. I did it a couple times before opting for honesty.

"She's here but she doesn't want to talk to anyone. The phone is upsetting her."

Now, we were constantly fighting. I didn't care. I felt a lot of contempt for her even though I still loved her and was in awe of her beauty. I walked around in a general state of alarm. Her behavior was so jagged.

She became very nasty to Sis at this point. I must've been eight and she, nine. Sis had allergies, and Ma refused to accept it.

"Stop sniveling!" *Smack.* "Go blow your f——king nose instead of sounding like a sickly little weakling."

Sis's eyes would bulge with unexpressed anger and sadness. The allergies helped hide her tears. Her hands were blunted by numbness as she attempted to dab her nose with the tissue. I now recognize that her body was checking out in an immediate reaction to Ma's snide attack.

These nasty interactions were accented by the fact that Ma didn't hit me at all and rarely ordered me around. This, I'm sure, was tied to the fact that I was willing to see her for what she was—mentally ill.

Sis and I still had plenty of fun. We spent many hours roller-skating behind the Catholic school in clamp-on skates or playing *Gilligan's Island* in the backyard. We still loved Ma and would make breakfast for her, walking it four blocks over to the gas station she worked at. Ed Kelly, her boss, a husky black man who wore two-tone shades and blue mechanic's overalls, always had a big smile for us. And besides . . .

I had my pogo stick. You could barely get me off it. I loved the rhythmic noise it made with each jump—that sound somewhere between a squeak and a crunch—1, 2, 3, 4. *How many jumps can I do in a row? One-handed? No hands?* No hands is not the smartest thing to try on a pogo stick. I still have the scar on my inner knee from that silly experiment.

Home because I remember one night in particular Ma was preparing for a party she was throwing. This was a big deal. We hadn't had a party in the apartment yet. What kind of people would come over? We hadn't invited anybody into our space, thus far, except horny men.

"Girls, please be good tonight. If you're quiet, you can stay up through the whole party. If you can show me how well-behaved you can be, I'll take you everywhere with me. That's a promise."

Now I had a goal. I wanted to know what went on in the world and solemnly vowed to be the best, quietest little girl possible.

And I was. I didn't make a peep. I sat in corners and watched everything with all-absorbing eyes. I found this suited me to a T. I liked watching people and was learning a lot as I listened to the chatter and took in facial expressions, some of which were not meant to be seen.

The company was pleasant enough—average people trying to look a little edgy and artsy. Most of them were from Laney College and Ma's ballet class. A few full-time musicians and jive-talkin' street men were thrown in the mix to add an air of urban authenticity. But that was it. Nothing outrageous took place. I enjoyed the scene and hoped we would do it again sometime.

Everyone thought Ma was so cool with all of her animals, her two mixed-race kids, the organic garden, and her home-farmed chicken and duck eggs. How sophisticatedly complex she was with this "organic, hippie s———t" coexisting next to her false eyelashes, glamour girl makeup, high teased hair, sexy chic clothes, and cosmopolitan ways!

Ma was giddy with the success of the party and her image. By the end of the night, she had been described as *deep, truly liberated,* and *a bad motherf———r.* And, now, she saw *us* as assets . . . commodities. We had further authenticated her coolness! The reward we got was more than I could've possibly hoped for.

Ma sat us down the next day. She told us what champs we'd been the night before. "Sweethearts, I didn't know you could be so polite. You can come with me almost everywhere." She meant it too. I was tickled beyond pink.

Our family outings were a blast! Ma was culturally very hip. We went with her to San Francisco to watch outdoor showings of the black-and-white films of Marlene Dietrich and Greta Garbo. We never missed Chinese New Year and even saw a few ballets. She took us with her to her dance classes where I found a new passion.

Helga, the ballet teacher, was short with a thick Slavic accent and a big stick she kept count with. She really made me feel like I could dance. That was the first time in my childhood I remembered feeling graceful. I was digging our new lifestyle.

We also went with Ma to her music classes at Laney College. This was especially exhilarating for me. I knew since age five that I was a singer/songwriter. I'd announced it to Ma back then and have never changed my mind since. That was my thing, period. My first song was a twelve-bar blues about a couch that I wanted: *There's a nice big table, a nice big couch, and I'm gonna move in this little old house. Oh, baby . . .*

Anyhow, the music lessons were a dream come true. I couldn't understand what the teacher was talking about, but just being there was enough. I sat in the corner with a music book busily copying all of the notation on the chalkboard. The teacher stopped mid-lecture. "Is that coming out of that kid's head, Mary Jane?"

"No. She's just copying."

Yeah, I loved traipsing around with Ma. We hitchhiked just about everywhere we had to go. Ma looked so cool now. She was going through her "tough" phase and sported a denim apple hat with her hair all tucked in, black boots, skintight jeans (she had to lie down to zip them up), a Danskin leotard, and one of her variety of vests. I was proud to walk into Fenton's Ice Cream with her and Sis and order our banana nut or pistachio ice cream cones.

Things got a little more stressful when Ma got another car. This time it was an old tan VW bug. Ma's driving was upsetting enough (can't forget that detached retina) without the added complication of a stick shift. She was running into or rolling back on everyone. And Ma was all fight. Even though she was at fault 100 percent of the time, she'd jump out of her car and get into the other drivers' faces cursing and making threats. She even backed up on the freeway, once, to follow a driver off an exit ramp so she could make her point. And she always got away with it, too—always. I literally had white knuckles driving around with her.

The only time her in-your-face style was ever challenged was during an altercation she had on foot while we were walking down a San Francisco street one Chinese New Year. Ma decided to try to break up a gang fight and, without hesitation, walked amid flying chains and knives to smack some guy in the head.

"Pick on someone your own size, *ass*hole!"

It was a good point. The guy whose head the gang member was kicking against the marble corner of the building was indeed smaller than him. At any rate, nothing really happened. They called her a few names, spit at her, and continued fighting until the cops came.

I started staying home more because of the car, the fights, and the piano—in that order. I spent hours noodling around on the keys. I didn't know what I was doing, but it didn't matter. My obsession with learning how to play was a much more productive form of escapism than the mindless hours I spent watching TV.

My favorite memory of Sis and myself is at the piano. Ma taught me a simple chord pattern with a catchy melody and easy words. With the tape recorder poised at the ready, I had Sis sing the song while I played. We did it again and again, adjusting a note here or an accent there, until two hours later she squeaked out a heartfelt version. *The wind in the trees is a wandering breeze coming in from the sea and the ocean . . .* I judged it to be "perfect!" and exaltedly announced, "That's it. That's the keeper!"

To my childish eye, everything was cool except for the men. The men were the problem. And the bigger we got, the bigger the problem got. It finally dawned on me that Ma viewed us as competition the more we started to look like women. She accused Sis of flirting with one of her boyfriends at age nine. I was right there and saw no flirtation of any kind happening. He had only said hello and given her a smile, but sweet Sis never heard the end of it for smiling back.

"Let me tell you girls something. All men are assholes. You can never trust a man. Use them and manipulate them because they're all a bunch of chicken s——ts. That's all you need to know to get along with them."

I was tall for my age. Gary down the block had asked Ma if I was dating yet.

"What did you do to make him look at you? Did you talk dirty to him? Did he come on to you? I don't want to hear any bulls——t!"

I didn't know what to say to her. I knew who Gary was because he was *her* friend and had a big pretty dog named Sesame.

"You girls better not be trying to get away with sexy s——t when I'm not here. I'm not going to have any little whores for daughters, *goddamnit!*"

Ma's eyes changed. Now they were filled with fear and distrust every time she looked at me and Sis, leaving me greatly alarmed. It was no small matter to be on this woman's bad side. I wanted to put her at ease but didn't know how. It was exhausting and sickening having to continually brace myself against her accusing looks. I wasn't doing anything wrong. Our growing bodies (what could we do about *that?*) were threatening her reign over sex and womanhood. Her wariness felt extremely primal and constant. The threat was real.

Sassing her would get me nowhere. My instincts told me it would be dangerous to confront her. So I transferred my simmering indignation into a bad attitude toward strangers. It was the one way I could safely let off steam.

Somewhere in all of this hullabaloo, we enrolled in school. I'm not sure how much school we had missed, but it was a lot. Thank God we were quick studies.

The first school was not so good. I learned to fight there—had to. Michael and his gang would've beaten me to a pulp if I couldn't fight back. My friends were Claudia and Luba. I was in third grade. The beaters were in fifth. At last my height was paying off. One teacher named Miss Kathy seemed to sense I was coiled like a spring. She gave me a special journal to write in. I would hand it back to her with tears every morning saying I just couldn't. The coil was too tightly wound to risk releasing. Still, her kindness and caring gave me a glimpse into another way of living. She looked so gentle, so sensible. It made a difference.

We switched to another school that had a program for gifted kids; I don't know if we were part of it or not, but Ma brought it up often to others in conversation, as if she were bragging. Every morning, we caught the College Avenue bus to Berkeley, transferred to the school bus, and went up the hill to Kaiser Elementary.

Sis and I had lots of friends: Kristy, Evan, Pam, Maurice, Allison . . .

Allison had the most beautiful hair, which ended up being at the center of a huge tragedy in her life. She was from the Philippines and had the most silky, straight black-blue hair. One day, she was swinging upside down on the monkey bars gearing up for a flip, her long lustrous hair blowing and flowing in the wind. All of a sudden, a girl from the special education class that was playing nearby became mesmerized by the beauty of Allison's shining black hair and wanted to touch it. She leaned over and grabbed Allison's hair with both hands tugging hard, which caused Allison to fall from the bars and land in a crumpled, unnatural position, her face a blanched study in pain, though she made not a sound. Teachers held us kids back as the ambulance came and somberly took her away. Sis and I weren't at Kaiser long enough to find out the end result of that horrible accident. But rumor had it that beautiful, serene Allison had landed in a way that stunted her growth for life. I hope it was only a rumor.

My best friend was Christine Larson. She brought out some of the bad girl in me (locking ourselves in the nurses' room, or scaring people with special effects at the Ouija board séances we held in empty classrooms). Smart, pretty, and sarcastically witty, she was a half-Italian girl with long luxurious chestnut-brown hair. When we weren't pulling pranks, playing tether ball, or in class, we were chasing boys and talking about Rod Stewart, Peter Frampton, or John Travolta (Vinny Barbarino). I'd go over to her apartment, and we'd listen to *Frampton Live* or the big hit *Tonight's the Night* and talk and giggle over our crush on John-John Robinson, the cute boy at school. This felt so fun and normal. I never wanted to go home to Ma's evil eye.

Orlando and his gang were the bullies in this school. I learned to run here. A more serious threat than anything I'd come across so far, Orlando was tall, mean, and hell-bent on hurting me and Sis. I can recall an incident in which he and his crew viciously chased Sis with pins, of all things! And they did it for nothing more than entertainment value.

He was large and in charge—Orlando with his cheap black jacket; dull, jaundiced eyes; and crooked, snarling smile—before I got him expelled. He and his crew were pounding me good. They had me backed in a corner. He was bearing down on me intending to put his full weight behind the punch. I ducked at the last minute, and he messed up the window frame, almost knocking out all of the safety glass. Because he busted school property instead of my face, he was expelled.

Ma was smoking a lot of pot at this point. She didn't even bother trying to hide it anymore. She left the paraphernalia on the kitchen table, her vanity—everywhere. One night, she was cutting my hair while high. She was so fascinated by how my hair kind of rolled off in fluffy balls that I was one-half inch away from complete baldness by the time she was done. The kids at school called me baboon face and beat me up until my hair grew back. This did not help my already strained relationship with Ma even though, to her credit, she faced them all in the principal's office and called them a bunch of chicken sh——ts on my behalf.

School was a little rough, but the teachers, the Mrs. Wong and Miss Kathy types, were very good for me. They brought me joy and made me feel like I was special and bright. I appreciated that greatly. They paid attention to me in a trusting, friendly, smiling manner unlike Ma. I am certain it was their presence that saved me from becoming irreparably bitter.

Yes, Kaiser Elementary was a bonafide school experience: My first talent show (winners: Me and Christine singing *Close to You!*); dances (popular songs: *Rockin' Robin, Kung Fu Fighting,* and *You Make Me Feel Brand New*); plays (I played a drug addict in some production); more singing, more dancing, and friends . . . I was actually getting comfortable enough to stop trying to be perfect. Kaiser was the place that taught me people could get mad at you and get over it. And because of this, a strong mini segment of history was built in my life as well as Sis's.

Even so, *I* was becoming a real asshole. As stated earlier, I had to let off steam somewhere. I needed my friendships badly and knew better than to test them with verbal abuse. So, my unexpressed anger was vented in all the wrong places. For instance, I said "F——k you!" to Mrs. Reynolds, another Kaiser teacher, because she was too prissy for my taste with her blonde Suzy-homemaker wig and swishy stride. Or I'd be riding the bus and an old lady would ask me for my seat. "F——k off!" I'd say, turning my back to her. I was starting to enjoy the fights at school, and my language had gone all the way over to the land of filth.

Luckily, I went through this neighborhood unharassed. No rapes or violence occurred in this house. Lots of weird neighbors dropped by whether Ma was home or not, but no one molested us children. Charles, the artist, was a druggie. His portraits were fascinatingly haunting and dark. Jim Parker, the skinny little pothead, white *nigga wannabe*, just bullsh——ted. He wanted Ma badly, but she wouldn't give it to him, and that ruffled his bantam feathers mightily. Big

Percy brought soul music into the house, and somewhere along the line, Ma started building a jazz collection.

I was getting heavily into music. I knew all the words to Ella, Billie, and Sarah's records. The soul music made me want to dance, and Judy Garland made me feel. Barbara Streisand in *Funny Girl* made me want to be a star, and Carole King's songs just made me smile. All this helped me escape Ma's paranoia.

The record player was in her room, so when she had company, I would watch TV in the kitchen as an alternative. I escaped into the worlds of *Charlie's Angels*, *Wonder Woman*, and *The Brady Bunch* religiously. This mindless TV actually was a very good thing. Before I'd had these distractions, I'd spent hours on end full of sadness or rage. Now I was relaxed and able to concentrate.

I was almost happy. My biggest superficial problem was that I went to school with dirty clothes on. Sis and I did the best we could, but we didn't have money. Though frustrating and embarrassing, it never occurred to us to wash our clothes by hand.

Sis and I were in band at school. She played cello; I, the saxophone. So, what did occur to us was the idea of making money for the laundry with our musical skills, amateur though they might be. This led us to the streets with our instruments. Now we could go see *Sinbad* movies at the Elmwood Theater and the Kurt Russell surfer movies at the Alameda Theater. We'd even go to the man-made Lake Temescal to swim with Gina from across the street. We never did get around to the laundry. Priorities.

Nonetheless, Sis and I were developing inside and out on many levels. But Ma's eternal childhood persisted. I tolerated her whims and tirades with silent exasperation that looked like patience. If any sweets were brought into the house, we would immediately divide them into thirds. We actually had to hide our portions from Ma, so she wouldn't eat them. Sis took to licking her share for extra insurance. We were developing horrible eating habits. We'd divide a pack of Oreos into thirds. I'd eat mine in one sitting to avoid the risk of having to get even angrier with Ma for eating them. Ma was either pigging out or on a five-hundred-calorie-per-day diet. Eating was not just about nourishment and flavor in our house. There was a storm brewing.

For "unparented" kids, we were hanging in there pretty well and staying fairly productive. One very upsetting occurrence for me happened across the street at the Catholic School. A bunch of us neighborhood kids were playing hide-and-go-seek, and home base was right next to a window. I was so busy watching the kid who was "it" chasing me, I missed the base and ran through the full-length plate glass window. My arm was split wide open only half an inch away from that very important vein in your wrist. You could see my bones and everything. All the kids ran screaming. Sis tried to find help. Ma wasn't home, so we went to our neighbor Agnes who gave us vanilla ice cream every Sunday. It was left over from her shriveled-up old husband, Warren, who visited every weekend from jail where he was serving time for tax evasion. Poor Agnes fainted. A stranger ended up taking me to the hospital to get my sixty-two stitches. The doctor wanted to graft some skin from my butt to my arm. I was already freaked out enough without entertaining that unpleasant thought. I wouldn't let him do it and still have the scar to this day. That's how I learned my left from my right.

Home because there are too many memories to jam into this chapter. Apartment number six was, without a doubt, a tapestry of rich and royal hue.

We had another big dose of health while visiting Kristy and her family at their house. Kristy was Sis's good friend from school. Her parents, Judy and John, fascinated me. They were two incredibly beautiful people that were clearly in love with each other. I had never seen such a thing! Ma would drop us off, or (miracle of miracles!) we'd actually visit them as a family, and that felt great. No evil eye . . . merely laughing, and talking, and sharing.

So, just as life was beginning to establish a manageable rhythm, just as I was beginning to let my shoulders down for at least a third of the day, things were about to change yet again.

It was during our final week of unsupervised time. Ma had gone on a trip with Bill Ganslen, an older well-established San Francisco photographer. I don't know what happened while she was on that trip, whether he had talked to her or if some kind of parental instinct started kicking in. But when she returned home from that particular trip, Ma looked at things realistically for the first time in a long time, and made a good very grown-up decision—probably the best one of her life thus far. She decided it was time to get out of the city.

Not only did she decide this, but she actually had the where-withal to plan the move a month ahead of time and tell us about it. This was unprecedented! Granted, it wasn't a lengthy plan, but for Ma, it might as well have been a year.

As with most kids, we were opposed to the move. As eccentric as it was, we did have a routine and had made friends here in Oakland. So, even though I knew from past experience that whenever there was a complete break in pattern a total change was going to take place, I opted to remain in denial. I did not allow myself to worry. I mean, what were the odds of our depressed, disappearing, paranoid, sex-crazed, narcissistic Ma getting organized enough to actually follow through? I found out when she pulled up one evening in a rented Ryder truck.

You tricked me. I don't know who or what I'm dealing with anymore. I don't have the luxury of feeling deeply hurt by your deceit. All I have time to do is prepare for the war that is about to take place. This is difficult because I'm not a soldier by nature.

CHAPTER 7

Culture Shock

Astonishing it is, how five hours can change the course of events in one's life. That's how long it took us to drive to the Ojai Valley. The last forty-five minutes of our journey were filled with the perfume of orange blossoms and smudge pots as the sea air slowly wafted away. We were winding down into horses and houses. Downtown, although I shuddered to call it that at the time, was one street of red-roofed adobe—one street of perfectly manicured middle-class money. We were still in California, but this did not look like the kind of place where people put wheat germ in their orange juice or protested the paving over of old ladies' gardens. I harbored a desperate hostility toward Ma for bringing us here. Why *here* of all places?

We took a right turn onto Old Creek Road and drove past the feed store on the left, which faced the town art center on the right. Half a block further and we were presented with our new house. It was nondescript—white, single story, just kind of . . . there. The first thing I did was turn Mousy loose.

Oops. I shouldn't have done that. The landlord was showing us around, where the fuse box was, etc. He went out on the back porch by himself for a minute. All of a sudden, we heard a curse and a whack! He thought Mousy was wild and had killed him in one fell swoop. Mousy's untimely death added fuel to my fire. I saw it as an omen. I was not going to cooperate with this move come hell or high water.

We picked up right where we had left off in Oakland; only now, we were in a more appropriate environment. We didn't have to build a chicken coop because one already existed. The cats were free to come and go from the house as they pleased, immediately bumping their lives up to humane. I anxiously eyed the acre of land the house sat on, praying that Ma would not feel compelled to recreate her garden. I hoped in vain; however, a couple of days of our comic attempt to cultivate the land with a hand spade and hoe proved even to Ma that it was sheer absurdity. We were off the hook. So, by all means, I should've been happy. Things were better, right?

My whining continued. I missed the Lantern, my favorite Chinese restaurant in San Francisco. I missed my friends Christine, Kristy, and MaryJo. I missed seeing the cars parked overnight in a line at the gas station due to the fuel shortage and the people in a line circling around the block to see the thriller *Jaws*. I missed the smell and feel, the hair grease and cigarettes, the hard shoes on pavement clicking out the rhythm of a strut. Where was the tired maternal voice soulfully hollering in the night for her son to come in? I missed the glare of TVs in lonely windows and drunks or junkies "sleeping" like babies by the curb. I was supposed to adjust to this change of scenery?

No! I couldn't and wouldn't rise to the occasion. I wasn't a country girl or even slightly rural by any stretch of the imagination. "Awkward" was the only adjective I could apply to myself that was anything other than negative in this situation. My discomfort ran deeper than the mere adjustment of moving from inner city Oakland to out-of-it Ojai. It's clear to me now what my problem was. But back then I couldn't pinpoint the unidentifiable emotion, which made me feel the need to repel this new place with something akin to disgust. It was the inability to blend in or see myself reflected that I found so estranging. The mélange was gone. I was surrounded by the energy of medium to small white people, most of whom were middle class or rich and completely invested in the safety and softness of their norm—*soft* being the operative word. Simply put: I did not fit in, in any way, shape, or form. Worse yet, I stuck out like a sore thumb in every way possible—physically, mentally, and emotionally. What a rude awakening!

I was a freak, a sideshow in this five-foot-four-inch blue-eyed community. No special effort on my part was needed to achieve this status. I didn't need to have an over-the-top personality or a deformity. My five-foot-nine kinky-haired caramel-skinned existence alone merited all of this special attention—and understandably so. Add to it my dark, heavy emotions and the intensity of my hyper alertness . . . people could not help but stare. I had to stare, too, at myself for the first time. My defenses went up as high as they possibly could.

It was all Ma's fault! I blamed her for her insensitivity, not "them" for their obvious curiosity. How could she casually throw us into this magnifying glass of an environment? Couldn't she have foreseen the obvious? My conclusion: either she didn't care, or she was trying to train us to be white.

We didn't have any discussions about the difficulties that might arise or insecurities that could be bred being the ink spot on the white shirt. I didn't have the skills to hang on to my own self-worth. To me, the entire situation translated into one lousy message: *I don't care who you kids are or what you're about; I'm tired of the city, so we're going rural; and because I'm tired of black people, just pretend you're white.* I felt deeply betrayed by her fickleness. I now know this was not her intention, but, honestly, I couldn't see it from any other angle at the time.

And the way it went down—it was such an affront. We had spent the last five or six years essentially unparented—left to our own devices. And we developed, accordingly, with a higher-than-average level of independence. Now, she was stepping in and rocking our whole world on what appeared to be another one of her fanciful whims. Yeah, I love you, too, *asshole!*

Off to school we trekked. I didn't sense the presence of evil or hate in this place. We were greeted with polite racism, stupid racism, if you will. Most of the kids had never seen black people up close and personal before. The dumb questions were natural.

"Do you have to wash your hair?"

"If you scrubbed for a long time with soap would your skin turn white?" *(Giggle, giggle.)*

They'd call us jungle bunnies and several other *fun* names like that. Thanks a lot, Ma. This is the life for me. (*Hardy, har, har*).

It was interesting, all right. Mixed in with their naïveté was mildness, a mediocre quality that threw me for a loop. These kids had no fight in 'em. And I was so ready for a fight and making noise. Resorting to violence only when provoked, I was completely beside myself with confusion and rage. No one was trying to beat up on me! Nobody swore. All I got were the stupid questions and that basketball of stereotype tossed in my face accidentally and consistently, hurting like a motherf——r—but what could you do?

These kids weren't seeing *us* when they stared. I could tell by the look in their eyes that they thought we were stupid, klutzy, and freaky—not ugly, but alien or perhaps a different species. Sis and I took it as a challenge of sorts.

Our reactions were quite different. Sis was visibly upset and became deeply introverted, escaping into her books and the pursuit of excellence. The way I saw it, I now had a job. It was my duty not only to undo all the insulting stereotypes going on in their sheltered, unenlightened heads (condescending attitude firmly in place). But I also had to make them feel stupid while simultaneously becoming friends with them (I'm in control).

I set my plan into action and proceeded to go out of my way to become unavoidably present at school. Now, it was all about good grades, theater, and laughing way too hard.

This laugh I developed was the best cover and release for my pain and nerves. It was a laugh that would rack my body and inspire others to double over in their own fits of mirth. But mine wasn't coming from joy. It verged on hysteria, this laugh of mine. No air of insanity echoed through it. But if one listened very carefully and threw out all preconceived notions of what laughter was, only one conclusion could be drawn: this laugh was the essence of fear. The rapid-fire bullets of sound shot from my lips and hit the air like explosions of nervous sweat evaporating in the sunshine.

It took about three months for me to completely win over my fifth-grade class at Topa Topa Elementary. I became teachers' pet and was hanging out with the "in" girls and even singing a solo (*Ain't it fun to do what you don't have to do?*) in the musical version of *Huckleberry Finn*. Unfortunately, I didn't get any sense of relief from my victory, the aforementioned actually enhancing my self-doubt.

Every goal I set for myself was so easily achieved. I wasn't certain I had duly earned it. I discounted the *A*s on my report card; my teachers surely had given them to me out of pity. The kudos I got for singing must've been false; they probably didn't want to hurt my feelings. The constant verbal approval (*This kid has what it takes . . . She's Harvard material*) and pats on the back must've been based in sarcasm. I wanted to crawl in a hole, not to die, but to begin again without a contradiction at every turn.

None of this cheerleading was new. I'd received lots of affirmation at other schools. But I couldn't handle it here. Something was messed up inside of me. I felt ugly and slow, and thick, and worthless. Sis was also heavily praised, but we didn't compare notes or, for that matter, interact much at all while at school.

We did spend a lot of time together at home—more than any place else we'd lived thus far. We made a tire swing and took turns swinging on it for hours. I found this exceedingly pleasant. The tree from which we swung was in front of the house on an easy hill, so when you kicked your legs up and went forward, you quickly got further and further from the ground reaching a surprisingly dramatic height. The wind created by the motion gave a moment's relief on hot, humid days. The tinny ringing of tennis balls shooting out of a machine and the dull *puck* sound of a person's racket making contact created a ritzy, recreational backdrop, as if we, too, were members of the country club behind our house. Sis would swing and sing, *Apricot pie, Apricot pie, Apricot pie, oh me, oh my. Please tell me why I like Apricot pie. Please tell me why. Oh, what a state of bliss. Almost as good as my first kiss. If I go on like this I could miss my piece of Apricot pie*—a song inspired by Apricot, the little orange kitty Sis adored.

Perfection was swinging until dusk, all hot and lazy from the sun and filthy with dirt and sweat. Reluctantly, our fingers, perhaps stained with a bit of pomegranate juice, would let go of the swing. Our feet would shuffle us slowly back toward the house. How bittersweet were those fleeting moments, hating to give up the autonomous joy but ready to as soon as the crickets broke into song warning of less friendly nocturnal creatures.

Sis and I really played together in this house—badminton, Monopoly. There was an old car on the property that we would pretend to drive, or we'd go explore the creek bed. We'd had fun back in Oakland, but here it just felt different. Maybe it was our age, me eleven and she twelve, or the fact that we were so out of place. I'm not sure. All I know is that I became much more aware of my sister. I saw what she looked like. She was pretty and much softer in appearance than I. She liked writing, and I believe she had an affinity toward the animals, which I did not share.

I only liked two kitties, Mellow and Ocelot. They were both male, brothers, and bigger than the rest. Mellow was tiger-striped and nothing bothered him, hence the name. I could flip him over on his back or squish him into the tightest ball possible, and he would just look up at me with his calm yellow eyes and purr. Ocelot was named so because his markings resembled that particular type of wildcat. He was beautiful, black and silver, and surprisingly buff for a domestic kitty.

The two were inseparable. I loved watching them lope across the property or stretch out together on a big rock in the sun. We had an exclusive agreement, those two kitties and I. They only let *me* pet them, and, in return, they'd bring me dead squirrels and birds as love tokens. The Ponderosa comes to mind as I recall their ways—Ben and Hoss Cartwright to be more specific.

Oh, no! It was happening again. The place was filling up with animals fast. The cats became so numerous they actually started eating their own kittens. Ma added geese to the brood and rented out the field next to the house to Jerri for her retired polo pony / race horse, Moomba.

Moomba was a big Thoroughbred. Suffice it to say, she did not have a very good temperament. She had been taken off the racing/polo circuit because she'd kicked around a stable hand. In fact, she was on her way to becoming glue when Jerri saved her. One of Moomba's favorite tricks was to take the opposite end of the field and run at you full speed, only to stop on a dime two inches away from your face, snorting and wild-eyed—her polo training, I guess. She had my utmost respect.

The duck population went up to a dozen or so. Now, Ducky had lots of girlfriends, as well as some competition. Those ducks were always screwing or fighting. But Ducky still found time to bite my toes.

Mom solved the gardening problem by hiring an old eccentric named George Higgins. He was skinny and leathery with eyes permanently squinted in protection from the sun. The deal was he'd tend the garden to earn his fair share of vegetables, which he promptly made into juice. Being an extreme vegetarian, he eventually ended up in the hospital for not eating solids, but he was with us for a good long while before his proteinless palsy set in. The garden was hard work, but with George pulling the majority of the weight, it wasn't so bad. He was also a good planner, so our work hours were maximized, and we felt a sense of accomplishment.

Life was becoming an odd series of juxtapositions. We now had a mini farm, but Ma still walked with her city strut. I left for school every day in miniskirts or jeans with a low-cut tank top and a face full of makeup even though it alienated me further from the norm. Now that we lived in a place safe enough to leave the doors unlocked at all times, I was afraid. The rural silence was an unknown entity. It kept me up at night.

The thorn in my side here was Jaime, the seventeen-year-old boy-devil next door. He liked scaring Sis and me with his BB gun. The rest of the next-door family was average: a pretty, conceited daughter; a doormat of a mother; and a yelling dad complete with a crew cut and beer belly. It's funny how there's always one of those kinds of men around no matter where you go.

I acclimated by the time I was about to hit junior high. What else could I do? Ma was less annoying because she was working more, and she wasn't bringing men home. All I had to do when she got home was go outside to avoid the consternation I felt listening to her ramblings. She worked at the post office and the Holiday Inn, leaving her no peace from her enemies and future murderers. I spent most of my time avoiding her paranoid verbal onslaughts on the tire swing, fantasizing about being a superstar.

This undoubtedly was the best period with Ma because though she wasn't around much, you could perceive her attempt at being responsible, and we kids desperately needed to feel that. She was never gone overnight anymore. That gave us some sense of continuity, more so than if she'd been there during waking hours. Things were fairly peaceful, and I was numbed out to my complex set of emotions associated with school. Everything was just fine.

My God! Ma was relaxed enough at that point for Sis and me to actually throw a party at the house. And, even more shocking, it was a success! Ma kept her cool. All the kids showed up. The music rocked. And it was all fun and innocence. The only racy moment was when Sis caught Drew, a boy we both had a crush on, kissing mournful-faced Karen in the backyard. I didn't mind because I'd already had my first kiss, ever, with Drew under the mistletoe at the Christmas dance. But Sis still liked him and wanted Ma to make him leave. We'd always had that problem of liking the same boy because we were so close in age.

We were in Matilija Junior High, now, in seventh and eighth grade. Nadia Comaneci was on the verge of becoming passé, and Michael Jackson was on the verge of becoming larger than life. I was your typically depressed teenager too busy feeling sorry for myself to notice others around me were going through a similar discomfort. I had really caved into and embraced self-pity because I blamed the race issue for everything.

True, it was more pronounced here in junior high. There were a few hateful racists, in particular, a big bully named Stan. His nastiness created a more academic Sis and a friendlier me. I told myself that since my peers needed to be cruel, it was my duty to bear the brunt of their ridicule because they didn't know any better. And I did (implosion almost complete). Problem was I could not take it.

Now, nothing seemed to make me happy. Every good time I had was temporary relief from my chronic distress. Ma tried to assuage my anger a bit. I painted my room a light green this time, and she and I made a special trip to the mall where I picked out and bought a "field theme" bed spread. I liked it so much with its little white tassels and the pattern of green grass and flowers. It kept me happy for a week or so, but I was the champion moper and quickly returned to my woeful ways.

Sis and I got jobs at the Ojai Valley News Press as inserters. We worked hard stuffing the sheets of advertisements into the papers, our fingers dry and black from the constant contact with the newsprint. The job was mindless, and we'd chatter about stupid teenage stuff to make the long hours pass or have speed races with the other inserters. We'd leave at dusk, our satisfied faces streaked with traces of ink. Most important was the paycheck from that job.

I now got on the bus every weekend and went to Ventura Beach. I'd leave at nine in the morning and not come back until five or six at night. Most of my time was spent in the water body surfing. I'd treat myself to a soft-serve cone about midday—vanilla with just a hint of coconut. The way the ice cream melted on my tongue mingled perfectly with and softened the bite of the sea salt.

The best part of those weekends was the emptiness that my mind and spirit experienced. The only thoughts I had were sparked in reaction to the beach. *Whoa! That was the best wave I caught all day. S——t! That was too strong. Aaah, warm sand. Hot, hot, hot! Where's the towel? My toes can't stand the heat. It's weird how everything looks gray when I open my eyes. I love the wind. I don't care how cold it gets. I feel wild and beautiful and strong. Look at how dark I'm getting. Funny how I don't sweat out here. Too rocky here . . . better move over. Here's the perfect spot, no seaweed or rocks, and the drop-off's only two feet.*

It didn't matter how many people packed the beach. I was alone and at peace. The water understood me and said all that needed to be said, leaving me no option but to remain silent.

The bus ride back was soothing, as well. I loved how the air changed as we passed Devil's Gorge where the off-road four-wheelers and dirt bikers recreated. That was the dividing point where the sea breeze turned into valley humidity. My cold body welcomed the suppressive hot air as I searched with my eyes for the wild mustangs that sometimes appeared just past the gorge on the left. Even walking past Libbey Park down Old Creek Road was wholly sweet; the unpaved roadside tickled the soles of my bare feet, gently coaxing my spirit out of the waves and back into my body. And home was fine, too, until I had to speak. Then, and only then, did I reenter my inevitable overwhelming grief and worry.

CHAPTER 8

The Accuser

We moved again, this time to the far end of town, onto five and a half acres at the end of San Gabriel Lane. I knew this would not bode well for Sis and me. We were able-bodied young ladies now, and good old George Higgins was no longer there to lead the way. The land, completely untended, had Ma's eyes getting big with all the possibilities.

I walked home from school every day with Sarah or Kelly. It was a long hot walk, but we'd talk and stop for orange-flavored Frosties at the Foster's Freeze, which made the daily trek seem a leisurely jaunt. Surrounded by mountains, trees, and horses, it felt safe and satisfying to be completely drained from the heat of the day in this peaceful environment. Turning into the final two-block stretch before I reached the front door, I felt I had earned the right not to think or feel anything.

Going through the door was easier these days because I had the attic. The attic was my sanctuary, my escape, my focus, and my hope. I would ascend the stairs to the attic, lock the door with ceremony, and turn on the tunes.

The songs were to me what I imagine drugs are to others, and, man, oh man, would I go on a trip! Donna Summers, Michael Jackson, Olivia Newton-John . . . I would lip-synch "Last Dance" or "Macarthur Park" and live a whole concert fantasy. I was a superstar/ superhero leaping and bounding onto the stage, singing from great heights with green fluorescent lava light cascading down as I looked over a sea of people while catapulting and spinning through the air on the "Oh, noooooo" part of the song, then vanishing altogether at the end of the concert in a burst of silver flames. I was experiencing quite a phenomenon in that attic—rapture in the rafters in the little town of Ojai. Music to do homework by was *Peaches and Herb* or the B side of Michael Jackson's *Off the Wall* album. I can't tell you how many A papers I wrote jamming to the tunes.

I received a portable radio for my birthday that same year. The radio, about the size of a letter page including its handle, always looked cheerful because of its short fat stature and bright golden color accented by the black tuning dial. The plastic always smelled new and important—even over time. It meant something to me.

Every Sunday I'd make sure I was awake in time for *America's Top 40 Countdown* with Casey Kasem. This was serious business. I made detailed charts and graphed the journey of each pop hit, accumulating books and books of Top 40 research over the next few years. The complete picture of concentration until Andy Gibb's "Shadow Dancing" or Cher's "Take Me Home" came on, I have to admit I was a disco child at heart and would boogie away if the beat hit me just right. The attic was a very productive place indeed.

But now I had reached the point in my young life where it was time to enter reality or break. And I did both. My several worlds started to noticeably separate, which meant collision would soon be inevitable. School life was where I looked smart, reliable, and well-adjusted; I was Heather the super student. Attic life was pulsating, sexy, rewarding, intense, and all-powerful. Home life was where I completely and utterly failed.

My failure coincided directly with my mother's first and only solid attempt to enter our lives as a hands-on parent. It was too late. Me and Sis were fourteen and fifteen, and very used to doing whatever, whenever, and however we wished. Ma's effort was valiant but off base.

Her idea of parenting was to raise her voice and accuse us of bad things, which we weren't doing, and then to try and catch us in the act of committing these imagined crimes. As a freshman (at Nordhoff Senior High School), it was more than humiliating to have

Ma following me in her car as I made my way to choir practice on foot or by bicycle. She would duck in and out of the cars parked a few blocks back, thinking she remained unnoticed.

Ma routinely insisted that Sis and I were flirting with everyone regardless of what sex they were or how old they were. She would go into major rages over trivial things like a broken glass. Everything was an unforgivable tragedy to her. And our whorish, careless, useless ways were something she took extremely personally. We *must* be trying to disgust and humiliate her with our lack of character and shameless desires. I had no tolerance for her need to control. And as her snide, martyred self-righteousness intensified, my main goal in life quickly became how to get Ma to *shut up*!

To say being falsely accused is not a good feeling would be a gross understatement. My logic was short-circuiting from the barrage of her paranoia. She wasn't rational. Coming to terms with Ma's continuous onslaughts sucked away all of my energy. I would try to have sensible conversations with her about it (how could I be a straight-*A* student if I spent my time doing drugs, and guys, and girls as she accused me of?). I tried laughing off her attacks. Not making any headway, I resorted to senseless arguing, banal invectives flying through the air on both our parts—a contest I couldn't possibly win. Ma meant and believed what *she* was saying; her eyes looked at me as if I was born of the devil. The only other option was to shut myself down completely.

This crescendo of delusional magnification happened over a six-month period. Another side effect of Ma's deciding that we needed to act like a family was the fact that I was no longer allowed to go from school directly up to the solace of my attic. She wanted me to do my homework downstairs, and for us to have dinner together, and hang out in general. Now, she was messing with my only source of guaranteed sanity—my sanctuary. *Sorry, Ma—I can't stress it enough—too little, way too late.* Her request for family time took the balance out of the phrase. Things escalated, and only one dynamic was possible: CRAZY LOUD!

How can I convey to you how horrific it is to have to kowtow to a mentally ill person that is trying to play the head of the house? Certainly, it isn't any less dramatic than being asked to cheer on someone running a 220 with an uncast broken leg. They'd hate you if you didn't cheer them on and condemn you for letting them run when their bones started shattering and piercing through the skin. The panic that sets in when you have to participate simply by proximity . . . no way to please her, no way to help her, no chance of peace, no simple escape.

I was afraid to express *anything* because of her overreactions. *Everything* sent her into a rage. She and Sis didn't have good chemistry. Sis and I weren't allies. Ma and I liked each other, but I never knew who was going to show up—Jekyll or Hyde? I viewed her as an incredibly competitive, jealous, foot-stomping, impatient, impudent, conniving, oversize child.

Shutting down—yes, that was the only solution.

A brief interlude from her suffocating presence mercifully presented itself when it was time to build our latest version of the farm—a diversion made bittersweet by my lack of enthusiasm. How easily and quickly I was distracted by my own whining. No words can accurately describe my frustration at being forced to be a *farm girl*. I had fully embraced my identity as a poverty-stricken, gritty ethnic city girl. I liked feeling tough and urban. But Ma was determined to have her farm, and therefore, so were we. For Ma, our toughness translated into brawn. We should've toned down our protest a bit. Perhaps, a little less rebellion would've spared us the honor of being extensions of her arms and legs.

This time when Ma said "Go build a chicken coop," we ramped it up to a whole new level. First, we had to clear brush from the designated area, ten yards by ten yards, which was dangerous due to the high population of black widows and small scorpions. No, they weren't fatally poisonous. But you couldn't convince me of that. It is safe to say that my fear of bugs reaches the height of phobia to this very day (so much for toughness). Step two was a trip to the feed store where we bought a supply of nails, wood, cement, posthole diggers, three different kinds of wire, and a dozen or so seven-foot-high, four-by-four posts that had to be driven a good one and a half feet into the ground and braced with cement. Did I mention I was a city girl? What the . . . ? I tore my hands up good with that posthole dig-ger as I concentrated all my anger, fear, and indignation into busting through the earth and clay.

The shed where the chickens slept at night is a sore memory, as well. We got it for free. All we had to do was disassemble, move, and reassemble it. This was not a small shed. It was at least six feet by ten feet and sturdy, made of wood and tiles. We took it apart and moved it all under Ma's supervision one wheelbarrow at a time.

The fact that neither Sis nor I had any stock in all these projects was what fueled the continual whining that spewed forth from my lips like an endless fountain. *We* did not want all these animals. *Ma* was the one with all the enthusiasm, but *we* were the ones doing *all* the work.

Once everything was built, we put all the poultry out including those damn geese, as well as our new addition to the family, Rodney, the Saint Bernard Ma brought home. He was supposed to cure me of my fear of dogs because he was so big.

Forgive my repeating myself, but have I made it clear that I did not take to all the animals? It was too many at once with too much responsibility. I didn't even want a pet for God's sake. And, besides, I was terrified of the geese, and they knew it. They'd hiss and snap at me. I would hang back as far as I could, while throwing them food, and turn tail at the last minute running. Every now and then I'd get a heel snapped. I detested those geese with a passion. As for the dog cure, let me just say that Rodney walked *me* and his favorite hobby was attacking other dogs.

No, I really didn't appreciate spending my after-school hours this way. With all the household/farming chores, dog-walking duties, and dinner as a family unit, attic time was now pushed back to at least nine or ten o'clock.

Now that the "farm buildings" had been erected, Ma needed a new focus. It didn't take Ma long to start her let's-hate-the-neighbors antics. The catalyst this time was Moomba, the retired Thoroughbred. She died suddenly, causing Ma to charge Pat, the next-door neigh-bor, with her murder. The scene was quite dramatic because a horse is a big thing, and Moomba lay dead in the car turnaround for a couple of days before whomever you call to pick up dead horses came to take her away to the lye pit. Of course, Ma disposed of the horse without the owner Jerri's permission.

When Jerri got the double dose of news that her horse was dead and had been tossed into a lye pit, you can imagine how furious she was! Ma tried to distract her by relaying her murder theories. The scene turned from mournful to surreal as Ma delivered the news with a child's level of hysterical delight. Too well-bred to yell, Jerri sobbed noiselessly while Ma rattled on in awe of her own telepathic powers of communication with animals. She claimed that she could feel the horse's pain as if she were dying herself. Ma went on and on about how she went through all the stages of nausea and chills simultaneously with Moomba.

"I understand her language. Moomba said that it was *Pat* who poisoned her! *Pat*, the *neighbor*!"

Unfortunately, now that the body had been eaten up by lye, there was no way to know the actual cause of death, not to mention the fact that Ma was missing the whole point. Jerri was upset about Moomba being thrown in a lye pit, the very thing she had saved her from. Her anger and shock were further compounded by finding out all this horrible news on the spot. The poor woman had just come up to visit and drop off supplies.

The horse incident seemed to accelerate the impending meltdown in our house, and the din of Ma's uninterrupted paranoia turned up yet another notch. She now exuded a turbulent, rabid, distressed version of craziness that was snowballing into God only knows what. Ma was always a mess, her sex appeal buried under her thunderous rage and fear. She only looked presentable for work. At home she wore the same button-down oversize men's shirt for days on end and a pair of flowing purple pants, reminiscent of her more glamorous days, now snagged and stained with oil spots and dirt. A "franticness" hung about her. She felt cold and clammy, feverish, her breathing was shallow, and her face unsettled, one moment drawn and pale, the next, red, the tension visibly rippling through her clenched jaw.

She was scared. Ma was ready for war. In her mind, everyone was against her. She searched obsessively for ways to stay one step ahead of her enemies at the Holiday Inn and the post office. Our landlord was on her "wanted" list too. She insisted he was manipulating her brain, and that rays shone out of his eyes, and that we mustn't speak to him because he would turn us against her. Her only allies were her psychic and her astrologer. Only they could help her ward off evil.

I had only one moment of compassion for her the whole time we lived in that house. She was pounding away on the old piano, now relegated to the toolshed down by the chicken coop. I walked in, and she was sitting there playing piano amid the spiders and their webs and cages of cooing fancy Jacobin pigeons (another pet whimsy) that couldn't walk correctly because of the hardened mud balls on their feet. You could see the thick dust in the air and the haphazardly packed storage boxes skewed here and there with no particular order. But there sat Ma, working on a song she was writing:

> *I'm what they call—a liberated woman doin' everything they say,*
> *Workin' at a full-time job, bringin' down my own pay.*
> *I'm a father to my daughters, runnin' things my way.*
> *I'm a liberated woman until the end of day.*
> *Then I'm so lonely. Who do I talk to?*
> *Who says, "Aw, honey, everything is gonna be all right?"*
> *Who says, "Don't worry?" And where's that touch?*
> *I'm a liberated woman, but, baby, it ain't enough . . .*

Wow! An actual human being not knowing what to do or how to fix things. If only her fear didn't become so perverted in the translation. The sane human response behind her sickness was so incredibly valid. It made my heart ache for her. But . . .

The more I interacted with her, the later the nights became in the attic. I wanted with all my might to take the power out of her distorted world by laughing at her outlandish claims. Her distress was so heightened and so righteous; I would get all tangled up in the heat of her emotion and forget the nonsense thoughts that had caused her anxiety in the first place. It was just too much to take in. I needed to escape her busy, paranoid mind at all costs.

Soon, I wasn't sleeping at all—literally. Sleep was no longer a part of my life. I'd stay up all night and study, daydream, and completely obsess on being a superstar/superhero, or anything that equaled calm and victory, right up until it was time to go to school.

I was still able to perform quite well. I got to class. My grades were perfect. I aced every test because I spent my sleepless nights memorizing the materials, sometimes verbatim. I made it to work and participated in track, drama, choir, etc. As long as I had the attic, as long as I had me, as long as I had a place to be me, I didn't need sleep. I don't know how long I could've continued to function in this insomniac state. I never had a chance to find out.

Ma's accusations got worse and worse. It got to the point where she was following us everywhere. She didn't even try to hide it anymore. She in her car, a menacing presence crawling along five feet behind me or Sis or us together, oblivious to the fact that she was holding up traffic, her eyes set in a narrow accusing squint. I used to think of her in a movie as a female version of Clint Eastwood waiting for one false move from the person she was just looking for an excuse to blow away. How else could I make sense of all her lurid thoughts? Order had to be established somehow in this operatic twilight zone. Somehow . . . someway . . .

It wasn't working. I had shut down but was unable to shut her out. I finally came up with what I thought was the most logical solution to the problem. She thought I was bad, right? Well, why not put some truth behind her charges? Then everything would make sense.

Ma started working the graveyard shift. After my sister was asleep, I would sneak out of the house to meet Dean Anders on a back road in his pickup truck. He was a trombonist from the band at high school. I don't even remember how we started talking or who suggested these late-night rendezvous. We weren't really attracted to each other. He was pretty much the only boy in school tall enough to date me, and because I needed it to be a secret, he had the built-in advantage of not having to tell anyone he was dating the black girl.

So, we would meet between two and five in the morning. He'd smoke a lot of pot and try to convince me to have sex with him. I'd say no and feel very grown because of his crude passes. We eventually did have decidedly unpleasant, uncomfortable sex in the front seat of his pickup. I didn't want to, but I was trying to be grown-up. I definitely felt a lot better when Ma accused me of having sex. Now, she was right! Cringe-worthy though it was, Dean and I did "it" twice, and "it" repulsed me both times. Instead of Dean and then the attic, I just went back to the attic.

The first hints of my eating disorder started showing up at this time. I was always a little chunky. Now it bothered me. I became obsessed with looking perfect and started trying to fast away the weight. No food, no sleep, tons of activity, exercise, and stress—something was going to have to give.

The weight would come and go. I really liked the way I looked whenever I lost five or ten pounds. I thought I faintly resembled a black Farrah Fawcett. That made me very happy. I didn't realize I had the potential to look that foxy. And I became more determined than ever to look like an Angel; however, my efforts were unsophisticated at best, and I was incapable of starving myself with any level of consistency. I needed advice, but this wasn't something you could talk about with people. Come to think of it, I didn't talk about anything with anyone. All I was good for was a laugh and an A.

Suddenly, Ma decided that we needed to live closer to her work. Inside of a month we had gotten rid of almost all of the animals, enrolled in Ventura Senior High School, and moved into a little one-story Spanish-style house on Anacapa Street. Boom! Just like that. *Goodbye, attic.*

At first I was happy with the move. Ventura was more of a seaside city. The school was racially mixed. We also lived walking distance from the ocean.

I became a fixture on the pier—the tall, dark, and silent mystery woman-child, lean and sleek in my string bikini, dancing my private dance with the waves. People would smile and nod. They quickly learned not to bother me with small talk. I was merely a presence.

School was interesting this time around. It was a little bit more urban than Ojai. Instead of just choir or band, there was also a performing arts class where we could work on popular songs and dances. There was even a girl from Australia in the class. I was in awe of her relaxed, way-cool vibe.

This more varied mixture of students created another new, highly unexpected development. There were boys of all different ages, sizes, and colors, and they all seemed to be interested in me. I hadn't experienced firsthand male sexual aggression before, and these boys were aggressive. Completely inexperienced in such dealings, I was clueless as to how to handle them. I wouldn't dare talk about this with Ma or Sis. I walked around simultaneously flattered and flabbergasted, more confident and more insecure, more proud and more ashamed. But nothing could detract me from my studious joy.

My favorite class was an elective I signed up for—television production. Mr. Evangeline, the teacher, was a short stylish man with a New York accent and a head full of loose curly hair. He was another curiosity for me. I had not been exposed to East Coast energy before. Once, after the third or fourth class, my interest in TV technology emboldened me to the point of action. I snuck back into the lab when no one was there and started messing around with the cameras, lighting, SEG, and sound board. I heard a voice behind me and turned to face Mr. Evangeline, just waiting to absorb his tirade of anger. The look on his face assuaged my fear. He wasn't mad at me. He was thrilled!

"Amazing! You just did everything right. You're a real natural."

I soon became his prize student, and he secured a paid internship for me at the local cable channel where I was being trained in every capacity from cameraperson to talent. In no time, I was taping all the high school and college sporting events, editing, and even assistant directing. I loved it!

I was also becoming very high profile in track, volleyball, and the performing arts class at school. My grades were up and I was well-liked by the teachers and students. I even started taking private piano lessons, something I'd always wanted to do.

A strange aside started developing in my family life at this point. Ma started another extreme behavior that put a constant question mark over my head.

Ma's astrologers and psychics (now plural) were giving her lucky numbers, which we immediately played in Vegas. She'd get the numbers and we'd hop in the car, school or not, and make the five-hour trip to Las Vegas any time of the day. Children aren't allowed near the gambling tables, so she'd drop us off at the Circus Circus Hotel for hours on end while she went and played her numbers.

Sis and I would dress in a manner that made us look at least nineteen. We wore long backless dresses with slits up the side that we'd made ourselves or bought from thrift stores. Too many episodes of *Charlie's Angels* informed our fashion sense. We would don these dresses, our faces fully made up, and Ma would drop us off leaving us completely unsupervised. Ma would let us sit at the bar and talk to men with absolutely no imputations, reactions, or consequences from her whatsoever. It was a recklessly bizarre mixed message. And, in my mind, it sealed the lack of logic I experienced in my mother's reasoning. The more I tried to rebel by acting grown and even embracing my sexuality in this particular environment where it actually could lead to very real scenarios, the more Ma seemed to be perfectly unconcerned.

Though they puzzled me, I loved these times with Ma because they were so easy, exciting, and fun. They were a welcome snag in the tightly woven fabric; however, the minute we got home, Ma would revert to her routine of talking about what liars we were, accusing us of every deviance under the sun, and following us everywhere. It was almost as if she'd forgotten all about our Sin City outings altogether. I was truly baffled.

At this point two things sent me spiraling out of control: number one, a Phil Donahue episode I really could've stood to miss and, number two, a big lie I caught "the accuser" herself in.

Now that there was no attic to retreat to when Ma came through the door, the only way I could filter out some of the verbal finger-pointing was with the TV. I became a complete TV head. I knew all the programming around the clock and watched whatever I could whenever I could.

My musical fantasies were not to be witnessed. They were too important and too revealing. Ma would've have soiled them and had the power to hurt me deeply if I opened up that much in front of her. So my songwriting days had to be temporarily over, along with the fantasy concerts and cascading lava. She knew about my countdown stats on Sundays and that I enjoyed singing, but that was it. I started keeping a journal instead. Ironically, it seemed much less personal.

The walls started to close in quickly in this small house. Ma's paranoia was magnified. You couldn't say anything to her without getting a huge overreaction. She was quite a sight. Her face would turn completely red and her voice would get louder and louder, her body language more overbearing. The threat was never physical. She never actually hit me. Ma had only tried that once back in Ojai in the dining room on "the farm."

She had been ranting at me about something I hadn't done and furious at my refusal to accept responsibility. She raised her hand, her intention very clear. I grabbed it in mid-punch, our eyes locked.

"I wouldn't do that if I were you," I said, holding her hand until she backed down.

The look in her eyes told me she was surprised, not expecting that reaction at all. I turned and went up to the attic. I had surprised myself. I believe I would have tried to beat the hell out of her if she had actually hit me.

This was extremely out of character for me. I was so angry at being falsely accused of things and tired of her dragging my thoughts into the gutter with her ludicrous grilling sessions. I was sick of this unnecessary rigmarole. That physical confrontation was the first time it occurred to me that my anger toward her ran deeper than I knew. I also realized that I was not afraid of her, that I really thought she was crazy, and that I loved her and wanted to trust her. But her reactions to me made it impossible to be open or close to her. It didn't matter what I said or did. She would always make up some terrible sin for me. I could never please her or bring her peace of mind or have any myself. I was sad but determined to live my life in spite of her.

That interrupted punch melted everything down to one simple bottom line: I was not afraid of her. I perked up. I was not afraid of her. I smiled. All this time I had believed I was. What a discovery! As refreshing as it was, my newfound bravery gave birth to a newfound fear. Now that her bluff had been called and my tolerance level had peaked, I could no longer passively avoid or ignore Ma's unchecked tyranny.

I made a last-ditch effort to rationalize her way of thinking so I wouldn't be pushed to the inevitable—so I wouldn't be pushed to leave because I really had nowhere to go. We didn't have any solid family ties or close family friends. The few times I tried to express how uncomfortable living with my mother was to teachers or other outsiders, they just didn't get it. "All mothers are a little overprotective. Don't blow things out of proportion. Everyone's mom is a little crazy," they'd say. I stopped bringing it up.

To outsiders, she was interesting, feisty, and passionate—a woman to be reckoned with. She was so captivating. Her lifestyle put colorful thoughts in bored minds. To them she seemed harmlessly eccentric, even instilling jealousy in more cautious types with her seemingly carefree ways. This made me question myself and my perception of her behavior. Maybe I *was* overreacting.

Regardless, things were getting worse. I had a new philosophy now that I viewed Ma with such scorn. It was every man for himself. I don't know how Sis was doing. I couldn't afford to care. I just noticed that she radiated white-hot anger and was very unavailable. My only focus, my only goal was to keep Ma out of my face as much as possible until I was old enough to leave.

The majority of daylight hours were taken by my busy school schedule. The days she was working were fine; our interactions were limited to somewhere between fifteen minutes and two hours. These points of connection were always agitated, but I knew roughly when they were going to end, so I could manage them with a fair amount of grace. I would head to the beach as soon as she left for work. That was my new attic, my ocean, my sand, my sun, my stars, and my turf.

Her days off were another story. She'd pop her head in my classes or drive in circles around the school. More humiliation. If I talked to anyone, she thought I was having sex with them. As a teenager trying to be remotely cool, she was mortifying me. She'd grill me in front of my friends, and I would act like it was no big deal. If a boy were talking to me, she'd threaten him.

"Don't let me catch you talking to my daughter again, or I'll call the cops! I can get someone to come and beat you to a pulp at the snap of a finger, and I will!"

She'd call all night long at my workplace to make sure I was there.

At home she was yelling all the time. At first I tried responding in a very quiet, calm voice. She would just get more in my face, an inch away, "Stop lying to me!" her eyes bulging, a vein popping on the right side of her red face as she tried to squash me with her body language. Man, I was really sick of this sh———t.

My logic circled back around to letting her believe that everything she thought I was doing was true. If I concurred then maybe she'd back off quicker. I'd come home to a barrage of accusations ranging from sex, to stealing, to lying, to whatever, and now my pat answer was "Yes, you're right. Sorry."

It seemed like the perfect solution at first. Her face would relax into an *aha!* and she'd say "I *knew* it!" And that was it—end of conversation. Everything was cool as long as she thought I was the worst kid on the planet. I'd found the formula. She just needed to be right—end of discussion.

Then things changed again. Ma changed her hours at work to coincide with when we got out of school. She became omnipresent. Now, I always had a distrusting eye looking my way. We'd listen to her for hours on end as she spewed forth her rotted thoughts about the evil, mind-control people at the Holiday Inn trying to brainwash her. I'd glaze over and tune out sitting silently through her deviant charges so as not to encourage her with reactions.

My in-depth relationship with the TV turned up yet another five hundred notches. It was my best friend now. Phil Donahue came on one afternoon with a particularly fascinating subject. The topic was eating disorders.

I paid very close attention. First they paraded the anorexics across the stage. I already knew about starvation and knew that I didn't have the discipline to starve myself like those girls on the TV. Then they brought out the compulsive eaters. I figured my mother belonged in that category. Next were the bulimics. What a brilliant concept: eat all you want and never get fat! The possibilities seemed endless . . .

Can I hide myself somewhere until it's safe to come out? I'm failing miserably at this feel-no-pain game. The shutout has not been complete, and I don't know how to swim in these waters. Help . . .

CHAPTER 9

Enter and Break

What an obvious solution! It took me approximately one month to get going full force. At first, I was afraid to make myself throw up. I thought it would hurt and that I would feel nauseous, as if I had the flu. Starvation was far more attractive, but it was impossible for me not to eat.

Then it happened. We had spaghetti for dinner one night, and I ate entirely too much. My tummy was stretched tighter than tight; I felt unbearably laden and grotesque. Now was the time. I told Ma and Sis that I was going to take a bath, and went into the bathroom, locked the door, ran the water, bent over the toilet, and stuck my fingers down my throat.

It was terrible! Most of the food came out of my mouth, but some noodles and ground beef went up my nose. It hurt. I was coughing and hacking, my nostrils burning . . . There was a horrible, acrid taste in my mouth. What a ridiculous, self-imposed ordeal! My fingernails were scratching the back of my throat. My stomach contracted so hard I didn't think it would ever relax. There was spaghetti sauce and chunks of ground beef spattered on the wall, toilet, and floor. Unbelievably, no one heard me. I cleaned everything up and got in the tub thinking, "I'll never do *that* again."

My throat still hurt the next morning. Curious, I got on the scale. I'd lost a whole pound and a half! I was impressed. Success was mine all day. I was snug and smug inside my clever little secret.

The weight came back on over the next few days. Desperation convinced me to try throwing up again. This time it was pancakes.

This time, it was no problem. One big glob of food came out in a matter of seconds—no fuss, no muss, no pain, and no noise.

I was sold! All I had to do was figure out what to eat. If I had spaghetti for dinner, then tons of ice cream for dessert would smooth out the process. Cake was easy. Bread you had to let digest a little first. Stay away from rice and spicy foods. I had it down to a science—food combining for neurotics.

It seemed as if Ma and Sis had no clue (later I learned that was not the case). I had to be careful that my meals didn't look too strange. After all, who eats sloppy joes with oatmeal? Soon, the need to be thin outranked caution, and I was throwing up every meal and could not care less what people thought of my food combos.

I started crossing over into even more extreme behavior when our performing arts class had to sell Swiss chocolate bars for a fundraiser. This is when I willingly and utterly succumbed to my addiction. You see, I had all these candy bars in my room. How could I resist? I'd get up in the middle of the night and eat seven or eight . . . a dozen bars at a time and then toss 'em up.

At first, I paid the money for the bars but quickly ran out of funds needed to support my growing habit. Instead of legitimately restocking, I now stole them from the school closet and had an endless supply for about two months. The teacher was outraged and wanted to know who was guilty, scolding the entire class. But Miss Straight-A Quiet-Serious Girl was never suspected. There were no consequences.

My existence at this time was all about obsession and anxiety. I was literally throwing myself up into the toilet four or five times a day. Now that I had this secret I had to keep from home and school, I became more of a reflection of my mother. I too was hypervigilant, ceaselessly on edge, and had a hard time deciphering what was real. I became obsessed with sit-ups—eight hundred per day. I was obsessed with a size-four skirt. Where I got this skirt from, I don't remember— probably a thrift store—but I loved it and needed, urgently, to fit in it for my own approval. I succeeded, and, at last, the size-four pencil skirt with the starburst print and contrasting black background hung just right off my newly protruding hip bones.

I, now, bought into my own bluff. I was pretty, thin, smart, popular, athletic, talented . . . I even fancied I gave the appearance of coming from money and had the elitist attitude to go along with it. Looking back, the pathetic figure I cut inspires nothing but pity. All my self-worth lay in everyone thinking I was amazing and on top of the world. And everyone *was* impressed with me. A life-or-death determination infused everything I did because I couldn't let anyone down.

There was a boy in my TV production class that had a crush on me. I liked him too, so naturally, I avoided him like the plague because his advances embarrassed me. Besides, he was a bad boy at school, and I wasn't sure exactly what that meant. He, Dave, was a big roguish Irish boy—eighteen and mischievous—with black hair, a devilish smile, and an endless supply of playfulness in those sparkly blue eyes of his. I was very mean to him whenever unavoidable contact forced me to respond to his flirtation.

He convinced Mr. Evangeline that he needed me as a tutor. Now it was my *duty* to spend time with him. He actually came to my house to study a few times. My mother didn't seem upset with his presence at all. Huh. Maybe it was because he was Irish. Maybe it was because I was so snotty to him.

Eventually, we cut the crap and started seeing each other. It wasn't long before his primitive charm convinced me to cut class. To have someone who doesn't seem to care about anything pay attention to you is very flattering. What did I have that the rest of the world didn't?

It was easy to rationalize the absentee notes I wrote, forging my mother's signature by tracing it off her canceled checks. Fate would have it that my little white lie accidentally helped me catch Ma in a lie of her own.

There, at the bottom of a stack of canceled checks, lay one that had never been cashed. It was dated back to 1976 and drafted to my mother. The signature at the bottom—Jesse Hayes. I didn't react. I put whatever thoughts or feelings I had into the small freckle on the inside of my right wrist. That was a safe place for them. They only snuck out once.

We were watching the World Series with the Milwaukee Brewers and the Saint Louis Cardinals (Willie McGee and Ozzie Smith, the short stop, were my favorite ballplayers). We were having one of our more successful evenings as a family, getting excited over the game, cheering, and yelling. When it ended, a conversation sprung up that led Ma to sing her own praises.

"I've had to give up a lot for you kids. I've played mother and father to you, and—"

"Don't say that."

I wasn't shouting. My voice, loud like a shout, was more emotional. The words, barely able to form through my hyperventilation, seemed to be coming directly from my heart. It was as if my chest cavity had opened to give direct access to the power and truth in them, thus removing all chance of superficiality or misinterpretation should they lose one iota of energy traveling up to and escaping from my mouth.

We polarized to opposite sides of the room like two magnets. With a quick glance and a small wave, Ma told Sis not to interfere. I had my back to her. My eyes were averted.

"Where is my father? Dead men don't write checks."

It's as if Ma and Sis evaporated into thin air. I only heard indecipherable, detached whispers as I walked to my room that were quickly drowned out by the thud of my own heartbeat heating up my ears. I never did get an answer. An occasional excuse would come up, while we were at the grocery store or in the car . . .

"I thought it would be easier if you thought he was dead. He had a family . . ."

Whatever. She could tell me anything. It didn't matter. There was no truth in this house. *She* was the liar. No wonder she was so paranoid. She thought we were as bad as her.

Surf was up! Now I had the beach and Dave. I felt a lot of real joy when we spent time together. My laugh was natural. I could talk and he would listen. He never accused me of anything. Though he drank and smoked cigarettes, I didn't care. He was fun, exciting, warm, easy . . . I was desperate for this kind of company. He was the big sloppy light in my day.

We were such an odd couple at school. Suddenly, I was cool because I was hanging with Bad Boy Dave, and he got a little prestige hangin' with Ms. Smarty Pants. It must be true love.

We started talking about the future. We started sleeping together, mostly in his mother's car. I was very pleased with this. Truthfully, I didn't feel a whole lot of sexual stimulation, but I was very excited about the fact that I actually wanted to sleep with him and was doing it.

Ma didn't know. I don't think she wanted to.

Her behavior toward Dave was completely out of context, just like the Vegas trips. She was almost normal. I still haven't figured that out.

Simply put, Dave became too important to me. He was the only place where I could go and relax. My shoulders were down around him. I didn't waste my time with him talking about the insanity at home. I reveled in each precious moment of being accepted and wanted. This newfound warmth, cushioned with laughter and silliness, was just what the doctor ordered. My guard was down . . . nonexistent. That didn't last for long.

He got comfortable with me, too, and started an incessant teasing, all of which I took to heart. This teasing . . . I could not process his calling me names and making fun of my long legs and big feet. I get it, now. He felt close enough to me to endearingly try to get a rise out of me whenever possible. I did not get it, then. I was horrified at what I perceived was constant criticism and meanness. What changed things? Why was he doing this? My insecurities reached a new height. In the blink of an eye, I was lost, despairing and clinging, my smiles and laughter, once again fake and full of wariness. It's sad to think how little I thought I had to offer him. At any rate, he was no longer a safe place to go to. Still, it was much better than life without him.

I did a strange thing right around this time.

One day after school, I went home to the usual routine, and it just got to me, like I was a stranger walking, unknowingly, into this Pandora's box for the first time. That afternoon, I felt the cells switching around in my head. I could not play the game anymore. The next morning, right after Ma left for work, I sat down in front of my bedroom door and methodically rammed the doorknob into my eye repetitively for about five minutes. I got up, grabbed my books, and went to school. I felt cold, numb, out of touch . . . gone.

My eye swelled up, and a few of my teachers asked me what happened. I said, "Nothing."

I was tired of putting up the front I had created but was incapable of being responsible for my own pain. I didn't premeditate—I'll give myself a black eye and then someone will help me—on a conscious level, but it was a clichéd cry for help.

Mr. Evangeline had my mother hauled into the school counselor's office for questioning. I didn't know about it until after the fact.

Her behavior changed markedly as a result. She said less . . . much less. But her eye was more accusing. This was, clearly, the calm before the storm. The school questioning didn't make her afraid. It challenged her reality and, literally, drove her deeper into crazy. The cells changed around in her head too. I could see the pressure building. When she did speak, it involved less finger-pointing and became more and more about going away from society to live in the mountains so people would stop trying to brainwash her or make her accept their evil as the norm.

Dave continued to tease me about my clothes, my hair, and, now, a new routine; he kept talking about how he was going to cheat on me. I mean he'd really play it up for all it was worth, which, in turn fueled my overdeveloped sense of inadequacy to reach an even higher plateau. My panic soared, and I went into a childish form of self-protection.

"If you cheat on me, I'll cheat on you" was my comeback. I couldn't think of a better one.

This back-and-forth betrayal ribbing got out of hand. Why were we doing this? We'd been together for about four months when, one night, he said, "I'm going to cheat on you tonight."

"I'll cheat on you first" was my response.

He laughed. I laughed louder.

We said goodbye after school the following day, and I was on a mission. I meant it. I couldn't live if he really did that to me. I needed to know the hurt would at least be even, or I would've had a complete meltdown.

I walked out the back door in my favorite size-four starburst power shield, took a left on Main Street, and redefined the meaning of the word "strut." It was a strange mentality to be in—very instinctive. I don't know where I was strutting to, though I had purpose and destination in my stride. My journey's end, apparently, was the front annex of *Betty's Fabrics*. I stopped when I got to the main entrance of the fabric store, as if the scent of quick meaningless sex hung in the doorway.

Fate exited the shop about a minute later in the five-foot, six-inch forty-six-year-old body of a man who would soon introduce himself to me as Jack. He came out, looked me up and down, kept walking, turned the corner, and a couple of minutes later, drove up in a new white sedan. He rolled down the window and said, "Hi, my name's Jack. You want a ride?"

I hopped in, told him my name, and he turned on the radio.

Not much in the way of conversation transpired. We commented on the weather. It was a warm cloudy day. He didn't even bother going through the motions of asking me where I was going. We arrived at his house about seven minutes later.

It was a nice little place in a lower middle-class neighborhood. He was a car repo guy. For some reason, I thought this was funny. I hated his bad haircut; it was an early Beatles style bob, but he had a beard. I liked the idea of a beard. I liked the idea of f——king a forty-six-year-old man with a beard.

This calculated sex thing was coming quite naturally to me. I marveled at how easily my fifteen-year-old mind went from being afraid and longing for love to being turned on at the idea of having sex with a complete stranger because I could. I realized that I thought he was ugly and was enjoying the challenge of trying to find something stimulating about him just long enough for me to stand his ugliness and the mismatch of our pheromones. Where was this coming from? What I'm trying to say is that I was a real natural little whore to my complete and utter astonishment.

We went in his room and got naked. He was pure pasty white bread, not skinny, not fat, not in shape, not flabby—average. At least he had a decent-sized dick and strong-looking hands. Was this *me* thinking like this? I couldn't believe it!

He lit some candles, put on soft music, and started trying to sweet talk me in the most respectful way. I was getting pissed off. He was ruining my turn on. I didn't want a soft, lovely experience. I wanted to feel the crudeness of this situation—the reality of it. I asked him to turn off the music—much better.

He started petting me softly, lightly. At last, I found the point of concentration: his hands. I didn't like the way they were touching me, but I liked the way they looked against my skin. His hands looked old and perverted touching my young, taut body. His hands looked like they were salivating with lustful hunger. I could see the reality. I could see the truth.

I wanted to feel that truth and instinctively started adjusting my vibe to bring it out. I didn't return his touches and made sure to keep my eyes cast down. When he kissed me, I didn't kiss him back. He started kissing me harder to invoke a response but to no avail. Finally, he said, "Kiss me," and I did. "With your tongue," and I did.

He liked the sound of his own voice telling me what to do. It lost the sensitivity and got very gruff, but not loud. His hands started to act as they looked. I did whatever he told me. I remember thinking, *Not very imaginative,* or, *Wow, I'm really doing this,* or *I don't like the way his sweat smells,* etc.

Right in the middle of the actual f——king part, there was a knock on his bedroom door.

"Dad?"

"Come back in about forty minutes, son."

The kid left. He walked right by the windows. I saw through the sheer curtains that he was a boy I went to school with. He was a couple of grades ahead of me. He was seventeen.

Papa Jack finished about ten minutes later. He wanted to hold me from behind for a while. I let him. This was disturbing to me. I didn't want to be there with him in this manner. I held my breath, it seemed, for the next fifteen minutes, as he held me and stroked my hair telling me how beautiful and wonderful I was. Finally, he got up to take a shower. I threw my clothes on and left.

I was feeling pretty smug. I'd done it with a much older man. If Dave had a cheating story for me, well, I would have one for him. I thought my story was sure to be more impressive than his because I'd f——ked an old man with a house and a son almost as old as Dave, so there.

My walk home was more of a confrontational strut. I was ready to fight the world! Seven minutes in a car translated into a one-and-a-half-hour walk.

I came home to my red-faced, angry mother. Three feet away, "Where have *you* been? I thought you were in the backyard." Two feet away, "How *dare* you pretend to be going out back. You *knew* you were leaving. You are such a *liar*! You were probably seeing that *Kim* girl." One foot away, "I know you guys are touching each other! Do you let boys *watch* when you do that?" Six inches away, "Look me in the eyes and tell me the *truth*! Are you high? I'm *sick* of your bullsh——t!" Three inches away, "Who've you been bending over for today?"

Me looking her straight in the face with the most calm voice: "Well, actually, Ma, I went out, picked up the first man I saw, went home with him, and f——ked his brains out."

Touché!

"You little condescending *bitch*! You think you're real *cute*. I know when you're *lying* to me. Now you're making *fun* of me. You're lucky I'm your mother and that I *have* to put up with your"—one inch away—"worthless *lies*. What a *chickensh——t*! Unbelievable! You're gonna end up *nowhere*. It makes me *sick*—sick with *pain*. I give up *everything* for you kids, and all you do is *lie*. Helluva way to *be*. Helluva lot of *character* you have. Go on. *F——k up your life*. See if I care!" Squinting, "*I* know you snuck off to see Kim, and *I* know the dirty little *games* you play with each other. You are *such* a worthless piece of *sh——t*, and it makes me so *mad* because you could be so *special*. *Thanks* for realizing your potential, *sweet daughter*. I love you *too*. I'm right, *goddamnit*, and *you know* it."

I back my head up to three inches: "Okay, Ma. Whatever *you* say. Sorry."

And there you have it: one of the sweetest, most satisfying moments of my life.

Dave called later that night. We got into our usual laughing, joking mode. I was waiting for the cheating thing to come up. I didn't want to be the first one to bring it up. I didn't have to wait too long.

"Well?"

"Well what?"

"Aren't you going to ask me if I went through with it?"

"Went through with what?"

"You know, *it*."

"Well?"

"Well what?"

"Did you go through with *it*?"

"I don't know if I should say."

"Why?"

"Because if I *did*, you probably wouldn't handle it so well."

"I'm cool. I can handle it either way."

"How about you? Did you do it?"

"How do I know if *you* can handle the answer to that question?"

What seemed like endless silence . . .

"*Oh* my God. You did it."

"What do you mean?"

"I can tell by your voice. You really did it. Oh my God."

Click.

I didn't dare call him back. I'd heard the horror in his voice. I was really confused. He had started this cheating garbage. He *always* talked about it with a straight face and *never* said, "Just kidding." I didn't know what to do or say. How was I supposed to handle this disastrous situation?

If I told him the truth, we would be finished. He was the only warm fuzzy in my life. I needed him beyond reason. It would more than devastate me if he left. And if I lied and told him I didn't go through with it . . . ?

Contrary to what my mother thought, I lacked the sophistication of a well-seasoned liar.

I had no one to talk to about this. My sister would be horrified, and everyone at school thought I was perfect, and happy, and well-adjusted. I couldn't admit my dilemma to anyone there. I also knew I would be greeted with shock or judgment by my peers. I didn't know what to do. I didn't go to school the next day.

Dave showed up at my house around one o'clock—no smiles, no hellos, an extremely accusing eye, a very different feeling when the accusation isn't false. What was left of my one bright spot was crumbling rapidly. I went into a paralyzed panic.

"I didn't go through with it and *never* intended to! What kind of person, no, monster, are you that you could actually *do* that or even think that I was serious? Oh, my *God*! Don't *even* talk to me. I can't even *look* at you. I can't talk to you for at least a week. I'm going to *try* to forgive you for this. Just look me in the eye, and tell me. Did you do it? Did you cheat on me?"

I was at a complete loss as to how to answer. I just wanted to say whatever would make it okay, whatever would make him love me. What is the right answer? What's the answer?

"No . . ."

"You told me *just* what I needed to know. *Liar!*" His eyes screamed at me. But all he said was "I'll talk to you in a week. Goodbye."

I knew in my heart of hearts that goodbye was a lot more final than one week. That whole week hurt more than anything I can describe. I ate and threw up everything. I did a thousand sit-ups a day. I ran. I swam. I walked the beach. Nothing numbed this pain.

My mother was no help. She scrutinized my hurt relentlessly.

"What's the matter?"

I hadn't shown her any emotion for so long. She gobbled up my grief like a starving, mangy dog.

"You hurting over your poor little boyfriend? You're *stupid* enough to shed that many tears over some little fool? Do you *cry* like this in front of him? Aren't you being a little *sickening*? His dick couldn't have been *that* good. I know you two had sex, so don't even *try* to deny it. He ain't shedding any tears for *you*. He's probably been messing around with all *kinds* of girls, so why do you keep blubbering and carrying on? I want you to stop this right *now*! You're *weak*! You're being *ridiculous*!"

I didn't go to school all week, and finally, school called Ma at work and told her about all my absent marks. She came home furious.

"You've been *deceiving* me all this time!"

Blah, blah, blah!

You know how your foot feels when it's fallen asleep and you start to get sensation back right before the pins-and-needles stage? You know—that kind of numb, tingling sensation? Well, that is how my entire head and spine felt. I was losing it big time. I couldn't even hear right; my tears and her noise were all a blur.

Dave didn't call me for ten days. When he did, we set up a time to meet.

He came over, and I had a spark of hope. His eyes were friendly. He held my hand. We sat on the couch. I just kept crying and apologizing. He pulled me up against him and gave me one of his big warm hugs. I leaned against him lapping it up, warm and happy for the first time in a long time. He started kissing me, and I kissed back with so much love and appreciation. We started having sex. My whole body relaxed into a sigh of relief. I was his. He was mine. We were gonna make it.

I opened my eyes and looked up into his. Something was terribly wrong. With each thrust his eyes exuded more contempt, disgust, anger, ice—no love. He came, and while he was still inside me said, "I don't love you. I never did. We're never going to be together again."

I started crying and searching his face. How could he be this cruel? He pulled out fast, ferociously discarding me like I was garbage. He threw his pants on, and walked out the door without looking back.

I couldn't think or feel a thing. I was in shock. I put my clothes on and ate and ate. Ma came home.

"Well, it's about *time* you stopped crying. Good girl. You've got to be a bitch to get through life. Showing people your weaknesses just gives them better tools to *hurt* you with."

I went to work, came home, went to sleep, woke up, went to school, went to every class except the one he was in, came home, showered, and changed. I put on my favorite midnight-blue over-size cowl-necked sweater with the dolman sleeves and my favorite rose-colored straight-cut corduroys.

It was January. It was drizzling outside. I decided not to take an umbrella because work was only four blocks away. I didn't take a purse because the shift was only two and a half hours and I didn't need money for anything. I said *bye* to Ma and Sis. I had told Sis about an hour earlier that there was something I had to do.

"What?"

"I'm not sure, but I have to do it."

I had no clue as to what I meant or why I was saying that.

I walked out the door and pointed my feet toward work.

God answers prayer even if you don't know him by name.

CHAPTER 10

※

Liar, Liar

As I reached the door to Cable Channel Six, instead of turning left and entering the building, I walked straight past it. It felt, literally, like there were hands at my back pushing me forward. The hands were strong; the grip, firm. Immediately, I surrendered to their authority and felt a great sense of relief—an almost ecstatic bliss.

I suppose this was the "something" I had to do. I was embarking on a journey, destination unknown, and felt incredibly lighthearted at the prospect.

I took a right onto Thompson Boulevard. All I could feel was the rain on my face. There was no sensation in my arms or legs. Wow, was I excited! Newfound bravery and strength pulsated through my veins. My stride became purposeful and rhythmic. I was into this, truly enthusiastic for the first time in a long time. I walked about forty minutes from Thompson to Telephone Road. Slowing I turned left on Telephone Road, as if compelled. This was the route to Dave's house. A horn sounded.

"Do you want a ride?"

It was David's mother of all people.

Her sudden presence shook me up. I didn't want to deal with her, or be stopped, or have to explain myself. I couldn't allow her to take me back to Ma. And I didn't want to have to come out of this powerful, purposeful state of inspiration. To maintain a sense of normalcy, I hopped in her car, my brain scrambling for ways to get rid of her.

She started saying how sorry she was for Dave and I—that he told her we had broken up. I started crying. She took me to lunch. Most of what she said went in one ear and out the other. I was crying through the whole meal, not for Dave, but because I was afraid of being stopped.

"I understand how upset you must be about breaking up with my son. You'll get over it, sweetheart. You just need some time. I know he was your first real boyfriend and how special that must've been. He did the best he could."

This was great! I didn't have to say a thing. I just sat there and played with my food, shedding crocodile tears to reinforce my incoherence until she felt she had done her duty.

"Where were you headed anyway? I'll give you a lift."

It was time to stop crying. I needed to be clear. We got in her car.

"Uh. Just going up to the mall—Ventura Mall."

She didn't believe me and wanted to take me home. My fear, again, gave me the tools I needed to finally convince her otherwise. Shopping would distract me from my sadness. It was my way of reaffirming that I was worthwhile. It would help me stop crying and I needed to do that for at least an hour or two. With a knowing nod and a sympathetic squeeze of the hand, she started the car and took me to the mall. I got out of the car and watched her drive away, a self-satisfied smile playing across her lips; her work was done here.

And so was mine. Yay! I was free. I hadn't been stopped!

It was cold now. So what? I was on my way. Not wanting to risk any more chance obstacles, I left the mall, walked to the nearby freeway entrance ramp and stuck out my thumb. Los Angeles became my immediate goal.

A rusty, noisy turquoise Dodge van pulled to a stop. I could feel the heat and smell the mingling odors of sea salt, sweat, and reefer as the door opened. It was full of long-haired surfer/hippie boy-men in their twenties. Intuition told me they were harmless enough, and I felt adventurous, so I got in.

Conversation was at a minimum. They were totally loaded. Five minutes passed, and still they weren't talking; they were, however, looking at me very intensely and sexually. Unnerved, I asked to be let out because I wanted to go shopping.

They asked me if I wanted some pot or booze. This question caused me to keenly judge the olive-colored shag carpet on the floor. Olive and turquoise do *not* match. Nervously, with a little shake in my voice I said, "I just want to go shopping. That's all." Nervous laughter.

The hard edge broke, and I could feel the change in their attitude. I think they realized I was a scared little girl even though I was five foot ten and fully developed. Laughing, they took the next exit and dropped me off, unscathed, at the Esplanade Mall in Oxnard.

I made a mental note to be a little more cautious. It was very clear in my mind that as a young female wandering off to wherever, I needed to be wary of men. Nonetheless, I, being your typical know-it-all teenager, thought I was a pretty good judge of character. After all, hadn't I just handled those guys? I felt triumphant and powerful as I exited the van. I had won a battle. Actually, two battles if you counted Dave's mother. I considered myself to be very mature and wise—jaded no less.

Reality briefly took over as my feet hit the pavement. It was cold outside and still raining. No coat . . . no money . . . I was chilled to the bone and decided to go into the mall for a while. See? Even my cover story had been wise. My subconscious had made the best choice. Where else can you walk around for hours on end without causing suspicion? Was I on top of things or what?

I wished I *could* shop. Well, at least there was window-shopping to be had. I remember feeling physically happy—superlatively slinky, agile, and light as I browsed the racks of clothing—another mission accomplished.

Starting to relax because I was far enough away from home now, I thoroughly enjoyed my window-shopping expedition. Ma couldn't find me here for quite a while. I had no plans, no goals . . . I was just free. I could let my guard down. I wasn't even sad about Dave. Yay!

The bliss of liberty was fleeting. Being carefree was a new and, therefore, stressful experience for me. Apprehension slowly started taking me over. I wanted to be in Los Angeles, damn it! I left the mall and again headed toward the nearest freeway entrance, sticking out my thumb.

It was five in the evening. The sky was darkening and the rain was coming down harder. But I was no longer cold. I did not feel the weather. All I felt was good about myself and purpose driven now that I was in motion—onward to LA.

A couple of cars stopped. My instincts told me not to get in, so I didn't. Finally, a fortyish-looking man stopped with his ten-year-old daughter. They were happy-looking people. I hopped in the car without a second thought. It was a fun ride. They hadn't seen each other in a long while. Their reunion was upbeat and boisterous. I happily and thankfully joined in all the merriment.

This is the exact point in time when my constant lying began—survival mechanism now firmly in place. I had entered such a happy scene. I didn't want to be a downer or feel the strangeness of my situation. I wanted to imbibe in their infectious joy and add to it if possible.

They asked me where I was headed. I made up a dramatic story about having some kind of musical opportunity in LA, the audition of a lifetime, and that my ride had canceled on me at the last minute, and how it was a do-or-die situation, so I had to get there no matter what. They thought this was fantastic and kept asking me for details. Within fifteen minutes, I had created an exciting adventure of a lie, which was so convincing even I believed it. It did not feel like a lie. It felt exhilarating. The little girl was looking at me with stars in her eyes, and the man was so enthusiastic and supportive. I loved all of this attention.

They took me as far as they were going and sent me on my way with congratulations, good luck wishes, and smiles. I was feeling ten feet tall as I watched them drive off in their little pod of joy.

Feet on the ground equaled my bubble quickly bursting. It was now completely dark, and the rain was falling even harder. The freeway was safer than this unknown neighborhood. I left the gas station they had dropped me off at and went back up the entrance ramp, very aware of the fact that I was nowhere near Los Angeles.

The night scared me. I was shaking from the cold, but I didn't feel cold. Perhaps I was shaking from the dark. I walked along the shoulder of the road for a while, but the slow pace made everything seem nebulous, as if I were going nowhere. More fearful of hitchhiking in the dark, I struggled with my caution as I plodded along leaning into the night. After an hour or so, my night anxiety prompted a decision. It was time to take a risk, so I halfheartedly stuck out my thumb.

Instantly, a black Camaro pulled over. In it was a macho mustached Hispanic man looking self-consciously cool in his black leather jacket. I knew right off the bat that he would make a pass at me, but something told me he was okay. I got in.

He asked me my name. I made one up. He asked me why I was hitchhiking in the middle of the freeway in the dark. I made up some story about my boyfriend and me fighting and him kicking me out of the car on the freeway.

It never ceased to boggle my mind how every time I made up a story it felt so authentic as I told it. I didn't miss a beat. The whole tale would just roll off my tongue feeling like and ringing of truth. I would have the emotions around it, too. As I was describing this fictional boyfriend, I started to experience real anger, pain, and despair. It was an amazing phenomenon.

The pass I had anticipated started to manifest within the first five minutes.

"You have beautiful eyes, beautiful skin. I love your body. You must have beautiful thighs. I want to love your beautiful body and make you feel better."

While he was talking he kept alternately rubbing my cheek and thigh. At first, I was paralyzed. Part of me was fearful, but the other part of me was curious and flattered. I was, again, getting so much attention. I liked being told I was beautiful and sexy by a "semicool" grown man.

He asked, "Have you ever had a man want to please you? I want to make you feel good."

Somewhere along the line, he pulled off the freeway and stopped the car. He started kissing me—long, deep, sexual-feeling kisses. The curiosity was gone. I was frightened.

An innate self-protective measure kicked in. I knew not to fight or say "Please, don't." I started crying and begging with my eyes for him to stop. He stopped abruptly, his pride utterly wounded.

"You don't want my loving?"

"No."

He looked at me with stunned disbelief and sped back onto the freeway, tires squealing from the sudden acceleration, mumbling to himself, "What am I supposed to do with her? I can't just drop her on the street . . . can't make love . . . [something in Spanish]," and yelling at me, "Why did I ever pick you up? Now I have to worry!"

He turned the music up so it was blasting. I felt so bad, so guilty, and so very much in the wrong. I had told a bunch of lies, given this man mixed messages, been trying to act grown-up, and I had not been able to handle it. I felt worthless . . . like a complete loser. I asked him to let me out. He refused to and told me to shut up. Shame usurped my fear. I needed to get away from him because his presence magnified that shame to an intolerable degree.

We traveled without talking for a while. After a nerve-wracking twenty minutes, he turned the music back to a normal level. He looked at me, and I could see the anger had left his eyes, that everything was okay again. He made small talk. I gladly chattered away, pleased that I had been forgiven.

I was so grateful when we hit LA, I almost dared to reenter my former know-it-all status. After all, my goal had been LA, and here we were. Hah! Señor Amor drove me to the vicinity of the Greyhound bus station. There were several cheap, sleazy motels stacked in a row down one street perpendicular to the main thoroughfare. They looked dirty and threatening. And the people in the doorways appeared despondent and hostile. He pulled up in front of one of the buildings.

"I'll get you a cheap room," he said. He got out, leaving me in the car. After a few minutes, he came back to escort me in.

The place was strange in an otherworldly way, veiled by a dull, gauzy aura. It reeked of urine and cigarettes. There were a lot of people listlessly standing about or leaning on the staircase cutting ghostly figures. They were all poor and black. Their clothes were dirty and torn, hair was a mess, and alcohol and cigarettes were everywhere.

I was not welcome. The men looked at me with lust and contempt. The women looked at me with unmasked hatred. No one said a word. I was inundated with an intimidating, hostile silence.

As we warily maneuvered the stairs, I became keenly aware of how huge the contrast was between this environment and me. I seemed so neat and clean in comparison, both physically and spiritually, kind of saintly or something. This surprised me. Fear and fascination played equal parts as I took in the scene.

We entered my seven-dollar room. The light was incredibly bright, emanating a high-pitched buzz. It must have been a hundred-and-fifty-watt bulb or more. There was a bed with an old stained sheetless mattress, and a sink—no chair, no table, nothing but starkness. The oversize window was stuck wide open. Neither of us could get it closed. It was freezing in there, the mix of bright light and cold air making the atmosphere seem two-dimensional, like a photograph.

Señor Amor had sex on the brain again. He started trying to fondle me and kiss me. Now I understood how to make him stop. My brain said with confidence, "I play dead equals he stops." The word *no* was taboo with this man. It would've turned him on in this environment; however, my mental state was complicated by the fact that I couldn't possibly say no, even if I had to. I would've been guilt ridden if I verbalized my unwillingness. My logic went thusly, he got me a room and drove me to LA; therefore, I do not have the right to refuse him. Regardless, I became a rag doll not responding on any level. As planned, my silent indifference offended him, and he quickly lost interest.

So, instead, he opted to vent for an hour about his wife and family. He said she was nice but not beautiful or exotic like me—that she had lost her figure and was always yelling at him.

I remained silent throughout his complaints. What could I say? I was past feeling flattered. Cold, hungry, sleepy, and anxious, I wanted nothing more than to be left alone but was afraid to be left alone, there, in that motel. I couldn't decide what would be worse, him leaving or staying. Finally, he got tired of bitching about his life and left saying he would return.

When he left, I became jumpy. I was afraid of the night, the cold, and the open window. I heard people arguing and screaming at each other down the hall. Every now and then, the man verbally attacking someone with his unending diatribe of profanity would hit the wall for emphasis. It sounded like he was right there in the room with me. The walls were so thin. Yes, I became extremely jumpy and wide awake. I sat on the bed in constant anticipation of someone breaking in and hurting me.

Señor Amor came back with a blanket. He made one last attempt at getting laid. This time he was frustrated with me and, half-jokingly, scolded me for being so selfish and such an unappreciative taker. He looked around the room gesturing with his hands.

"You didn't even say thank you!" He laughed as I cringed with guilt. "Relax. I'm just kidding."

It was too late. I had already taken all he said to heart, the kid in me at last coming fully to the surface. I started to cry and apologize over and over again.

"Stop being silly. I'll be back in the morning."

He left.

I didn't sleep all night. I was in a strange physical and mental state, afraid to move, or think, or do anything. I sat on the bed in the same cross-legged position all night with an empty mind. The only thing I was aware of was every single noise and my fear. The bright light made everything seem surreal, like I was looking straight into the sun in the middle of the night. The bright light and the gloom and misery of this place just didn't jive together at all. I didn't dare turn out the light.

I'm paying attention, but I don't know what the lesson is. Is there a point here?

CHAPTER 11

First Day of Freedom

Morning came. I no longer felt cold or hungry, just numb and reptilelike. My eyes seemed permanently stuck open. I was very far away.

At ten in the morning, Señor Macho knocked and entered.

"So . . . ? Where do you want to go?"

I didn't answer. I had no idea.

He held my arm as we walked down the staircase that looked and felt exactly the same by day—same gauzy aura, same stench of pee and cigarettes. The sounds of the city smacked us unceremoniously as we opened the door and exited. That and the gray daylight of LA winter were a welcome normalcy.

We crossed the street and sat on a bench outside the Greyhound station for a couple of hours staring at a carload of men that would be heading to Tijuana as soon as it filled up. He explained that they were illegals going to visit their families. He thought I should go with them. This didn't appeal to me at all.

"Why not? Why are you so against it?"

Still elsewhere, I didn't respond. His gesticulations and sales pitch were too exhausting to cooperate with.

"What's wrong with you? It's the best thing!"

I saw a bus pull into the terminal marked *San Diego* and came to.

"I want to go to San Diego."

This made him turn red with anger.

105

"I *can't* have the car stop in San Diego," he said, his voice dripping with exasperation. "The police'll be suspicious of a car full of Mexicans and give them a hard time."

I checked out again—flipped off the switch. He noticed the bus marked *San Diego*, connected the dots, and pulled out a twenty, which he threw at me dramatically.

"Fine! Go catch your f——king bus!"

Off he huffed.

Relief set in as I reentered the present and immediately proceeded to pat myself on the back checking off my list of accomplishments:

- I'd made it through the night.
- Señor Macho was out of my life.
- I had a new destination.
- I had the resources to get there!

My game of playing grown-up began at the ticket counter.

"I'd like a one-way ticket to San Diego, please."

"That'll be ten dollars, Miss."

I emphatically slapped the twenty down on the counter with immeasurable glee.

It was exciting to have money to spend! And my excitement was nourishment enough. I went into the gift shop, cheerfully looked around, and bought a cheap little notebook, gum, and soda. I was pleased with my purchases and tickled to the core that I still had a few bucks left over. The idea of going to San Diego had me pumped. Now, I *really* had something to look forward to.

I felt alive, beautiful, free, and cocky—arrogant once again. I recalled the seedy motel with amusement, erasing my earlier impression completely. How lucky was I to be having all these spontaneous adventures? Life was so interesting.

My bus arrived some hours later. I boarded, sat down, and oriented myself totally into the present. The seat was comfortable. I looked clean and intriguing. Overly aware of how other people perceived me, it was extremely important to me not to appear dirty, homeless, or unequal. A very nice-looking young black military man sat down next to me. I was thrilled.

I, overnight, was developing great confidence in my feminine appeal to men. I knew he found me attractive, and I wanted to have all of his attention. He struck up a conversation. My lying kicked in. I can't remember what I told him. My goal was to be flattered and desired.

He was a down-to-earth kind of guy—no bull. I immediately adjusted my approach and started talking tough and gritty. He loved it. I was flying high. Did I have this game figured out or what? He started complimenting me left and right on my looks, brains, common sense, and maturity . . . I was in heaven!

This time around I mixed truth with the lies. With him the lies felt like lies. He was an honest man and a good person. There was no need to lie, and he was not a threat. I think that's why the lying felt uncomfortable and my logic imploded. Because he was a good person, I didn't want him to see my vulnerability, which equaled failure in my eyes. I wanted him to think I was completely okay, self-sufficient, and happy. Apparently, my bluff job was good.

When he asked me for a date and my phone number, I made up a boyfriend and said I had a ride waiting for me in San Diego. I hated this. I wanted to be real so badly but couldn't show weakness or neediness in his presence.

"Well, you've got a lot of black in you, girl. Wish I could've gotten to know you." The bus pulled into San Diego. I got off, and he continued on to the White Sands Military Base.

Here I was in San Diego! It was a bright sunny day. I was hot in my sweater. What a nice feeling it was to be overheated. My excitement relaxed into a chilled-out nonchalance as I began my stroll through the downtown area. The city was not as I imagined it would be. It was big and ugly with unsavory-looking characters monopolizing the street. My casualness turned to surprise and then annoyance as I realized with each turn of a corner that it wasn't just a block or two of city hustle. This was not the clean-cut college town I had envisioned. Disappointment set in.

I was getting harassed by a lot of men. Their advances were crude and ignoring them didn't work. They were totally invading my person with their belligerent sexual energy.

I headed back toward the bus station. There I was able to attain a comfortable level of invisibility. I sat for a long while, hours, people watching. A janitor started talking to me. He was a fatherly looking black man with a gentle nature. I liked him. He didn't ask a lot of questions. He just talked on and on about himself and his friends. His tempered monologue washed over me like a lullaby.

He was planning a big trip to Las Vegas with some friends for the following weekend. His face lit up all over like a child's at the prospect. It was healing to watch. I remember thinking he should be leading another kind of life. He didn't belong in a blue, white, and red Greyhound jumper with a broom in his hand.

What made my encounter with him so unusual was the fact that it was totally non-stressful. He didn't ask questions. I didn't have to lie. It felt good, comforting, paternal, loving. I snuggled right into all the positive energy. He knew I was wayward, and this didn't offend him at all. I felt accepted and, dare I say, approved of just as I was—not because of some front I had put up.

I decided to walk around the block for some fresh air. This time I took a left instead of a right. It was incredible to me what a different impression of the city one got by walking in the opposite direction. A sharp contrast to the downtown area, this neighborhood was squeaky clean, stately, and beautiful. Things were looking up. I headed back toward the bus station with a bit more pep in my stride.

Just as I was about to walk in the door, a slim black man with beautiful eyes and a beautiful smile rounded the corner. He gave me this look of awe, his big smile getting even bigger, and said, "You're my angel come to watch over me!"

I laughed and kept on going. Something had really struck me in his tone, though. I didn't feel like he was trying to pick me up. It felt fanatically sincere. He followed me into the bus station. As a passerby, he was amusing; in my immediate space, he was too intense and logic told me he must want *something*. He was so smiley and enthusiastic about getting to know me, I found myself unsettled by his magnified presence.

I wanted everything to be soft and unchallenging. I didn't want to have to protect myself from anyone or any circumstance. I wanted to rest. I couldn't remember the last time I had really slept.

He left rather reluctantly after a short, stilted conversation. He was so excited to meet me, and certain I had been "sent" to him for some reason. I honestly didn't want to give him the time of day, but the attention fed my adolescent narcissism, so I tolerated his domineering enthusiasm. After he left and I'd been sitting for an hour or so, reality started to sink back in.

I was tired and hungry (but not hungry enough to buy food), aching from all my walking, and exhausted from having to maneuver through men and beggars. Curtis, the nice janitor, was too busy to talk. I continued to people watch, noticing all the criminal types, the families headed off to some fun event, and the good-looking college-age boy-men with their *laissez faire* attitudes.

My defense mechanism was to find this whole scene thoroughly abhorrent. I looked down my nose at it all. I wrote mindlessly in my journal, desperately trying to escape reality. Curtis came over and told me I should go in the bathroom for a while because the security guards would get on my case if they saw me hanging around too much longer. I followed his advice.

The bathroom kicked me right off my high horse. It was depressing. A weather-beaten, leathery heavyset bag lady sat on the floor leaning against the wall. She was pretty much lost to the world. She was so busy talking to herself or imaginary whoevers she was unaware of my presence. The floor was filthy; she was filthy. The other women that came in were bus station stereotypes. You know—either those really irate-sounding, loud black women (the kind with a constant edge in their voices), or those anemic-looking twenty-year-old white girls with thin blonde- or brown-feathered shags and anorexic, drugged-out-looking bodies wearing jeans and leather jackets. I would get the once-over from them all as they entered. The black ones generally did not approve of me. The white ones were indifferent or socially polite with an automatic half-smile in place.

This constant sizing up (me of them, not them of me) was stressful. I could not deal with it. I wanted to relax and be alone and not have to worry about being on guard or attractive. But pride ruled. I wanted to be equal, as pretty, or prettier than any woman that came through that door. I didn't want them to think I was homeless or dirty or wanting in any way. And I needed to make sure they knew I was not connected in *any way* to that disgusting bag lady!

I scrutinized myself in the mirror and made sure everything about me was flawless. Since I didn't have makeup, all I could do was neaten my hair, put water on my eyelashes, and keep my clothes dirt and lint free. My reflection greeted me with smug pleasure. No one would know that I was homeless or penniless.

The game quickly lost its allure. It took a lot of energy—energy that I didn't have. I couldn't handle the competitive pressure I'd created for myself. I had to be best, or I didn't count. I went into a booth and tried to sleep. It wasn't happening.

Curtis knocked on the main door yelling, "There's a new security guard on shift. Come on out. No one'll bother you."

He wrote his number down for me.

"If you're not busy, join me and my friends in Vegas next week. Just give a call. Ya hear?"

He went back to work.

I tucked his number away and sat down for a few moments. Bored beyond bored, I opted for another walk and found myself back in the ritzy neighborhood I had scoped out earlier. It was even prettier by twilight. The short loud siren of a police car froze me in my steps.

"Where are you going?"

"Just taking a walk."

"You must not be from around here."

"No. Just killing time till my bus comes. The Greyhound bus."

"Get in the police car, Miss." This was said with great authority and severity. I got in.

Suddenly he took on a more conspiratorial tone. "Don't you know that this is Klan country? You can't be walkin' through these neighborhoods at night. Be thankful you ran into me instead of one of these homeowners. I just saved your ass. I'll take you back to the station. You wait there until your bus comes. This ain't no game."

I found it hard to take the young black officer seriously. It seemed so far-fetched to me.

"San Diego? Klan country?"

"Oh, yeah. This is one of the most racist hotbeds in the country. Don't be so naïve, young lady. You stay in that bus station until your bus comes. Don't learn the hard way."

I was so incredulous I forgot to be afraid that he might want my ID or try to find out about my family. Luckily he did neither. He just tipped his hat and left me at the station.

Now boredom looked good. I sat back appreciatively glad to indefinitely pass the time.

After a while, something made me look up. Lo and behold, there was Michael, the smiling bundle of energy who'd claimed I was his angel. I was actually glad to see him. Interaction with him would distract me for a while. He was a lot less intense when he said *hello* this time, not nearly as demanding. Our conversation flowed easily enough.

What an interesting character! Now that I was willing to talk with him, I took in more detail. He really was quite beautiful. I couldn't make up my mind if his exaggerated thinness added to or detracted from that fact. And he was clearly "street," but very well-spoken in a natural way—a very refined version of Louis from Oakland and clearly much more intelligent.

I asked what he did for a living. He said he was a con man with as much pride as if he were telling me he was a doctor. He lectured about the art of conning and how to roll die so they would come up as you called them every time. Fascinating . . . I was hanging on his every word and really enjoying myself. It was early evening by this point. Earlier he had asked me to lunch—a picnic with him and some of his friends that I had turned down. Now when he asked me to join him for dinner, I jumped at the opportunity.

"Goodbye, Curtis." I waved.

He gave me a nice smile and a nod of the head. He looked at me, then at Michael, and then at me again. There was no judgment in his eyes, just a lot of compassion and good wishes. What an unusual man! His peaceful presence did me an awful lot of good, assuaging many of my subconscious wounds.

Michael's apartment was on the edge of another very chichi neighborhood. I was happy about this. The constant sight of dirt and depression was getting old.

When we entered I was surprised. The apartment was completely empty except for a bed, a boom box, and some cooking utensils in the kitchen. You entered through the front French doors into the living room, which had freshly painted white walls and newly laid beige carpet. To the left was the bedroom, also with French doors, white walls, and beige carpet. Entering the bedroom, you would find the bathroom off to the right; in sharp contrast, it was old and run-down with brown peeling linoleum on the floor and a crack in the glass window. The bathtub was permanently stained and had that old mildew smell, not to mention the mirror, which was full of rust spots and made you look a bit blurry. The kitchen, also run–down, was off the living room through a doorless entryway. Its floor was a tacky brown and white ornate linoleum; the walls, a glossy Navajo white, were full of grease and specks of food. It smelled like an old refrigerator.

Michael was juiced up about having me there. His energy was divergent, not sexual, but kind of clingy, like I was a special spiritual object of his. The word "fanatical" always comes to mind when I think of him. He acted like I was something sent to him from a higher power and he needed to walk on eggshells around me. My anxiety was high. How could I live up to that? He went out to get us some food.

Aaah. What a relief to be alone! I immediately collapsed into relaxation. I could feel how grateful my muscles were to rest on the springy new carpet. I sat with my back against the wall, my legs extended in front of me, my head turned, my cheek pressed to the cool, fresh white paint. It felt so good. I wanted time to stop.

Many footsteps passed the front door. I noticed other building tenants walking by out of the corner of my eye. It dawned on me that there was something strange about them. Curiosity made me sacrifice my perfect comfort. I got up and peeked through the minimal sheer curtains. To my astonishment, most of the passersby were conservatively dressed men with full facial makeup on. How odd. They had lipstick, false eyelashes—the works. This mystery entertained me and had me scratching my head quite a bit. I questioned my sanity for a moment and had to keep checking through the curtain for affirmation until the passing of much time normalized the circumstance. Darkness came.

I was no longer relaxed. The knowledge that Michael could be back at any moment overrode the enjoyment I felt at being alone. I allowed this to prevent me from completely letting loose. I wanted to lie down and stretch on the floor, perhaps dance around and sing. I stifled all these things for fear he would catch me in the act. Finally, he came back and I was glad to see him because this ended my dilemma.

We had a lot of fun. We ate ribs and corn and laughed and talked. He continued his con man lecture. He even demonstrated his die-rolling abilities. My hat is still off to him to this day. The die came up exactly as he called them, time and time again. He showed me how to do it on flat surfaces, carpet, ricocheting off the wall, on felt . . . how you suckered people in by not looking too slick and rolling the die wrong every now and then. He told me stories of how he had almost lost his life because he had won so much money.

This man did all of this so naturally with such passion, joy, and precision. He was in his element. It was a beautiful art form to witness. I loved seeing perfection. It thrilled me. Many hours went by in this manner. It got very late—three or four in the morning.

We had an unspoken understanding that I was staying there for a while. Conversation fell to the wayside. He told me to take a bath or sleep or whatever, to just make myself at home. A bath sounded great, and I locked myself into the bathroom, determined to relax if it killed me. I felt like a failure because I just couldn't. This created more inner turmoil. At least the hot water felt good. Somewhere in the back of my mind, I was starting to worry about the sleeping arrangements.

There was only one bed. I did not want to sleep with him or have sex. This worry quickly soared to the forefront of my mind.

How was I going to handle this? This man was not going to be tricked or manipulated. He was king at that. I didn't want him to feel rejected or angry with me. I had no idea how to handle the situation. I lingered in the bathroom for a long time. I was mentally harping on myself, *Would it really kill you to sleep with this guy? What's the big deal?* I couldn't talk myself into it, no matter how hard I tried.

I finally came out of the bathroom. Michael's whole energy had changed. He was sad, down, far, far away in some world of his own. He looked up at me, and I could see all of that in his eyes. His emotions were stunningly beautiful. He was in pain, and I lived vicariously through his display.

He was sitting on the edge of the bed. All the lights were out. The moon was shining bright through the window, its light hitting him directly, turning his skin a silvery charcoal blue. I was not afraid of this man. The pain he felt was too deep for me, a confused fifteen-year-old, to comprehend on a conscious level. I went over and sat down on the floor in front of him. He looked at me, looked through me. I was meeting his eyes with mine in fascination and a mix of complete understanding and not understanding at all. He kept his feet on the floor but lay down on the bed facing me never taking his eyes off me. He kept saying, "You are beautiful. You are an angel that has been sent to me."

He said this over and over again sporadically. I said nothing. He traced my face with his fingers for what seemed like an eternity. I just kept looking at him. He started tracing my arms and fingers. He commented on how long and beautiful my hands were. There was nothing sexual or ludicrous in his touch. It was very complimentary and savory. He was taking me in. It was the first time I had experienced this kind of poetical touch. I didn't say a word.

I sat on the floor and watched this man in all his pain and sadness taking me in. He was saying things like, "There was a time when a dark man like me couldn't touch a woman with skin like yours." He held my arm up in the moonlight. The vision of his strong dark hand on my lighter arm imprinted itself in my mind. It was an oddly meaningful experience. I watched him fall asleep. I remember the smells of sweat intermingled with a kind of fruity sweetness, soap, and human breath.

All my exhaustion and the need for sleep had been canceled out. I was incredibly high from all the extremes of emotions and experiences I had gone through in the last seventy-two hours. Sitting there on the floor that early morning, feeling the sun come up, and watching this man, I finally had some peace. *Aaaah . . .*

More lessons I'm too tense to learn. I need to relax, but there's a price to be paid when you do that. Maybe that's what I'm supposed to learn.

CHAPTER 12

House of Games

The sunlight brought an eventful, uncomfortable day. Practicality was the architect of all actions taken. Michael had to go make money. He asked me if I wanted to tag along just as he was walking out the door. I silently fell into step.

I was hopeful as we walked. I don't know what I was hoping for, but alas, it did not matter. We had walked back into the dejection of skid row San Diego, leaving me less than thrilled. Alarms were sounding off in my head as we immersed ourselves further into that bellicose organism. I couldn't breathe.

I spent the majority of my time standing in an unmarked doorway with some of Michael's friends. One young black man, Chris, seemed nice enough. He was your stereotypical jock, fun to have around, but not big on conversation. Lots of smiles combined with head nods and the phrase "Right, right, right," offered up entirely too many times either as a question or agreement—you get the picture. The Negro dandy that called himself the Ice Man—meaning he sold cocaine—was a caricature of himself. He was intolerably cocky, lecherous, and tacky in his feathered hat, stretch pants, and greed. I couldn't hide my disdain for him, and this fact drew him to me like a moth to the light. There was Marylou, a young black woman of twenty-two or twenty-three, who also got under my skin. In my eyes she was low-class—coarse. Her crowning glory was a black shoulder-length Supremes-style wig, which paired with her bright red lipstick and her eyes thickly outlined in black brought Halloween to mind. The makeup was crooked and uneven as if applied by a young child—very unrefined. Corruption oozed out of Marylou, pungent and slow like molasses.

So I stood there in all my puritanical loftiness—not easy to do when you're trying to "hang"—while Michael jive-talked with his crew and sized up passersby out of the corner of his eye. He was looking for a sucker and I knew the second he found one. His body convulsed from head to toe in an excitement-induced palsy. This was nothing less than a drug for him.

Michael took off after the "mark" like a chattering-teeth toy and began the art of his con. I didn't quite understand how he picked people. Chris expanded his vocabulary enough to explain how one spotted the guaranteed sucker. According to him, it was usually someone from an upper-middle-class neighborhood dressing down and coming to the high-crime areas looking for gambling action. They were easy to spot because they didn't look or act natural. They either tried too hard to fit in, exuded fear, or carried themselves with an arrogance that was not street-born.

Marylou tried to strike up a conversation with me.

"You f——ked Michael yet?"

"No! And I'm not *going* to!" I responded, embarrassed and indignant.

She pursed her crayoned lips and rolled her smudged eyes at me as if she knew better. I despised her. I didn't even want her to *touch* me. Ew!

Impatiently I awaited Michael's return. He was gone for hours, which left me fuming and highly agitated.

At last, Michael returned. What a relief it was to see him walking up the street! He had another young black man with him. This new guy was clearly stupid. He didn't use his brains, and he wore that fact like a uniform. He was hard, simpleminded, restless, and had an urgent, violent feel to his personality. I was not looking forward to spending time with him. My anxiety level went up.

Michael looked absolutely devastated. I didn't ask him any questions. He must have lost a lot of money. He, his new friend, and I walked back to the apartment in dead silence. I was nervous. Michael was berating himself. I upgraded my impression of his friend from stupid to out-and-out scary. The level of rage and violence that emanated from his person—he was dangerous and reckless. I had never been up close and personal to someone like him—someone like Derek. The newness of Derek's unfiltered energy was simultaneously terrifying and stimulating. This half-frightened, half-fascinated state of being, which I had experienced multiple times in the last forty-eight hours, was quickly becoming my norm, my "MO," my form of entertainment, my drug. We entered the apartment.

Michael and his friend were talking in the kitchen too low for me to hear what was being said. They were definitely arguing. I got the impression that Michael was yelling at Derek for screwing up the con that afternoon. About a half hour went by. Derek the Neanderthal left. *Good.*

Michael sat down on the edge of his bed without saying a word to me. I didn't try to converse with him. He was very far off inside himself again. He put on a Luther Vandross cassette and kept listening to "A House Is Not a Home" over and over again. This made me happy. I could relate to the medicine of music—not exactly the same as my superhero fantasies back in the Ojai attic but . . .

I loved sitting still and hearing the beautiful, soulful, sad voice. Listening to the song loop around again and again created a bubble of comfort around my being. I felt like the music sounded beautiful, soulful, sad, alone, and at peace. Though I was aware of Michael's presence, I did not feel like I was with anyone. I felt full and free to be. The slackness of relaxation slowly seeped into my muscles. The song played on.

After around six hours of hearing the song, I loosened up to the point of inhibition. The song continued to serenade me as I prepared and took a long, relaxing bath. It was better than the best.

I came out of the bathroom wrapped in a towel. Michael came out of his spell long enough to give me a sweet, lustless smile, and offer me a shirt and some pants of his. The shirt was a light smoky blue—my favorite color—and silky. It felt incredible against my skin. Seeing me in his clothes gave Michael an emotion that he worked hard to suppress in my presence. The feeling flitted across his face too fast for me to read but left me feeling mildly alarmed for a split second. I quickly convinced myself it had been in my imagination. Once I was all settled in, he sat back down on the corner of the bed to resume his stupor, the music easing him quickly back to that place . . .

Pretty little dahling, have a heah-har—t, don't let one mistake kee-heeheeheep us a-pah-ha-ha-ha—rt . . .

After many hours (it was early morning, two-ish), I felt the wonderful feeling of being too tired to keep my eyes open. Michael saw this and told me to sleep in the bed.

"Don't worry about it," he said waving me to the bed without looking my way.

I clahaimb the stehyah, and turn the key-ee-ih-ee, oh-ho-ho, palleeze be the-here . . .

I used the blue shirt as a nightshirt. Just as I was fading off to sleep, Michael climbed in the bed in his shirt and underwear. Tension stole my sleep as I froze with nervousness, hoping he would stay on his side of the bed.

Doo, doo, doo, doo, dooh [pause] duhm, duhm, duhm duhm, daaahm, duhm, duhm, duhm, duhmhayh . . .

Time stood still until I heard his breathing take on a heavy, rhythmic quality. Okay. He must be asleep. I'm not naked. It's gonna be cool. I exhaled without sound, shut my eyes, and realized I would fall asleep in . . . a . . . few . . .

But ah—chah—riz not a ha—ha-ha-haowusss, ennahowsiznotta-howme when thehzno-o wontheh . . .

I felt Michael cuddling up behind me. Tension again stole my sleep as I froze with hysteria. If I move away will he be insulted? Is he going to rape me? A few minutes passed . . .

Ah-hahmmm nnot mahnt to livaloho—ho-ho-ho—wnnh . . .

And I realized he was just cuddling. *Yes, yes, he's just cuddling.* I didn't like it, but that's all it was. *Go to sleep. Go to sleep. Go to sleep! You're fine. Stop being a silly baby.* I held my breath and exhaled when I absolutely had to without sound as slowly as possible. Time passed and I could feel that he had a hard-on. Survival mode immediately kicked in, which, in this circumstance, equaled inaccessible emotion and pretending to be asleep. He got out of bed (Yay! He's going to leave me alone.), turned up the music, took off his underwear, and got back in bed.

Wihyi—th mee-hee-hee-hee—yah-hah-hah—heh-heh . . .

He pushed up against me, and I could feel his penis against the back of my thighs. The newness of the sensation broke through my survival mode and I was temporarily able to feel. I felt breakable and young. I *didn't* feel womanly at all. I was a little girl that needed someone to be fatherly and nonsexual. I became simultaneously depressed and stressed. I froze with a hurt beyond tears. I held my breath to the point of bursting and exhaled in silent, quick pants that would not make my body move.

It's drahvin meh crayzay to think that mah baybay woulden bih still lin lahv— with mm mee-hee-hee-hee . . .

Survival mode quickly returned, now in the form of numbness, coldness, and the patience one has when one doesn't have many choices. In my feigned sleep I started inching away from him in miniscule increments. Just when I would achieve my goal of creating space he'd pull me closer than before and try to slowly push himself between my legs. I'd freeze-frame for five minutes then again start my microcosmic journey to the edge of the bed over and over again, just like the song.

Are you gonna beee, say your gonna bih, are you gonna bih, sayyaw gonna bih, ah you gahnah bih, sayyah gahnah bee-yee-yee—, wehl, wehl, weahll, way-ay-ay-eh-eh-ehlll . . .

I kept inching away; he kept pressing closer commenting out loud, "Damn, girl—what you so uptight for? I just want to be close." He kept releasing frustrated sighs and persisting. Tension numbed me into robotic repetition. Inch by eternal inch I won the battle just as day was breaking. Sleep was slowing down Michael's efforts, and I had inched halfway off the bed when I heard the undeniable sound of snores.

Stilllihiihnh—la-ha-haaa—vuh, wi-hhhh-hi—th . . .

I turned the music off.

Now I was on guard duty sitting in the middle of the new beige carpet, arms wrapped around my knees. Michael slept from five to nine in the morning. When he awoke, I pretended that I'd gotten up just before him. He was all smiles and sweetness. I followed suit and did not reference the night's disquietude.

Out loud, that is. Internally I could not stop thinking about it. I had been traumatized. I so much wanted to be a little girl. Something broke in me, filling me with an overwhelming sense of sadness and disappointment. Externally, I smiled politely and made him breakfast.

This time when he went out to run a con I stayed behind. When I was alone I didn't know what to do with myself. I was wide awake. I had this compelling desire to be a really good girl. Paranoia and panic pervaded my being like waves of nausea. I didn't want to be distrusted by Michael or suspected by others of being a female leech. I guess this was my way of taking some control of the situation. It was my job to prove I was a good, clean person. It was not my job to feel broken even if I was.

I scrubbed the apartment from top to bottom. My natural curiosity kicked in as I cleaned. No one could live in a place as stark as this. There weren't any personalizing factors to be found. The only hints of humanity were some massage oils I discovered on the top shelf of the bedroom closet in the right-hand corner. Oddly enough this brought up some feelings of jealousy for me. I didn't want to be sexual with Michael, but I didn't want him to be sexual with anyone.

When Michael returned, he was in a great mood. He sat me down and told me the whole story of how he'd conned the hell out of some guy. He was so happy and animated; I was mesmerized by his persona and the delivery of his words. He presented as so much larger than life, it took me a long while to actually hear what he was saying.

By the time I was able to digest the content of his stories he had moved on to the subject of the massage oils. Like a psychic he stood up, went to the closet, and took down the oils to show me.

"I've got this friend that comes over sometimes. She's good to me. Makes me feel real good." He paused waiting for my reaction. I gave him none.

"It's not love, and she ain't attractive. It ain't like that. She's just good to me."

I met her one night. Beth came by when he wasn't there to drop off some more oils. My presence didn't upset her, and she didn't upset me. The idea of her is what had bothered me. In person she was a warm, friendly, plump black woman—one of those "mom" types that makes you feel taken care of and as if everything is all right. The first impression she made on me was beige, like the carpet. She came and went.

So the first three nights and days with Michael were pretty livable. During the day, I would do things around the house to lessen my feelings of guilt and worthlessness. Early evening was filled with the wonderful void when Michael was lost in himself, accompanied either by silence or Luther's lush voice singing, yes, the *same* song. Then came the mesmerizing stories of con and the drama with which he told them.

That was my favorite time. I could relax in those sunset moments. I could also truly enjoy my late-night baths because I knew my privacy would be uninterrupted. If I came out of the tub and found Michael sleeping, I would sit with my back against the wall in a state of conscious sleep. I imagined this is how wild animals must rest with their eyes wide open. If his breathing pattern changed at all, I would tiptoe to the bathroom and stand at the ready to act as if I had just gotten out of the tub. If he caught me before I made it back to the bathroom . . .

"Aren't you going to lay down?"

I would lay down for the dreaded four-to-six-hour game of inchworm; I treated it literally like a nightmare. By day I refused to anticipate or recognize it as reality because I couldn't afford to let it compromise the waking hours.

Things were different by day four. Michael left as usual to run his con. But he was back within two hours with Chris and the stupid mean guy in tow. Their silence was heavy with doom. Something had gone terribly wrong. No one said a word, and Chris didn't make eye contact or even wave goodbye when he left a few minutes later. Michael and Derek were absolutely livid with each other. They didn't speak. It seemed a fight could break out at any moment.

Hours passed like this with the curtains drawn and no one speaking. I could not stand it because I didn't know the "what" of it. I knew better than to ask. Michael began murmuring things under his breath. Derek heard this, and his anger accelerated. I was scared. He didn't lash out at Michael or anything; he just sat there looking ready to explode, not breathing—eyes darting. He was being blamed for whatever had happened, and they were both in big trouble.

Chris came back that night with some food. They told me to go into the bathroom so they could talk. I tried to listen through the door, but everything was unintelligible. They talked through most of the night, and Chris left in the wee hours. I came out and sat in the corner against the wall for the rest of the night. I wanted to make sure Derek understood that Michael and I were not having sex. No one slept. Michael sat on the edge of the bed while Derek paced. Both men jumped at every neighborhood sound. What the hell was going on?

The next day felt a little better; we made breakfast. That was normal; some of their anger and tension had died down. Good. Derek left for about an hour, and Michael was friendly but not talkative—one more step toward the land of "okay."

Then Derek came back with a whole mess of people: Marylou, Ice Man, Chris, the heavyset chick, and one or two other young guys. Crap! They were laughing and acting carefree—*acting* being the operative word. You could cut the tension in the air. I was seething. I didn't want to deal with these people, especially in such close quarters.

It's funny how intuition works. My anger was born from the intrinsic knowledge that these people were going to be around for a while. I was right. They stayed for three days. The two women were the only ones free to come and go. Everyone else was hiding out from somebody—cops, cons gone sour. Who knows who was after them?

From that moment on, I did not sleep at all. Ice Man was not to be trusted, and Michael changed. He put on a big macho front—acted like Mr. Cool. All that was bright and beautiful about him vanished. I was disgusted. Stress consumed me.

Still, no one would tell me what was happening. Everyone was very condescending to me. The women made me ill. Marylou was still made-up like a clown, bending over in front of the guys, pushing her ass and breasts in their faces. The other woman, Beth, was neat and tidy like a nurse (hair stuck back in a bun, nylons, loafers). She wore a tailored tan coat that she never took off. It was the only thing that distracted my mind; why did she always wear the coat? It was her job/role to mother all these people. This disturbed me emotionally for some reason. Her maternal nurturing seemed lurid . . . incestuous. I couldn't shake off how inappropriate it felt.

Beth had brought a bag of groceries with her on the first day. We were to ration these out.

It was strange how these people operated. During the day, they were noisy, animated—bullsh———ting with one another. At night, all lights were out except the one in the kitchen, and no one talked. Tension and fear ruled. Tempers were quick to rise and nerves were maximally strained; the smell of human sweat filled the air. I did not understand. Why was night such a threat and day so carefree?

By day three their presence unhinged me. I couldn't stand warding off Ice Man's advances or hearing Michael's macho bull anymore. I hadn't slept or even lay down since their arrival. My body was numb, and I recall always feeling cold.

My hunger became irrepressible that third night. Everyone was sleeping. I had already eaten my ration for the day, but I wanted more. I quietly went to the kitchen and cooked a potato and half a hot dog in some grease and ate it as fast as I could. I had somehow convinced myself that no one would notice.

Michael woke up.

"What are you *doing*? Get up! Get up, everybody! Look at what she's doing." He looked so betrayed and disappointed.

Chris felt for me. "Mellow out, man."

The rest of them were filled with glee that the Goody Two-shoes had fallen from grace, and they jeered at me with full enthusiasm. I felt so bad. I wanted to crawl away. No part of me could stand up for myself. I was weak.

I didn't speak to anyone the whole next day and was constantly reminded of my selfish behavior.

"Who the *hell* are *you*?"

"*We* don't need to eat?"

As it turned to evening, Michael and stupid mean Derek decided to chance going out to try and earn some money for food. Michael said I should go with him since I'd taken what wasn't mine. I welcomed the idea. I could rid myself of some guilt and get out of the poisonous atmosphere in the apartment at the same time.

So the three of us went. The fresh air felt good, and we were all temporarily happy as we walked. I was laughing so heartily, releasing days of anxiety through that laughter and chatter. I didn't even notice that Derek wasn't in step with us anymore. If Michael noticed he sure didn't make it clear.

We had been carrying on for about ten minutes when we heard footsteps running up behind us. It was Derek. He looked nervous, excited, and triumphant . . . he was rushing off adrenaline. He had stolen a purse. I was horrified. Michael was pissed. Derek looked at us incredulously as though we were the most ungrateful people on the planet.

"It's money, you fools!"

He opened the purse and turned it upside down shaking the contents out on the sidewalk for dramatic emphasis. Now he was incredulous for an entirely different reason as he sat on the sidewalk counting the money in disbelief.

"Only a f——king $1.85! Mm, mm, mm. It was two white girls. I was sure they would have more."

Michael was beside himself. This guy had complicated things once again over less than two dollars.

"Go!"

He pushed me back in the direction of the apartment as he hissed at Derek, "Now we have to worry even more about the cops! You *want* to go to jail and *take me with*!"

I headed nebulously back in the direction of the apartment in a state of . . . I can't describe the emotion. It was something I hadn't felt before. It was not anger, fear, or shame. This made my skin cold and my heart beat slowly. My feet couldn't move in a straight line.

After walking awhile, I saw the two white girls up the street. They weren't moving very fast. I could see that one was upset, kind of sniveling and dry heaving. The other was comforting her, cursing *niggers*, and running off at the mouth. It felt surreal as I walked past them on the opposite side of the street. Everything was moving in slow motion. Then *bam!* It really hit home that I was with someone who had just robbed somebody. It made me feel low to the ground, useless, and slimy like discarded motor oil. A small part of me was also amped up on all the drama—this roller coaster ride of action and feelings was pretty intoxicating. Reality focused my walk, and I moved toward the apartment with more purpose.

When I got there, it was a strange feeling to be happy when the door opened. Wasn't this the place I couldn't breathe in filled with people that disgusted me? They all knew something was wrong immediately because I was alone. Suddenly I was very important. They pulled me in, bombarding me with questions.

"What happened?"

"Where's Mike?"

"Why are you alone?"

I was holding court and relayed the whole story. This was the first time these people listened to me. I felt special, necessary, and exhilarated. We all speculated as to what could've happened until we heard a key in the door. It was around four in the morning.

I was excluded from the conversation as soon as they entered. Now Michael and Derek were the focal point. This angered me. I was *there* for God's sake.

They hadn't brought back food. Everyone was on edge. Michael was the only one giving Derek a hard time. I guess if there had been money in the purse, the others would've praised him. The conversation worked its way back around to me again in the worst way. They were on my case because I had eaten that extra ration.

"Maybe if you give up that pussy, I'll forgive you."

Shut up, Ice Man. So tired of hearing your sh——t! Wish I had the nerve to say it out loud.

This energy felt like death. I was spinning out in space. I couldn't take it anymore.

Relief came the next day. Ice Man was gone, the two women were gone, the young guys were gone, and Derek was gone. It was just Michael and Chris.

They were full of smiles and jokes. We went out to breakfast. I don't know where the money came from. We drove around in Chris's car. I was happy and fairly relaxed. Things were as lighthearted as day one for a while. Unfortunately, they felt the need to start talking macho smack. I became indignant. They had started talking about the two of them being together with Marylou and all the crazy things she did to them. No detail was spared. *Ew! Gross!* When they parked, I exited the car in a seemingly casual manner and walked all the way back to the apartment in a huff and sat at the front door. They showed up about two hours later.

Chris apologized for being so rude. "Sorry, man. We weren't thinkin'."

Michael and I were not getting along. Seeing the show he had put on when people were there had completely disillusioned me.

"Okay if I take a walk?"

"You can do whatever the f——k you *wanna* do. Fine with me."

I walked down the block and called Curtis collect from a pay phone. He was leaving for Las Vegas the next day. I asked if I could go along for the ride. He liked the idea. We made arrangements to meet at the end of his work shift at three in the afternoon back at the bus station. I felt free and hopeful. His goodness hit me like perfume through the phone. It gave me strength.

On impulse I called Kelly, my friend back in Ojai. She was worried about me.

"Where are you calling me from?"

I panicked. "Can't say, but I'm not in California and I'm okay."

I was still terrified, and very paranoid that she would tell Ma where I was. She was my friend, but I knew that in her rule book, home would be better than me being out here. In my rule book that was not an option. I would rather die than go back. It was not okay to be talking to her, to be in the immediate past. I got off the phone quickly.

Click. I was in the present. Anticipation of the trip to Vegas took over my world. I was almost delirious with anticipation.

I went back to the apartment after the phone calls and tried to act nonchalant. Michael the con artist knew something was up. Chris was easier to deal with so I focused all my attention on him. He and I had fun jive-talking with each other. I was having a good time. He left in the early afternoon. I had no idea how to act around Michael. I just about hated him at this point. He was trying to be friendly. I was not doing a good job hiding my contempt and the fact that I was bursting with a secret.

When night came I got in the bed and slept real sleep for the first time. I don't know if he cuddled up to me or not. I was truly out. The next day had me feeling uneasy and very excited. I was not looking forward to confronting Michael, but I would have to in order to make that three o'clock rendezvous. Luckily, the perfect circumstance presented itself.

Around noon, Chris came over. I had to contain a smile when Ice Man sauntered through the door around twelve thirty. This was going to be easy. Sure enough all the guys started their pissing contest almost on cue. Michael was in particularly fine form. At about two o'clock, I grabbed my stuff and said, "Hey. I'm leaving now."

"Okay, cool. Bye." Chris and Iceman were still laughing and carrying on about some sexcapade.

I left. At the door, Michael's eyes met mine long enough for me to see he was upset. I felt bad, free, and happy at the same time. The concrete became my focus the moment the door shut. As I walked down the street to the bus station, I had a much lighter step.

CHAPTER 13

Out of the Frying Pan

Curtis was there. Wow, was I glad to see him! The feeling was definitely mutual, to my surprise and relief. I guess I expected some kind of lecture on my being so stupid or him telling me I had changed or something. I thought he would be able to see all the *yuck* on me or telepathically know where I had been and what I had done. I expected judgment and rejection. Nothing. He smiled and patted me on the shoulder.

"Glad you made it. I'll be done real soon. Just hang on."

That was it. Hmmm . . . I sat in one of those gray bucket seats where you can put in a quarter to watch the TV built into the chair arm. I thought it was kind of amusing, the built-in TV, even when it was off. I watched Curtis's every move as I waited for him to finish his work. I was looking for a sign of anger or disappointment. He would sporadically look up from what he was doing and beam at me like a proud, protective father. Hmmm . . .

He finished up and was practically skipping as we left the bus station and walked to his car. When he opened the door, it was apparent that he had only recently made an effort to clean it up. The car was free of debris but far from clean as evidenced by the lingering smell of ketchup, mildew, and hair oil. For some reason I loved this. The aroma worked like magic, and I immediately became a kid bobbing my head to the tunes on the radio as we drove to his house.

His house was tired looking on the outside from the faded olive color to the rusted screen door. It was obvious he only kept it looking passable so the neighbors wouldn't whisper. As we entered, my mind started conjuring up visions of how the car must've looked the day before, and I had a newfound respect for Curtis's efforts. His house was dirty, messy, and beyond comfortably cluttered. The kitchen floor was caked with dirt, leaving the actual color of the linoleum in question. I detected the same odors—ketchup and hair oil, Afrosheen to be precise—among many others. You couldn't even see the dining room table or the counter space; there were so many dirty dishes, bills, car parts, half cups of coffee, etc., everywhere. He had shelves upon shelves full of books and clothes pressed on hangers thrown carelessly over chairs, or should I say thrown carelessly over piles of stuff on chairs.

"Here."

He cleared me a chair by unceremoniously brushing its contents to the floor with the side of his arm and put me in what looked to be the living room.

He talked to me in a rushed manner out of the side of his mouth while concentrating on the tasks at hand. "Have a seat. Make yourself comfortable. The others will be here soon. I've got to get my stuff together. Please, answer the door when they come. Thanks."

I nodded. The whole scenario tickled me to no end. There was no way I could make myself comfortable in the living room; it was so crowded. The floor was covered with tools and junk. I found myself sitting completely upright with my feet tucked under me because there was no place to put them unless I stepped on something. He stopped packing for his trip just long enough to bring me a cup of hot tea. All conversation ended. He was busy.

I had a hard time not bursting into laughter as I watched him bustling around getting things together. The neat, orderly manner in which he packed his things panned out in hilarious contrast to the state of his house. It was obvious that Curtis didn't travel much. He was excited like a little kid. I found him very endearing and refreshing. He actually sprayed cologne inside the suitcase before he put his clothes in—anything to separate the specialness of the trip from his everyday life.

A carload of people pulled up: two colorful "present" black women in their midthirties or early forties and a heavyset good-natured black man who waited by the car while the women came up and rang the bell. I was afraid to answer the door. I thought they might think I was a tramp or a pain in the neck; however, Curtis had asked me to get the door, and I didn't want to disappoint him. I opened it shyly.

"Well, who are *you?*" asked this very serious *sistah* as she and the other lady pushed into the house. I could tell she had put her outfit together for the drive to Vegas. Oversize two-tone sunglasses, a lightweight sleeveless faux lamé knit turtleneck, three ropes of beaded costume jewelry around her neck, golden lipstick, French manicure, and a pixie-blonde wig. She meant business. The only problem she had with me was that I might slow down how fast they got out of the house and on the road.

Before I could respond to her question or the other woman could get a word out of her mouth, Curtis came buzzing into the room, making quick introductions.

"Ladies, ladies, please! We have to get moving. Say your *hellos.*"

The two in unison: "Hello."

I said, "Hi."

"We're giving her a ride to Vegas. Now chop, chop! We've got to get a move on."

Curtis linked arms with the ladies and steered them back outside to transfer all their suitcases from their car into his car. It was funny to watch them argue and holler at one another about the best way to make everything fit into the trunk. The men exchanged a conspiratorial smile. They seemed to be *misloading* the suitcases on purpose just to get a rise out of the ladies who were waving their arms, shaking their heads, and barking orders. They were having such a good time jiving and bullsh——tting. It made me smile. I liked this kind of bull—Comedy Central right here.

Everybody came back in huffing and puffing, harassed, and glowing with sweat. Now his ladylove was affectionately harping at

Curtis because he had a few loose ends to tie up. "Curtis, get your dress jacket, baby. This is *Vegas*! *Please* tell me you are not wearing *that*."

Everyone laughed. He rolled his eyes, grinning quickly to show it was in jest (he was either very kind or slightly afraid of his ladylove) and ran off to change. The other two were making loud comments about Curtis and his girl. Good-hearted camaraderie continued to dominate the atmosphere.

And no one was paying attention to me. That felt wonderful. They weren't ignoring me. It was as if I was part of the family and didn't need any special treatment. How warm and relaxing! I loved it, relished every second of it.

"Come *on*, y'all. We *gotta* get this show on the *road*." Curtis shooed everyone toward the door.

They stopped joking around long enough to get in Curtis's car, which I now noticed was big, American, and burgundy in color.

I remained very quiet the whole time I rode with these folks. It was more important to soak up their warm, fun, good energy, and I greatly appreciated being part of the backdrop. It felt *neato*. They laughed and talked about gambling and shows all the way there. No questions came my way. I got through the entire five-hour drive to Vegas without giving my name or knowing anyone else's besides Curtis's. We stopped once because Curtis was tired of driving. The other man drove, and Curtis slipped into the back seat with his friend's girl and me. I kept stealing sideways glances at him because of the joyful anticipation on his face. His cheeks were rosy for God's sake, and his eyes gleamed so much they almost looked crossed. It was adorable.

When we reached our destination, he asked me casually under his breath, "So where are we dropping you?"

"Um . . . the Flamingo Hotel," I told him. I had always thought that was pretty when I used to visit with Ma and Sis. We pulled up in front. It was still pretty, its fuchsia, pink, orange, and golden lights all ablaze. In fact, it was intimidating—*gulp*.

I got out of the car. He gave me a big loving smile and grabbed my hand as if in a goodbye handshake; he had slipped me twenty dollars.

"Thanks . . ."

"No sweat. Happy to give you a ride. Take care."

The car door closed, and I watched them drive off. I was on my own.

I watched the burgundy back end of the vehicle driving away until I couldn't make it out anymore. I tried to recall all the light-hearted, sassy energy of these people and embody their spirit so I could come up with a plan—no such luck. The best I could do was keep a stiff upper lip.

I turned and looked directly at the Flamingo Hotel. I just couldn't make my feet step toward the door. It was so beautiful, so daunting. Instead, I decided to take a walk and started heading up the strip.

The sky was gray, not quite fully dark, but it was warm outside. I was nervous. I felt like an intruder and very see-through, as if everyone knew I was homeless and wandering. I remained intimidated by the big glamorous hotels and the many people walking up and down the strip. Everyone seemed so energetic and adult. I walked until I found myself in front of the next familiar place, Circus Circus, where Ma, Sis, and I used to always stay, then turned back around, and walked back down the strip on the other side of the street. There was nothing else to do but repeat my actions—back and forth. As the night grew completely dark, I shortened my distance, walking slower and slower. I always made it to Circus Circus, but after several hours, my nebulous trek went no further than the first two long blocks in the opposite direction.

At any rate, it was working. No one looked at me twice, and the number of people on the sidewalks did not thin out until about five in the morning. That was fine because the sun would be up fully by seven. So, I'd made it. I'd made it through the first night.

And during that night, my body kind of disappeared. I wasn't hungry or thirsty, hot or cold. I didn't need to use the bathroom. Nothing. I even kind of stopped hearing. I felt the presence of the people brushing by like ghosts on the crowded sidewalks. My feet kept moving, and my eyes liked sparkly things—the neon signs, jewelry in windows, street signals.

But now the sun was coming up. And with that came the return of my mind, feelings, and sensations. The heat was strong. I took off my Dolman-sleeved navy blue sweater, which I'd had on over Michael's smoky blue silk shirt. That was better. But I was self-conscious carrying the sweater in the bag with my little red journal. It made me feel truly like a young runaway kid, homeless and embarrassed. My embarrassment started morphing into alarm and fear. What was I going to do? That damn sweater in the grocery bag was completely exposing me to myself. I was nowhere. I had no one. *Sh——t!* I couldn't handle feeling so scared and insecure, so my mind started looking for someplace else to focus.

I shoved my free hand into my pant pocket, felt the worn twenty-dollar bill, and immediately got very excited about it. Twenty dollars to spend exactly as I please! All I wanted was a change of clothes. I was convinced this would solve my dilemma of the sweater in the bag. Not only would I have fresh clothes but I would also have a clothing shopping bag instead of a grocery bag to carry the sweater in, and that would make sense and be much more together looking. I walked back down to a big mall on the right side of Caesar's Palace. I knew it was too early to be open, but I wanted to look in the glass doors and see what kind of stores were inside. It would occupy my mind, and I could plan.

I peered through the glass main entrance with both hands shading the sunny glare from my eyes. *Ooh, look!* The second store on the left was a *Clothestime* store! Their prices were always good. I for sure could find something to buy. Yay! The mall opened at ten. I just had to kill an hour or two at the most.

I re-embarked on my perpetual trek to back-and-forth land. My job was to find out exactly what time it was. That was all I needed to have a little more confidence, some reason to do something. I was still too nervous to talk to people directly. I didn't even feel comfortable walking into a convenience store to gaze at a clock. Why this meekness? I don't know. I was not going to have any problem walking into *Clothestime* when it opened. Not sure why everything else was totally off limits . . .

The heat was harsh. I needed to walk very slow and take breaks so that I wouldn't sweat up the silk shirt. I meandered impatiently. Now that I had a goal, I was in a hurry. The sun became even more formidable. I was squinting, and everything had a gray faded-out hue, like it did when you were at the beach for too many hours.

A short shiny black man came into my peripheral vision just as I was about to pass Caesar's Palace and the entry to my new obsession, the mall. He was very dark and skinny, with his hair all slicked back. His hair was shiny, his clothes were shiny, his skin . . . *He* was shiny. Smiling, he said, "Hey, sister, you're beautiful! What are you doing?"

Stupidly flattered and full of bluster I said, "Walking the strip." I realized what that sounded like as soon as it left my mouth, and I saw that he took it that way.

He fell into step with me and started relating to me like a partner in crime. I listened to him go on and on for a while. He was hinting at *this* and *that* but never saying anything too specific.

"You wanna get out of the small time? Go in with me, and we can make a lotta cash."

I was very offended. "You've got the wrong idea, *sir!*"

The sun played off the folds in his shiny, satin shirt emphasizing each gesture and the word it went with as he talked. "But you *said* you were *walking* the *strip*, babe!"

We argued back and forth. My meekness had disappeared. Goals were useful. There was no way I was going to let this shiny little man interfere with my shopping. That new outfit was gonna save my life, and I was ready to fight to the bitter end for it. Mercifully, he laid off.

He backed up with his hands in the air. "Okay, okay. You're just lookin' good, and I wanted to offer you the opportunity of a lifetime. That's all. Ain't no thang. But"—he looked me up and down—" . . . damn. How about a picture? Can I take a picture of you by the palace here?"

"I've got errands to run." I turned away, and if I could've flipped my hair, I would have.

I stomped toward the mall, and miracle of miracles, the main entrance was open! It must be ten o'clock. I zoomed into *Clothestime* getting ridiculously happy at the sight of all the sales racks—half-price here, 60 percent off there, pink tag sales . . . a shopper's paradise! I was going to take my time and stretch that twenty as far as I could. I went through each item on each rack very carefully to make sure I didn't miss a thing. I tried on sweater after sweater. Anything that was eleven dollars or under and fit me, I tried on. The saleslady was young and indifferent. She sat behind the counter filing her nails with an expression on her pouty face that showed how put out she was by her job. Good. I wanted to enjoy my process privately.

I found a lightweight baby blue V-necked sweater that looked perfect for $6.99. This made me realize I might be able to buy some pants as well. I went through all the pant racks, but everything was just a little bit too much. Then, there they were: one pair of tan corduroys marked down for the fifth time to nine dollars. They fit perfectly. I put on the baby blue V-neck. They looked great together! Not to mention the fact that my moccasin loafers went perfect with the ensemble. Wow, I had done it—a whole new outfit with money to spare!

That should've satisfied me. But it didn't. My mind kept going back to one red and white T-shirt I had tried on. If the sales tax weren't much, I may be able to get it as well. I did the math in my head. If my calculations were correct, I was only fifty-six cents short. Only fifty-six more cents and I could have everything.

I became fixated on the red and white shirt. I felt I must have it. I looked on the floor of the dressing room. Maybe somebody had dropped some change or a dollar. No. My wheels were really turning.

Knock, knock, knock. "Everything okay in there?"

"Yah, yah. Just trying to make up my mind." I heard her walk back to the register.

I had never shoplifted before. I thought once wouldn't kill me. Jasmine, one of the most popular, coolest girls back at school in Ojai, used to brag about shoplifting. I kept rationalizing, and soon I found myself putting on the red and white T-shirt. I tried to wear it under Michael's silk shirt. Too snug. Couldn't even get my arms through the sleeves. I put it over the silk and under my navy blue cowl-neck sweater, which was roomy but also dark with a loose weave. I could see hints of red through the knit of the sweater. I was feeling sick. I just *had* to have that T-shirt. You don't understand. I *had* to.

Conversation in my head:

The only reason I can see the red is because I know I'm wearing the shirt. She's too busy filing her nails to notice. Besides, I don't look like a thief. It's just a stupid shirt to them, less than five dollars. She won't care even if she figures it out.

"Miss?"

"Yes. I'll be right there. Can't quite make up my mind. Two minutes. Just have to get dressed."

You can do this. People do it all the time. If you have this shirt you can wash out the others and rotate your clothes and then you'll be able to get a job and save money and get an apartment. You have to do this.

Aha! There was the motivation. Shirt equals three days' worth of clothes so I could get a job and save money for my place. Now I had nerve. I walked up to the sales counter. I was hysterically nervous. I put on a fake smile and put the pants on the counter with the light blue sweater.

The five-foot-eight sales clerk with her dirty-blonde ponytail looked up and then stiffened. She said without hesitation, "I'll have to ask to see what you are wearing under your sweater."

My hands started to shake. I was sweating. I was looking at the floor. My voice was just above a whisper.

"I'm sorry. I'm sorry. Please don't turn me in. I've never done it before. Please!"

I was breaking down. My body was shaking. Tears were in my voice. I couldn't go back home. If the police came I might be sent back home.

She was looking down as well in the same stiff pose. "Can you pay for it?"

I took out the twenty dollars and trembled it onto the counter. "This is all I have. I'm . . . not living anywhere. I need a change of clothes. That's why I wanted the extra shirt." My voice was thin. I tried to look up but couldn't.

"Go take off the shirt." She was in the same stiff pose.

I went back into the dressing room and took off the shirt. I was relieved. She wasn't going to call the police. *Thank God!* I was so ashamed. I didn't want to face her again. But I had to in order to leave the store. If I didn't leave the store soon, she *would* call the police. I came out after ten minutes. She had already rung up my two items and put them in a bag. She handed me my change and looked toward the door. "Now leave and don't come back." Her voice was even and devoid of emotion.

"Thank you." I looked at her. "I'm sorry. Sorry. I'm so sorry."

She pointed toward the door without making eye contact.

I hesitated for a moment needing to see that she understood I wasn't a bad person. She refused to look my way. I grabbed the bag off the counter and left the store. I couldn't breathe right. My heart was pounding so hard I thought it would burst.

How could you do that! You're weak! She should've sent you to jail! You little . . . sniveling . . . I hate you! You deserve to be hurt! Idiot! Fool! That's not you! Why would you try such a thing? Un-f——cking-believable. What a dolt you are!

And so the self-berating went. I was so into it, I didn't even notice my shiny skinny little fellow had returned until he took hold of my elbow. I gave him all my attention—anything to get my mind off what had just taken place.

"Just a picture, sis. Just one."

"Oh, okay."

We went in front of Caesar's Palace, and he took a few pictures of me. I couldn't have smiled any bigger. I was so grateful for the distraction. Then we started walkin' and talkin'. I was almost feeling like my old self. We had walked into a big department store, and he started talking about big money and how it was to be had in this town. Here we go again.

"Come *on*. I'm willin' to share this opportunity with you. People would *kill* for somethin' like this. A sister like *you* shouldn't mind gettin' your hands dirty with a little drug money."

I was furious. He still thought I was a hooker! I gave him an angry look and started walking the other direction. I wouldn't speak to him.

"I don't mind what you do. Why are you so teed off?"

I got so mad I started to cry. This time he didn't back down. He kept talking his sh——t. Finally, a bus was passing. He hailed it.

"You can't fool me, but you can keep foolin' your*self*."

He got on the bus, and that was the last of him.

I let his words really sink in. Now I saw myself as even more stupid, weak, cheap, and low-class. I felt I deserved punishment and hardship. I also thought I should've seen all of this coming. *Am I really this big of an idiot?*

The day's insistent heat demanded my attention. I exhaled. I was glad to be alone again. A shift was occurring inside me. I was back in the present. Oh yeah! I had a new outfit in a bag in my hands. I walked for a long time in search of a filling station. I was still too intimidated by the glitter of the big hotels to think of changing in one of their public restrooms. I finally found one.

I went into the restroom, changed my clothes, and promptly forgot all my problems. I looked really pretty in my baby blue V-neck and corduroys. I would've been perfect if it weren't for my hair. The heat and lack of hair products was starting to dry it out. At any rate, I was once again feeling giddy, free, and adventurous.

Now I walked up and down the entire strip, slowly going in and out of every external nook and cranny. I was subconsciously pumping myself up to break into the major leagues of the big hotels. I was still afraid of their grandeur. But my new clothes made me feel like I had the right to participate a *little*.

I sat down on bus benches and listened to people's conversations. I ended up in conversation with several people myself. I learned that from the Barbary Coast up was the prostitution section. According to some, the price went up block by block. I watched women pick up men.

I was captivated by the homeless older men. They were babbling—drunk or mad, I don't know which—about how they'd lost everything. I could stare right at them, and they would go on and on unaware of my presence. It was like watching TV.

My favorite time of the day was when it was just turning dark and all the Vegas lights went on. The sky was an electric blue. The air was hot and dry. The people were ready to live and let live.

I've always been a night person. The darker it got, the more confident I became. Having regained a small portion of my teenage cockiness, I thought I was pretty smart coming to Vegas, the twenty-four-hour town. I figured my plan was foolproof. Yeah, that's right, I said it—my "plan."

Now that I was adjusted and ready to enter the big hotels, I found that I had not foreseen the obvious. I wasn't in the Stardust for more than five minutes when the security guards were on me saying, "*No* one under twenty-one allowed." I hadn't counted on that. Sis and I had never been bothered on those past trips with Ma even when she had left us alone. I tried a few other places. Sometimes I wouldn't be noticed for half an hour or so, but I was always noticed eventually.

I started getting into that numb, slow-motion space again. My small bubble quickly burst. So tired and worthless feeling was I. Things weren't working out. I stopped thinking. I skipped right past worry to nothingness. I didn't feel anything. All I knew for certain was that I couldn't walk all night again.

At about three in the morning, I decided to give the hotels one more try. This time I went directly into the restrooms and into a stall. At last, I found a longer temporary respite. I couldn't fall asleep, but at least I could sit and rest my body for two to five hours before anyone would bug me. The hot lights, gaudy carpeting, or fake marble, accompanied by excited voices of women, young or old, coming and going out of the lounges maximized my feelings of worthlessness. They were on vacation, and I was hiding. The wallpaper changed patterns in the various women's lounges from hotel to hotel, but the voices always sounded the same. The voices sounded slightly inebriated with the underlying thrill of mischief in them—ladies looking for a little harmless trouble so they could feel like they had lived on the edge for at least a weekend. I felt so abnormal.

Come morning, I was back outside. The sun was up, and I was walking around as if in a trance. I didn't notice anything around me really. I couldn't feel my body. I didn't feel hungry. No one tried to talk to me. I passed about three or four days in this state. I wasn't sleeping, but at the same time, I felt as if in a constant state of sleep. I wasn't eating at all. I drank water in the hotel bathrooms when I washed my face, not consciously (you need to drink water in order to stay alive) but as a by-product of throwing water on my face.

On the fourth or fifth day, I suddenly "came to" for some reason. I was very hungry. I decided to walk downtown and go to the Golden Nugget. Ma, Sis, and I used to go there for strawberry cheesecake as a treat. I think it's strange that I didn't eat for three or four days when I had a couple of dollars in my pocket. My logic had short-circuited. Anyway, I went downtown drawn by the memory of the infamous Golden Nugget strawberry cheesecake. It was an extra-long walk—longer than I thought. By the time I reached the Golden Nugget I was back in that space of feeling too inferior to walk into such a fancy place. It had a little more class than the hotels on the strip. I stared at it for a while and left.

Initially I walked deeper into the downtown area, but it was ugly and scary to me. There were so many people and hardcore gamblers around. The intensity level reached uncomfortable heights. I felt violent things could happen more readily here and quickly headed back to the strip.

One smaller hotel/casino caught my eye on Las Vegas Boulevard because it was bright red and had a million dollars on display in a glass case, mostly in small bills, coins, and poker chips. It was called *Vegas World*.

In my self-hating frame of mind, my logic went thusly; because it caught my interest and I wanted to go in, I wouldn't let myself. I also wouldn't spend my money on food even though I recognized I was very, very hungry. I walked all the way to the farthest end of the strip to the Tropicana. There was a slightly smaller, less flashy hotel across the street from it. *Okay, loser, you can go in there.* I entered.

I located the bathroom immediately but lingered in the entrance hallway just in case it was remotely okay to do so. The security guards didn't kick me out this time. I inched closer to the tables. All was well. A little closer. No problem. I was excited and decided to watch the gambling up close—a welcome distraction, indeed.

Two men started talking to me. Their casual demeanor was very inviting. One was a nondescript brunet about six feet, and the other was six feet two inches, graying with a mustache, and a thin build accented by his vintage Hawaiian shirt. I found the latter one attractive and was thrilled that he was paying attention to me. Neither of them smiled once while we talked. This suited me perfectly. Their understated conversation was the only kind I could respond to without stress. The gray guy won a little money at craps. They asked me if I wanted to have lunch with them in their room and watch a little TV. Sounded great to me. We went upstairs.

It suddenly became very uncomfortable. There was a lot of tension in the room, and I did not know why. Not uptight tension. They were waiting . . . impatiently.

"Here. Get what you want."

I picked out a turkey sandwich from the room service menu. There were grapes and wine on hand. They told me to help myself and poured some wine. I had two grapes and stopped. I didn't want them to think I was hungry. We didn't talk. We sat in a row on the couch. All of our eyes were glued to the TV. The food arrived. We ate in strained silence. I ate about half of my meal even though I wanted the whole thing. I didn't want them to think I was a pig. And I couldn't really enjoy the food anyway because of the unease in the room that weighed heavier and heavier with each passing moment. My stomach was in knots. They kept pressing the wine on me. I finally picked up the glass and took half a sip. Why did people like this stuff?

I was ready to sit back and watch TV for a while. The fact that I wasn't walking anymore made it worth it to ignore the inexplicable apprehension. They asked a few questions. It felt strange. I knew they weren't interested in my life, so I couldn't understand. Why the questions? Then the gray one said, "You look tired. Why don't you go rest a while? Take a shower if you want. Everything's right around the corner."

Sounded good to me. I jumped at the opportunity and was all smiles at the kind gesture.

"Thanks so much. That's really sweet of you guys."

The hot water felt great, and I relaxed in spite of myself realizing how totally sleepy I was. I dried off and put the corduroys back on with my blue silky shirt, the one from Michael. I hadn't been lying there for five minutes when I felt French kisses, a hand pulling up my shirt, two hands around my hips, and a knee between my legs. I opened my eyes. I was terrified, speechless, and motionless. The gray one looked in my eyes and stopped. His friend stopped.

"What? Don't you know why we asked you up here?"

The other guy said, "Aww. Come *on! Really?*"

I said nothing.

"Are you really that stupid to think you were going to just watch TV?"

The gray one looked like he couldn't believe anyone could possibly be so dumb. They got off me. They were disappointed, disgusted, and angry.

"Get out of here. You were just teasing. Stupid little girl! I thought you knew what a man needed. What a f——king waste of time." Gray guy again. It was all he could do not to hit me.

I was humiliated. They went back around the corner and turned the TV on loud. I couldn't find my shoes. It was so awkward. Mercifully, I stepped on the pillow on the floor and felt my shoes underneath it. I grabbed my bag of stuff and walked out without saying a word or looking up.

I was mortified, frightened, shocked, and, at the same time, stimulated by the drama of the situation. What had just happened? I cursed myself for not understanding why they had asked me up to their room. I also realized I was lucky to get out of there without being raped. The close call of the situation was highly provocative to me. I knew if I had screamed or talked back, I would've been in a much different situation. The outcome would've been nasty. The whole thing scared me and excited me to no end.

I walked out of the hotel. I walked fast trying to put some distance between myself and the experience, to get it off my skin and out of my mind. It wouldn't leave; hence, continual self-criticism persisted and grew—and grew and grew.

The sights of the strip were no longer distracting or entertaining. They were old hack at this point. I needed something to focus my attention on. It was too painful to be inside myself with continuous torment and self-loathing. I kept stopping in restrooms to see if I looked pretty, happy, and normal. I was pleased with my appearance except, of course, for my hair. It was dry and breaking off, getting shorter and shorter. I tried to ignore it. I concentrated on what I liked about my appearance. I liked my body, my skin, my eyes, my lips . . . This would make me smile.

Getting exasperated by my own vanity, I turned my thoughts toward the weather. It was strange. The skies were cloudy and gray, but the temperature was warm and the air dry and still. The gray stillness was irrationally upsetting to me. I walked on with direction but not on a conscious level. I ended up in front of the one place that had caught my eye and the one thing at this point that could preoccupy my every thought: *Vegas World* with its million-dollar display.

How easily we forget. Distractions, no sleep . . . sleep . . . no food . . . food . . . just call me a sucker. I can't get rid of my needs. I am still human. How unfortunate . . .

CHAPTER 14

In Sheep's Clothing

How late in the day it was I couldn't tell. All I knew was that the sun was up, though behind clouds, and my legs were tired. I sat on the red padded circular bench surrounding the money behind the glass and distracted myself alternately with people watching and greed. This was one of those rare moments in life when inner certainty creates an almost gleeful smugness because you know for a fact the stars are aligning.

You see, I had stumbled upon the perfect distraction: unattainable money inches from my face; freaky people, in fact the whole world walking by for me to judge, admire, or make up fantasy lives for; a padded bench for my tired body to sit on; and a built-in game. There were a million dollars in that case, and I had nothing but time. The counting could go on endlessly.

I started with the ones . . . *one, two, three, four, five, six, seven, eight, nine, ten, eleven, twelve, thirteen* . . . I would've loved that money . . . *fifty, fifty-one, fifty-two, fifty-three, fifty-four, fifty-five* . . . All that was separating me from it was a thin piece of glass . . . *one hundred and seventy-two, one hundred and seventy-three, one hundred and seventy-four, one hundred and seventy-five . . . Is there any way to count the bills carelessly piled on top of each other? Hmmm . . . well, if I can estimate how thick a pile of twenty-one-dollar bills looks loosely stacked, then I can make a pretty good guestimate as to how many ones are in a two-inch stack. Not feeling ready for that yet. I'll switch and count pennies for a while . . . one, two, three, four, five, six, seven, eight . . .*

Life became mercifully simple for about five days. I'd get up and wander around a bit, and as soon as I got tired, I'd work my way back to the money display and count or just stare. The front of the hotel was open-faced to the sidewalk, so I was sort of sitting inside and outside at the same time. This mixed indoor/outdoor environment created an otherworldly effect. Reality was suspended. I also believe this is why no one bothered me or shooed me away. I was having a good time. I bought some *Red Vines*, my favorite candy, and would suck on a single piece until it was almost completely dissolved and then chew the last little bit. Aah, pure satisfaction!

Sleep did not come. I think my body was asleep and my mind was awake just enough to keep my eyes and ears open. I felt nothing, not achy, or tired—complete desensitization. When the darkness of night filled the outdoor backdrop, the whole casino would get a second wind. Sounds and "sparkliness" were magnified, stimulating me enough to help me stay awake. I was infatuated with this alternate painless, feelingless universe. My favorite nights were those when a dry warm wind would swirl through the casino. The breeze stirred up the cigar and cigarette smoke long enough to wake up my nose with their surprisingly pleasant odors before quickly disappearing. This brush with the melded environments, with this desert dreamland—it was a simply breathtaking zone to live in.

As the days went by it dawned on me that I was seeing some of the same people walk by. Obviously they were going to or coming home from work (not easy to tell in twenty-four-hour Vegas). Ah hah! Yet another layer of entertainment: counting the familiar faces. Six in particular always walked by: two female card dealers, one casually dressed fortyish fellow with a briefcase, service workers (maybe maids or bellboys), and one young man, maybe around twenty-seven. I couldn't tell what he did. Sometimes he was in a Hawaiian shirt and jeans, once in a blue mechanic's jumper, and once in a black button-down shirt and Dockers.

On the third day, the twenty-seven-year-old started to nod in acknowledgment as he passed. I nodded back. On the fifth day he spoke.

"Hello. Nice day isn't it?"

"Yeah." I turned away. Talking was not part of my alternative world.

On the sixth day he asked me to come home with him for dinner. I was crestfallen.

He talked on and on. I hardly heard what he said. His face came to life, and his teeth kind of flashed against his dark skin and black goatee when he smiled. I was protesting. My objections sounded monotone, and I reminded myself firmly, *No! Talking is not part of this.* I hushed and blearily observed the manic animation on his face in utter horror.

I was in a complete panic from head to toe. This wasn't going to be a safe place to sit anymore. Where else could I go? I hadn't finished counting the money. I wanted to finish counting. His thirty-minute onslaught ended abruptly with a shrug and him turning on his heels and quickly walking off. *Whew!* My heart was pounding dangerously like a fist thudding to get out of my chest. *Okay . . . okay . . . okay. He's gone. You're going to have to leave, but you can count the money for twenty-four more hours. He has to work, so you have one more day to count. It's okay. Have another Red Vine.* The artificial flavor and gummy texture worked like an IV sedative, and I slowly went back down into my tranquil state of *one, two, three, four . . .*

On the seventh day, I realized too late that I had not kept good track of the time as I saw *him* getting closer in my peripheral vision. I tried pretending not to see him, but he got directly in my face and started the whole dinner thing again. *No, no, no! Go away!*

I mustered up one wave of energy. "Get out of here! Leave me alone!"

I saw the color of anger come into his face. Passersby were ogling our exchange. He became more angry and embarrassed. I got up and started walking away, but he walked right with me.

He was deeply offended and more determined than ever. His voice shook with emotion. "Look, I'm not trying to pick you up. I'm concerned. I don't like seeing a beautiful young lady like you out here on the street. I'm a married man for God's sake! I'm looking at you like a daughter. If I had a daughter out here, I would hope some kind stranger would take her in and try to straighten her out. I've talked this over with my wife, and we just want to help you out. You could stay for a while, or call your family, or get a job. At least come have dinner with us tonight, and get some food in your stomach."

He seemed sincere and was upset to the point of tears. He hadn't mentioned a wife before. That fact gave off the scent of safety. I didn't want to go home with him. I liked the floaty peace I had found. But I also knew it was now permanently destroyed. It didn't exist anymore. *I want to finish counting the money.*

He was standing so close to me I could feel the energy emanating from his body and could almost smell the salt in his tears. The water in his eyes was different than the pathetic alcohol-laden tears Clifton had cried back in Syracuse. It stunned me. It shamed me. I dejectedly fell into step with him.

He was *so-o-o* happy. I was surprised how quickly I assimilated back into the here and now once I'd made up my mind. Now that I was *here*, I enjoyed it. He was very image conscious and was trying hard to be charming. The walk to his place was short and overloaded with content.

He and his wife lived in an apartment directly behind *Vegas World*. She looked less than thrilled when I walked in. She was a defiantly heavyset black woman who seemed to have forgotten how to smile—glasses, an old worn-out housecoat, and potato chips topped off the stereotype beautifully. Dinner was your standard soul food—fried chicken, corn on the cob, collard greens, biscuits, and gravy. She acknowledged me by saying to her husband, "Get her a plate."

My stomach couldn't handle a heavy meal. It felt like I'd swallowed a whole person. Now that I'd eaten her food, they both gave me their version of small talk.

Him, "How long you been in town?"
Her, "An' why you need a place to stay?"
Him, "Why Vegas?"
Her, "Don't you have a *family?*"

I sat there feeling sick and trying to answer their questions. Thank God they didn't ask in too much detail. I was nauseated. I was concentrating on not getting sick. I couldn't think up a good story. I understood in no uncertain terms that the truth was not an option. Whatever I told them they seemed to buy it. At last I was free to take a shower.

I turned the water up high for noise cover and heaved up dinner with full force, uninduced—much better. I can't explain how good it felt to do that. Light-headed and giddy, the hot water running down my body, I was in heaven. I was in a state of delirious high. I stayed in that shower for the better part of an hour and would've continued but for the shouts of Ms. Thang.

"Girl, get your ass out here. You ain't gonna be using up all *my* hot water!"

Ummmm, darn. My fun was ruined. I'd forgotten all about them and everything else for just a moment. I put on a terry cloth robe they gave me and came out. He had tea for me. It was the first time I had tasted black tea with sugar and cream—delicious. I only knew about tea with lemon. Cream and sugar had never occurred to me. Yum.

"I'll make a pallet for you to sleep on in the living room."

For some reason I really liked the sound of the word *pallet*. It sounded sophisticated, grown, so English or European. The child in me, Miss Make-believe, was coming out—me sitting here in a robe, sipping tea, waiting for my pallet to be made. I happily ran with my fantasy, escaping into its absurdity. He finished my little pallet. She forced herself to say "good night." He was all smiles and "sleep tight."

"Sweet dreams, sweetheart. Are you all comfy?"

I smiled.

They went to bed. I went to sleep.

Wow! Did I sleep! Not long, but deep and hard. I slept so hard it didn't even feel good. I felt like a boulder pressing with full gravity against concrete. I slept so hard it hurt.

And I woke up completely disoriented. The clock said five. The light coming in was that light, which could either be night turning into day or day into night. I felt paralyzed, literally stuck to the floor like a mouse in a glue trap. My body was so fatigued it felt like my eyes were the only part of me that could move. I wasn't cold or hot, but I could feel the sensation of air on my legs. This got me curious because I knew I was covered with blankets. I wanted to see but it seemed such an effort to lift my head up and look. I tried to see out of the corner of my eye, but all I saw were mounds of blanket, and just beyond that, I saw the couch with something big and brown on it.

I felt it took a lifetime for my eyes to focus and see what was there on the couch. It was him, and he had a big hard-on in hand which he was massaging with full force. He was staring at me with his eyes focused on the lower half of my body. I was too shocked to react and consumed by the heat of misery to the point of suffocation. He was concentrating so hard, he had no idea he was being watched.

You know when you have those dreams where you're trying to scream for help, but you just can't get a sound out or move at all? That's how I felt. I must've moved my head some because he suddenly jumped up with his finger to his mouth.

"Shh. Shh. I didn't touch you none. I was just looking at your pretty legs and your hot little ass. See what you do to me?" he whispered with a smile, pointing to the sticky glob of cum on his abdomen. "It ain't no thing. I really hope you let me massage those pretty legs sometime maybe as a way of saying thanks for helping you out. Shh. Shh. Just go to sleep. Ain't no harm done."

He scooted off to his bedroom. I heard them f———cking.

I pushed myself up on my elbows to see why I felt the breeze. The robe and blankets had been pushed up to just above my waist and my bare ass and legs were hanging out on display. I felt so degraded and humiliated for about ten seconds, and then I felt nothing. I had tucked away those bad feelings somewhere nice and neat inside.

They got up around eight thirty, and we had breakfast. Nothing was said. They bullsh———ted with each other, and I sat quietly nauseated by the food—waiting for an opportunity to purge.

On his way out the door he twisted and leaned back in, one hand on the door frame, his weight balanced on his back leg, and said, "I'm bringing my cousin back tonight, and we'll get you a job."

Flash of white teeth against the brown skin, his eyes drunk with some kind of imagined power . . .

I sat and watched soap operas with her. She was all sulky snot-tiness and refused to interact. Her attitude afforded me the luxury of judgment. I called her names in my head (*fat bitch, walrus, nasty-assed dumbass*). She left after about an hour.

I went and threw up my breakfast. I didn't keep one meal down in that apartment. I just couldn't. *Bvlaaah, bvlaaah.* And she knew I was throwing up. I could hear her bitching and moaning about it sometimes while I was in the bathroom heaving. *What the hell is wrong with this crazy bitch!* I didn't care. She never said a word to me directly or made eye contact.

That evening he came back with his cousin: a tall, lanky red-headed rooster, all silk shirts and hair gel. He was chewing me up with his eyes. I felt completely devoured.

"Hey, Rhonda, what's up? Dave told me he found somethin' on the way home. I *see* . . ."

His presence gave me access to my hosts' names.

"You start work tomorrow night at Chauncy's place."

"What'll I be doing?"

"It's a club. You'll be waiting on tables. Probably make some good money in tips."

I latched on to the idea immediately—once again, something to look forward to.

Bedtime that night was uneventful. Dave's cousin left, and I was unmolested. The reason I knew this is because I didn't sleep a wink.

The next day was a little more challenging. Rhonda went to the store for about twenty minutes. He asked me to get naked; he didn't want to touch but just look.

"No."

With anger, "You could show a little more appreciation since I got you off the street *and* a job, *et-ce-ter-aaaah*. And you'll be starting that job tonight. Yah. That's right. The job *I* got choo."

Silence.

He laughed. "Chill, man. I'm just joking."

I pushed my shoulders down a little and tried to appear unperturbed. He came toward me and grabbed my ass while pushing me to the wall with the weight of his body.

"Relax, girl. I ain't gonna hurt you. I just want to feel your fine young body. I love Rhonda, but she's starting to spread out with all that weight. Stretch marks everywhere and big saggy tits. Lift up your shirt and show me those pretty little tits."

I closed my eyes and a few tears squeezed out, my hands at my side.

He looked incredulous.

"What the hell you crying for? Ain't no one hurting you. Leave your *damn* shirt down then. Sh——t. I can see how perfect they are anyway. The perfect mouthful. Just enough to grab on to and suck."

His mouth was about an inch from my breast as he was saying this.

Keys in the door. Rhonda and a friend. Relief. He was in the kitchen before the door was halfway open.

"Hey, Rhonda, I'm going for a walk. I'll see you later."

"Make sure your ass is back here by seven because you are *starting* your job tonight."

I got out fast wandering aimlessly. Nothing in this situation was simultaneously scary and stimulating. That dynamic was gone forever. I had turned yet another corner, and I knew it. But I wasn't relieved and leaving. I'd gotten fixated on the job. And I recognized that I needed to do something. No, I wasn't leaving. That job was necessary. I could catch a bus or get a hotel room with the money. Teenage cockiness is resilient, so even though David was a threat, I saw that he was also a coward, and I thought I could maneuver that. Rhonda had some kind of hold on him that he would not jeopardize. Her hold and his ego would keep me safe. As long as he knew I wasn't interested, he would not do anything except make me uncomfortable.

It was only about eleven thirty, so I had lots of time to kill. Boredom set in fast. I felt worn and torn. That one night of sleep had reminded my body of its needs. My legs just weren't cooperating. I was also dodging people, men especially, and cringed whenever it looked like someone was going to say something to me. Indeed, all the worldly charm of my walkabout had left. Now it was all about the job—the job. I had a job. It was finally time to go back.

"Here." Rhonda tossed some mascara and rouge my way.

I applied it and got in the car with Dave.

We drove a long way past downtown heading west. Once you got past the strip, it was all over in Vegas. The neighborhoods we passed went from humdrum, to shady, to downright scary in a matter of minutes.

Dave was stoic and almost gentlemanly as we drove. Strange, how he seemed to need my approval. I didn't give it to him. I didn't want him to feel comfortable around me.

We parked in front of this decrepit-looking little bar with a couple of neon beer lights in the grimy windows. Once inside, it was bigger than it had looked from the outside though just as dingy. That was all the time I could allot to the décor.

All eyes were on us and then on me the second we entered. The eyes told me I was surrounded by rough customers, a sea of hardcore *niggahs*. I spotted the one straight shooter in the room, an older black man with a neat white afro, thick black-rimmed glasses, and overalls. He gave Dave an angry glare and said to me, "How old are you?"

"She's old enough for this place, Chaunce."

Chaunce rubbed his chin. He was weighing the risks.

"All right. Put her behind the bar."

Dave walked me to the bar with a comical level of swagger. What a joker!

"It's her first night. Chaunce wants you to show her the ropes."

The bartender gave me a neutral nod, opened the bar gate to let me in, and started my education. He taught me three drinks: rum and coke, scotch and water, and gin and tonic and, also, how to pour shots. My whole existence was caught up in learning these drinks. The *A*+ student was on task. I was myself again for those ten minutes.

"Okay. Good, good. Fill an order."

My first customer was a wild-eyed Negro with an untamed afro poking out every which way from his black baseball cap.

"Would you like something to drink?"

"You, baby. Why don't you climb up on the bar and give me a full shot of your pussy juice. Am I in heaven fellas?"

There was laughter all around.

The bartender hissed his frustration at me. "Who the hell *are* you? Girl, you can't be polite to these dicks. You better get tough quick."

He didn't look too optimistic.

After a few more indecencies came my way, my teacher signaled to Chaunce. "Man, get her out of here. I can't work and watch her at the same time. There's gonna be trouble."

Chaunce peeled me off a ten from a huge money roll.

"Come back tomorrow and wear something that makes you look a little more like you been somewhere."

David and I drove back to the apartment.

"Girl, you f——ckin' up. Don't you want this job? You better be straight tomorrow. No f——ckin' appreciation." He shook his head and tsk-tsked me.

I felt bad. I handed him the ten dollars for food or whatever. He snatched it and continued shaking his head.

"Why are you guys back so early?"

He walked past Wanda and pointed over his shoulders at me with his thumb. She was leaning forward with hands on hips, spitting her words at me.

"What's wrong with you, girl? Get it together. We can't take care of you forever so you better make this job work!"

Nighttime . . . bedtime. Two hours later the bedroom door opens. Out comes David. Hand over my mouth.

"Sshh. You're gonna show me some thanks. I'm sick of your f——ckin' bullsh——t."

Hands all over my thighs, my ass, getting too close to . . .

"David, where are you?"

"I can't sleep, baby. I'm upset at this kid out here who ain't even said *thank you* for all we done, and now she's f——ckin' this job up."

His fingers inside me rubbing his hard dick against my belly while he's shouting back to Wanda, "Maybe you can help take my mind off it, baby. Let me come in and show you all the man you got."

He pulls his fingers out of me and puts them in his mouth, giving me that knowing look like we have a sexy little secret. He goes into the bedroom and leaves the door open. I hear them f——cking. I feel nothing.

Morning—they came out and started telling me how ungrateful I was. At last she mentions my throwing up.

"Wasting good food. People are starving and you're in there heaving good food down the toilet. You f——cking crazy or what? Neurotic light-skinned bitch. Probably trying to f——ck my husband too. You don't deserve our help. Ten *goddamn* dollars. Probably pocketed fifty. David, why are you helping her? She ain't nothing but trash."

He gave her a fleeting kiss, put his arm around her, and turned to me.

"Because we're good Christians, baby. You better start praying, little girl, before God throws you away like your Mama and Papa did."

Ouch. That hit me squarely on the jaw.

"I'm sorry! I'll be back in time for work and try to be better."

I left. No food. No shower. No fight. No ego. No feelings. No energy. No good. Numb.

I was in a walking mood. It suddenly seemed I could walk for days. I didn't think I was going back. I walked to my favorite places on the strip: Flamingo, Stardust, Caesar's . . . I decided to go to the last hotel before one hits the desert, which, at that time, was the Tropicana.

The left-hand turn off the strip there looked interesting. It was a wide clean-looking street, and I wondered what was down it. *Hmm . . . distraction.* I walked down it. A row of newspaper machines, shiny and new, caught my attention. They looked pretty. I walked up to them for closer inspection. I noticed the date on the paper and realized that it was my sixteenth birthday.

My sixteenth birthday. Wow! I was beyond excited. *I'm sixteen!* I sat down on a bus bench and started tripping out on this sudden realization. I'd been wanting to be sixteen for the last five years. Cool, man! I was grinning deliriously from ear to ear having my own private party there on the bus bench. It took about an hour for the glory to wear off and the walls to start crumbling. They crumbled fast. I was sixteen. Today was supposed to be one of my most important birthday celebrations—sweet sixteen, friends, candles, cake, a special dress . . .

And where was I? Who was I? And how sweet was I? These thoughts set me off to tears—not weeping, panicky, or crocodile tears, but real tears. This was not the way it was supposed to be. I was in a bad place with no one safe to turn to.

I got up and started walking again. Maybe that would help me stop crying. It just made things worse. The faster I walked, the deeper I breathed. Soon, I was sobbing. I couldn't see through all the tears. I sat down on the sidewalk and surrendered to my emotional torrent. A big black car stopped and rolled down the window.

"You need some help, girl?"

The questioning voice scared me, and my startled body convulsed before I quickly and clumsily stumbled to my feet. I emphatically shook my head *no, no, no.* My voice was too choked with tears to speak. I crossed my arms, and started walking blindly in the opposite direction the car was driving. I knew I couldn't acknowledge my tears by wiping them away. That would confirm my weakness. I peeked back surreptitiously and waited until the blurred blob of car was out of sight and collapsed to the cement again. Honk! Honk! Honk! Honk! It had circled the block and was back. Damn car.

"Look, kid. I can't leave you out here crying like this. There are evil people out here. They can really hurt you. Please, get in the car, and get yourself together. Do you want to end up dead? Please! Look, I'll park the car and go. You can sit in the car by yourself and lock the doors until you stop crying, okay? Please! You can't sit in the middle of the sidewalk like that and cry. You're in Vegas, girl. Here, wait a minute."

He parked the car, not on the curb but perpendicular in a random driveway that led nowhere. It was paved up to the chain-link fence and then dissolved to sand in an empty unpaved, unkempt lot.

"I'll be back in an hour. The passenger door is open. Get in. Lock yourself in, and cry till you can't cry no more. Knock yourself out. Bye."

He left. I got in the car and locked the door. The smell of spearmint air freshener was overwhelming—so overwhelming it interrupted my despair.

How the *hell* could he stand to drive around in his own car? The car itself was cool, a nice big black Cadillac. I'd never been in such a nice car, and it was immaculately clean. But that smell . . .

And the man? He seemed strange. He had a big perfectly groomed afro, glasses, jeans, a navy blue T-shirt, and muscles, lots of muscles, but it didn't look right. I got the feeling that he was much less showy than his look, like he was really supposed to be small and quiet but had too much of an inferiority complex to let himself be so.

But back to the smell—the powerful spearmint scent canned my pain—all gone, no more tears. Little did I know how literal that thought would be. Those were the last tears to come out of my eyes for the next five years.

I decided I would sit there for forty-five minutes and leave before the man came back. The car was comfortable, but I had to address the smell. The windows were electric so I couldn't roll them down. I opened the door a little to let the air in. I kept it open by sticking my foot out. That was a little better. I started stressing because I didn't know how much time had gone by—fifteen minutes? Twenty minutes? What if I stayed the full hour by accident and had to deal with him? The car door opened. He was back early.

"It hasn't even been thirty minutes."

"I was worried. Thought you might be hungry. Here. I brought you some breakfast."

He handed me a takeout platter of pancakes, orange juice, sausage, and scrambled eggs—one of my favorite meals. I enjoyed every bite of it. We sat there with the car doors open, me stuffing my face and him sweeping out the perfectly clean floor on the driver's side with a whisk broom and emptying out the perfectly clean ashtrays. I finished my breakfast.

"Liked that, eh? Now, what're you crying about?"

"Today's my birthday."

This was a powerful moment because it was the first truthful statement I had made to anyone in the last month and a half.

"Well, happy birthday, baby. Today's your lucky day. Let's go celebrate."

"*No.* I can't. I have to go to work."

"*Oh*, you got a job? Well . . ."

I started getting all cocky and indignant saying I had a job and a place to live and Lord knows what else. I was improvising heavily at a cringe-worthy rate. The food was kicking in, and I felt strong enough to be Ms. Fifteen, no, sixteen-year-old know-it-all, again, for just a minute. He was highly amused by my self-righteous outburst.

"Ex*cuuuse me*, ma' am. I just got the impression that you had nowhere to go. You don't look like a bum, but those raggedy-ass shoes are making you look a little improper. You should come with me to my sister's house and borrow a nice dress to wear to *work.* That's all I'm trying to say."

Wooh! He had just struck a whole set of nerves. I really didn't want to look homeless. He'd wounded my pride more than he knew when he dissed my favorite shoes. Apparently, my love for them was clouding my vision . . . *borrow a dress* . . . If I had a dress then I could show David and Rhonda how serious I was about trying to do better and make them eat their words. A dress—then I would have three changes of clothes.

"Okay. Where does your sister live? And what's your name, Mister?"

"She lives down the road here, and just call me Slick. All my friends do."

How colorful. Just like a character in *Charlie's Angels* or *Barretta*.

Slick was an interesting person because I couldn't read him. He didn't act like other men when I met them. He wasn't full of compliments, and I didn't see any sex in his eyes. He seemed very casual, yet very alert at the same time. He had that look that people get when they're trying to memorize something. His vibe was totally nonthreatening. I think he was about thirty-five, thirty-seven years old. I was actually finding it hard to stay tense—a miracle.

We drove ten more blocks and parked in front of an apartment complex. He told me to wait in the car. He went up the stairs and knocked. An intensely irate but beautiful black lady answered the door. She had such a pretty face and nice loose curls down to her shoulders. I guessed her to be around twenty-eight.

She was mad as hell and letting the entire apartment complex know about it. She slammed the door in his face. He came back down to get me.

I was afraid to meet her. I didn't want to be an imposition. She seemed so angry. All I wanted to do was make her smile. He knocked. She opened up. She had wild, stormy eyes. She looked at me like an untamed animal trapped in a corner that I was shining a flashlight on. She really was something else—a wildly beautiful woman, mad and scared as hell. She didn't say a word, just opened the door wider and stepped out of the way. We entered. She slammed her way down the stairs running and stomping. Wow! If I were a man, I would've been in love with her big eyes, perfect tawny body, and more perfect coffee-colored skin and full rose lips. She'd made quite an impression on me.

Slick didn't give me any explanations. He walked me to the closet and told me to pick out a dress and some shoes and then went in the other room and turned on the TV. I was so happy. The closet was full of beautiful clothes, and this man wasn't going to even try to kiss me. I *could* relax. It *was* okay.

I tried on several things and settled on an ivory crepe dress with a turquoise floral print. It made me look incredible. I had never looked so beautiful. *Phenomenal . . . wow! Look at me! Woo hoo!* I grabbed some tan pumps. They were one size too small, but I was used to squeezing my big feet into shoes that were too small. I looked so damn classy and grown-up, I just couldn't believe it. I changed back into my old clothes and put the dress and shoes in a bag.

"Okay, Slick. I found something that'll do. Is it okay to take this?" I tried to act all casual and cool.

"Yeah, man. You need a ride home?"

He was sitting with his feet up on the coffee table, leaning back with his hands behind his head, the picture of relaxed normalcy.

"Umm . . . okay. No, wait. I have an errand to run at *Vegas World*. Could you drop me there?"

"Yeah, sure. Ready? Let's go."

He dropped me off in front of my home away from home, with the million-dollar money display.

"Okay. If for some reason you need a place to stay, I'm just letting you know that my sister's leaving town for a week, and you could chill out in her pad while she's gone. Here's my number." He handed me a scrap of paper. "Call if you need a place, and I'll come and get you. Take care, kid. There are bad people out here that are just looking for an opportunity to use up a young girl like you. Be careful, man."

"Thanks, Slick." It was heartfelt.

"Bye-bye, man. Hey, I'm gonna need that dress back at some point. I'm trusting you with it."

"I promise I'll get it back to you soon."

He laughed and shook his head as he drove off.

A plan started spinning in my head. I'd work at Chauncy's for a week, save the money, and stay at Slick's sister's place. When she came back, I'd have enough money to go somewhere, or rent a room for a week, or something. I didn't want to see Dave or Rhonda. I thought I had everything figured out and started getting really full of myself. I even got it in my head that I could find my way back to Chauncy's on my own and wouldn't need a ride from David. I started walking west with great purpose.

I got past downtown and through part of one of the boring residential neighborhoods to an ugly industrial area. A car stopped.

"Need a ride?"

The guy looked harmless enough. I got in. The day had turned into a hot one. He was blasting music and had all the windows down.

"Where are you going?"

"Far west side."

We had to yell at the top of our lungs to hear each other over the rock music.

"I'm not going way the hell over there."

"Well, just take me as far west as you're going, thanks."

He was fortyish, white, what I call a short-haired hippie—full beard, jeans, and a flannel shirt unbuttoned with a T-shirt inside. He was obviously an intellectual, probably a professional student, a philosophy major by my guess. I assumed he was harmless because he was white.

"Do I make you nervous?"

"No."

It took half a second for me to completely numb out and flat-line my responses. Survival mode.

"Are you afraid of me?"

"No."

"I can do whatever I want to you. This is Vegas."

Silence. Observant, survival mode silence. I looked closer at the light in his eyes. They were on fire. He was insane.

"I could turn this music up louder and shoot you in the cunt"—I noticed the gun on the seat now—"I could ram this gun up your ass"—he laid his hand on the gun, his fingers twitching in a strange nonrhythmic pattern—"and pull the trigger, and f——ck you, and chop you into little pieces, and bury you in the desert, and no one would know. Nobody would care. Am I scaring you now?"

No reaction. Ma had trained me well. Those early morning copper bracelet drills were coming in handy.

"See all that sand out there?"

I looked out the window at the sandy expanse.

"I can bury you. I don't even have to bury you. I could just throw you out there dead. You could scream as loud as you want to right now and no one would do anything."

We started slowing down for a stoplight and out the window I flew. It didn't occur to me to open the door. I just jumped out the first escape route I saw and started running. I don't know why he was talking all that sh——t to me, but I wasn't going to hang around and find out.

I ran until it was physically impossible for me to continue. Then I bent over gulping for air, hands on knees, a sharp pain in my side, squinting as I looked forward.

All emotions and thoughts were now checked. I would not register that interaction as reality. Next?

Sigh. It was going to be a long walk back to the strip. I kept thinking about how good I was going to look in my dress tonight, the dress that was in the bag I was still holding in my white-knuckled, death-gripping hand.

The dress was the motivation in my stride. Step, step, step, step . . .

At last, the money! I stopped and tried to rediscover the peace of counting. It was forever gone, but I did glean a minimal comfort from the familiarity of the money display. I walked behind *Vegas World*, took a deep breath, and knocked on their door. Dave opened it looking very disapproving and mad.

"About f——cking time!"

I walked in.

"I've got a dress to wear tonight."

"I told you she pocketed the money. How else could she have a dress?"

There was Rhonda throwin' in her two cents.

"Come on. You can change at the club. We've got to go now."

Dave and I headed out. As soon as he hit the gas pedal . . .

"What's wrong with you? I'm just trying to help you out. You're so fine and acting like you ain't never been touched before. I know you ain't innocent. I know you've been f——cked *real* good by a whole bunch of men, probably a few today even. It's natural, you lookin' so fine and all. Stop pretending like you're a nun . . ." and on and on.

We got to Chauncy's, and I went into the bathroom and changed. Smashing! I came out. Trouble. Chaunce wouldn't even look at me.

"Put her on the floor tonight instead of the bar."

Redheaded Rooster was there shooting pool. He looked up at me while he took his shot. His eyes never left me.

I tried to take some drink orders. There were hands on my arms, my legs, accidentally brushing across my breasts as I walked to the bar . . . I just kept smiling and trying to be businesslike. I came back with a tray of drinks. I had to walk by Red. He was making me very nervous. I placed another drink order at the bar and started making my way back with the tray full of drinks. Red knocked the whole tray out of my hands.

"Dance with me," he said pulling me close with his hands on my butt, squeezing so hard I thought he was going to pull my skin off. "You motherf——ckers go to the bar and get your own drinks. I'm gonna dance with this foxy lady now."

They all laughed.

I didn't know what to do. I just froze. No one was going to help me. He whispered all kinds of "sweet nothings" in my ear about what he was going to do to my creamy skin with his dick and his tongue and how he was going to beat the hell out of me 'cause "it would feel so good to hit such a fine bitch." He grabbed me all over with hard, heavy hands while circling us around like we were dancing. It only hurt for a minute, and then I felt nothing. I shut out all the touch. I saw his hands moving all over my body but didn't feel a thing.

"You gonna like it, bitch," he said, yanking my hair hard.

"You gonna love me by the time this night is through."

David sat at the bar watching and getting drunk. I . . . was . . . numb—didn't even know how to think. Red's friends were yelling at him to finish the pool game.

"No, no. I got my hands full—real full."

Chaunce came out of the office.

"Hey! That girl's got a job to do. Let her work, *goddamnit!*" Red let go, oh so reluctantly.

I picked up the tray and took more drink orders, all smiles. "Drink?"

Now I knew better than to say "*What* would you like to drink?"

An hour went by without any problems. Then some new guys entered the bar, six of them, f——cked up and clearly looking for trouble.

A little time passed and, all of a sudden, things were different. I don't even know what caused the confrontation. One minute I was filling my drink order at the bar, and the next, I was pulled off-balance from behind and watching a baseball bat slamming down hard on my right arm. I took a few more hits before I grasped the situation. I was so surprised the pain didn't register. Then guns—lots of guns—and I found myself kissing the floor, and the strangers were gone. The guy with the bat apologized, "Sorry you got mixed up in that. Weak motherf——cker grabbed you too fast."

Everything went back to normal. A couple of roosters were strutting and fluffing their tail feathers, but that was it. Chaunce came over.

"You can call it a night. See you tomorrow."

I cashed out—fifty-seven dollars.

Dave and I left. We got in his car.

"Pretty exciting night for you, eh, girl? Sure do look fine. I enjoyed that little show you put on with Red. Turned me on. Let me see those pretty thighs. I ain't gonna f——ck you. I'll just get me a few handfuls."

He had me pressed up against the car window. His alcohol breath was in my face, hands squeezing my ass and thighs, breath coming in short pants while he was trying to stick his tongue in my ear and mouth. His whole body tensed and arched. I was just lying there like a rag doll seeing nothing, feeling nothing. He started the car, and we drove back—no conversation, only the sound of the car engine.

We walked in, and I went straight to my pallet, burying myself in the covers. They were talking. I heard their voices, but the words weren't coherent to me. I was far away. I . . . was . . . numb.

Early morning came. I opened my eyes and rose from something that may have been sleep. I certainly wasn't rested; I certainly felt exhausted. My body was numb, but I was definitely in touch with one feeling. I was sick of this sh——t. Dave and Rhonda came out of their room. The coffee was on.

"Hey, did you make any money last night?"

I gave him forty dollars, secretly hanging on to seventeen for myself. He handed the money to Rhonda.

"Better, but still, she should be bringing home more than that, Dave."

There was Rhonda, throwing in her two cents again.

"She'll do better tonight now that she's getting to know the place."

"I'm not going back tonight."

"Oh, yes you are."

"No. I won't."

"What the hell is wrong wit' you, girl? You got a job, a place to stay, food to eat . . . You think you're gonna lay around here and be kept?"

There she was again.

"Absolutely no appreciation . . .," Dave said rolling his eyes.

"Did you tell her about last night?"

"What's to tell? You went to work and you got paid." He gave me a threatening glare. "Ain't nothin' to tell."

"Well, I'm sorry, but I can't go back. I'll find a job on my own."

"Yeah, right. How old are you? What city is this? I got you the only real job you can get and you're just throwing it away."

He slammed out the front door shaking his head. Rhonda stuck her nose in the air and turned into the bedroom with a slam.

I changed into my baby blue V-neck, grabbed my bag with the silk shirt and crepe dress and my little red notebook, and left.

Little girls shouldn't play with grown-ups. They're bad people. Remember, girl? Lesson number one, man, don't relax . . .

CHAPTER 15

Into the Fire

Unfortunately, leaving didn't make things better. I was no longer easily distracted from my thoughts, especially those surrounding David and Rhonda. Somewhere in the back of my mind, I felt I was better than them. I wanted to go back and show them that, maybe by getting my own job, or . . . I don't know. Nobody else on this adventure had rankled me like these two.

What a confusing form of arrogance. My teenage logic could not separate the issues. I felt guilty for my conceit, yet at the same time I was certain I was a higher quality person than those two. I wanted to squish them like the weak nasty slugs they were. Oh, well.

I was on the road again. And it had turned into a hot day.

Walking past the familiar sights felt simultaneously comforting and a bit unnerving: Caesar's Palace equaled little shiny man; mall equaled failed shoplifting humiliation; Flamingo equaled first time being kicked out by security for being underage . . . It was like watching a movie of someone else's flashbacks.

The last time I'd walked the strip, I had been in a food-deprived, dream state. Now, I was fed, alert, and disturbed. My anger at David and Rhonda was good for something. It had jerked me out of some of my apathy.

I couldn't find Slick's number. How could have I lost it? I turned every leaf of my little red notebook with forced patience, hoping it was stuck there somewhere between the pages. I shook out all my clothes, digging through every pocket—nothing.

Should I just show up at his beautiful sister's doorstep? No. It would look so pathetic. I had too much pride. Better to simply walk down by the Tropicana and loiter. Slick would eventually drive by. It could look like a chance meeting. I talked myself out of this as well—way too obvious. Oh well, I'd figure something out. No hurry.

I had seventeen dollars left. My spirits lifted. I had clothes, money, the freedom to do whatever I wanted, *and* I was better than at least two people on the planet. That day, the first trip into a bathroom where I caught my reflection in a full-length mirror elated me. Simply put: I was absolutely gorgeous and had a phenomenal body. No matter how much I wanted to down myself, I couldn't. I really did look the best I'd ever looked in my life thus far. I must've admired myself for over forty minutes—sideways, front, back, up close, from a distance—pure teenage narcissism in its full glory. The only imperfection was my hair. The heat was drying it out but not to the point of embarrassment, yet.

I almost skipped as I roamed around that day bouncing off the fluff of my inflated sense of ego. I enjoyed the Mojave heat and really felt my stride. I even enjoyed being complimented—no cringing today.

The first few hours of darkness were fun as well. I defiantly went back to the Vegas World money display, almost daring a run-in with David to occur. My ego bubble burst as soon as I sat on the familiar padded bench. The touch of the sticky red vinyl brought me into the moment immediately. My mind was temporarily clear and nonreactive. All fantasy states were on hold. I pulled out the little red notebook and began to write for the first time in a long time.

The past entries had been sparse, just a few short sentences from when I first left, about the breakup with David. They weren't emotional, just a sort of factual documentation: *David and I are no longer together. Told me he doesn't love me and . . . wonder what Ma and Sis are up to? I'm in Vegas now . . .* I had written the date down every day (up until February twenty-second) whether I'd followed it or not with words. Tonight I wrote, *Slick was right. There are a lot of messed-up people out here. Luckily, I haven't been hurt by any. It's either luck, or I'm pretty good at getting out of bad situations. I haven't told anyone my real name. I've gotten great at making up stories on the spot . . .* I went on in this manner for a paragraph or two and then put the notebook away.

It was enjoyable watching people go by. They looked happy and excited all in their dress-up clothes, going off to see shows. The Midwestern tourists looked strangely plain under the bright lights. You could spot 'em every time.

Yeah, this was a good night.

In my peripheral hearing, the sound of a car horn began to nag at me. I looked around to see where it was coming from. Whoa! There was Slick smiling and leaning out the window of his big black Cadillac on the other side of the boulevard. I was so happy to see him I didn't even try to act cool. My body language wagged like one big puppy tail.

"Hey, Slick!" I yelled at the top of my lungs. "Wow! Hey, I've got your dress. Thanks for the loan!"

I walked across the busy street with the dress in my outstretched hand. He laughed an "aw, shucks" laugh as he took it.

"Glad it came in handy. How've you been doin', kid?"

"Okay."

"Still workin'?"

"I quit. It wasn't a very good job. Had to leave where I was staying too."

"Sounds like you could use a hand. Hop in."

I did.

Whewee! There it was. The obtrusive mint smell was diffused a bit by the cologne of a couple of young hard bodies that were with him. He introduced them, but I couldn't hear their names over the loud music and the squeal of car tires as he accelerated.

"We got a few stops to make first, okay?"

"Sure, whatever." I had to shake my head at my own ridiculous attempt to sound casual. I wasn't fooling anybody, including myself.

We dropped the guys off at a house party. Now it was just me and Slick, and that loud sugar-sweet instrumental R&B music. We stopped at his sister's apartment. She wasn't there. *That's right.*

I remember. She's out of town. He threw the dress playfully in my direction.

"Put that dress back on so I can be proud of you."

It still looked greater than great though he didn't seem to notice. Off we went.

We pulled in and parked at a ritzy condo complex. Slick's face was contemplative as he shoved the gearshift into park and turned off the motor.

"Hey, kid, just be cool in here all right? And don't let Ice Man get you alone."

Another Ice Man . . . I knew what that meant. I was feeling very worldly. I was in with the hardcore people now getting an *A* in street smarts. I felt my jaw set with a little more confidence, the tick of the cooling car engine punctuating the subtle adjustment.

We got out and rang the bell.

A thin pale blonde dressed to the hilt opened the door. I was introduced to two more thin white women with perfect makeup and elegant dresses. Their clothes were more classy than sexy. They looked picture perfect but were very much nonpersonalities—diaphanous shadows. All I remember about them is their perfect skin, eyes, and hair, like life-size wide-eyed dolls, beautiful, pale, thin, and rich. I was fascinated by their ghostly, gauzy aura. They barely said "hello," and one was on her way out.

Ice Man was a handful. *Cockadoodledoo,* what a big shiny black rooster all dressed in white with a red feather in his perfectly tilted white fedora! He was sugar daddy, pimp to the bone with a diamond-studded gold tooth and all.

"All right, Slick. What you got for me here?" he said bugging out his eyes.

"She ain't for you, Ice. I just brought her by so you could take a look."

"Oh, okay, man. Ain't no *thang.* Does she have a name?"

"Naw. You don't need to know her name because you ain't gonna see her again. I'm keeping you far away after tonight."

"Well, madame," he said kissing my hand and then holding it up and away as if we were about to dance. "I can see you are clearly a prized possession. It's an honor to have such a perfectly beautiful woman in my presence. Please, make yourself at home, and if there's anything I can do to make your visit here more comfortable or luxurious, do not hesitate to ask."

What fun! I was feeling like a queen.

The condo was a palette of slate grays with white furniture and black and red accents splashed across the room. I was poured a drink that tasted like candy, a Tom Collins I think. I sat in a big comfy white leather chair while Ice and Slick sat at the dining room table talking and laughing. Their conversation was audible but indecipherable because of the constant hum of the air conditioner. The women would come and go. They never joined in. They were just on their way in or out, upstairs or down, haunting the house. Ice noticed me watching them. He spoke a little louder.

"Do you know what they're doing?" I shook my head "no."

"They're going out to meet men. They make a lot of dough. You are looking at some of the most exquisite, expensive call girls in the US, man. They make thousands of dollars in one night."

I could hardly believe it. They looked so classy. They looked just as perfect when they came back as when they had left. I couldn't believe they were out f——cking and sucking.

"*You* could be making that kind of money, girl, real easy. My clients would turn cartwheels over a sweet, fine, young thing like you. You see how these women are living?" He stretched his arms out for emphasis. "They get the best of the best. And they ain't f——cking no junkies. It's high-class, man, politicians, doctors, stars . . . Slick, you shouldn't hold this chick back, man. Let her make some *real* money."

Slick just laughed and shook his head.

I took it all in, in amazement. I would never do such a thing, but the fact that I could and was being offered the opportunity made me feel super grown-up and sophisticated—very powerful feelings for a fifteen, no, *sixteen*-year-old girl. There are none more powerful at that age.

"Well, I've had enough of your bullsh——t for a while, Ice. We're going now."

He stood up to leave, and I followed suit.

"I'll be right back."

Slick went to the restroom. Ice was on me like glue.

"What would it take for me to have that perfect body of yours? How much? I can make you feel real good. I got a big dick, baby."

He grabbed my ass and pushed up against me throwing me off-balance into the wall. He looked like a little devil cartoon in his white hat with the red feather, the hanging lamps below eye level, the slate walls absorbing all the glow of light, leaving only his greedy little beady eyes to shine.

"You feel all of that? I want it to be yours for the night. Slick can't do *sh——t* for you. *I'm* the man and don't you forget it."

Slick was back. "Get off her, man."

Ice raised his hands in the air, backing off.

"You can't blame a man for trying. She's too fine." To me he said, "Remember what I told you. Think about it."

Off we went. Slick's quiet protection drew me to him. No drama. He never raised or lowered his voice—just an understated intensity that was clearly respected. I had never met people like that.

I was happy, a little buzzed off the drinks, and smug because I was a woman and sexy too. I glimpsed at Slick's watch as he drove. We had been at Ice Man's place for more than six hours. It had only felt like two. *Chauncy's* and David and Rhonda seemed like a bad dream now. Wow, did that seem long ago and far away. We drove back to his sister's house.

"I'm staying here tonight because the sun'll be up soon. We'll set you up with some groceries in the morning. Sleep tight, kid."

He pointed me to the bedroom and flopped himself on the couch. I felt perfectly safe as I drifted off to sleep. What a nice normal feeling. I've never enjoyed falling asleep more in my life.

The next few days were wonderful for me. I spent most of my time alone in that apartment. Slick would stop by once a day for an hour with some friends, always men. The guys treated me like a kid sister. They would come in noisy and joking with each other, turn on a ball game, and yell and scream at the TV, or we'd go to the park and I'd watch them play ball. Somebody always had a big smile or a friendly punch in the arm for me. They'd bring chicken or pizza and then leave, asking me if I needed anything.

When left to my own devices, I lounged. I would lie in front of the TV with chips and pop and be completely immersed in whatever show I was watching. I slept, and slept, and slept. The bed felt so good on the back of my calves. I wriggled my toes a *lot*. I started writing in the little red notebook every day, silly, stupid entries about the shows I was watching or the worn-down nap of the carpet.

I loved the nondescript little apartment and had no desire to be anywhere else. This was a departure from all things challenging, which I embraced with full enthusiasm. I didn't like it outside and refused to think of what I would do when the week was up—this week so reminiscent of the one I'd experienced long ago in the Gulf of Mexico with the lobsters in the fridge and Oreo cookies every night . . .

However, Slick easily enticed me out of the apartment by taking me to a few shows. It was a very special and exciting time. I dressed up in a silver-blue long sequined gown and got my hair done at a salon. My hair! Can you *imagine* my joy? I looked so adult and elegant.

We saw Siegfried and Roy and Wayne Newton at Caesar's Palace. The security guards didn't even pay attention to me now—if they only knew. I hated Wayne Newton but loved Siegfried and Roy and their tigers. It was a dinner show, and we were sitting at a long formal table with strangers. This was the best game of dress-up I had ever played. Most of the women looked a little unnatural in their gowns and most of the men were a little plump. Everyone was friendly and smiling though. It made me feel even more beautiful, if that was possible. And the best part was not having to talk. I watched the shows and enjoyed the fact that etiquette required silence in this situation, which enhanced my fantasy state. Just two more days and the week would be over. Sigh.

The next day Slick stopped in by himself for fifteen minutes. "Oh, by the way, kid, my sister will be gone for another week so you can stay."

Yippee! was what rang out in my head while I silently nodded and gave a placid smile.

"But if you've got to go, I understand, or if you want to try to get hold of your family don't hesitate to use the phone."

Jeez! It had never occurred to me to even think about the phone. I scanned the room and located it for the first time on the wall by the kitchen counter. Come to think of it, it had never rung and I hadn't seen anyone talk on it all week. For some reason I felt guilty that I hadn't noticed it until now. Why? I wasn't going to call anybody. But the knowledge of the phone was extremely unsettling.

Week number two was not so good. There was a gradual change taking place. Nothing I could see, just a feeling. Slick always had the same four guys with him now, no new faces. It got so that Slick and at least two of them would fall asleep in the living room every night. I began to feel afraid, like I was being watched or guarded. I would try to talk myself out of it. *Am I being paranoid like Ma?* They were still being very nice and laid-back. But my fear persisted, becoming constant and stronger. I decided to face it and test it.

"I'm going out for a walk, Slick."

"All right. Keep her company, Joey."

Each day I tried to leave for my walk alone.

"Hey, Slick, I want to be alone and do some thinking."

"All right. Al, drive her over to the reservoir so she can walk and think."

I began trying to leave without saying anything, but someone would always fall in step with me. I'd get up at three, four, five in the morning and come out of my room just to be greeted by Slick's smiling awake face.

"What's the matter, kid? Can't sleep?"

The constant guard slowly started to feel thick with hostility. The pleasant smiles started to look rabid. I started to realize I felt threatened. I started to realize I wasn't being paranoid.

I stopped trying to go for walks.

The week passed and nothing changed. No sister came back. No one mentioned it. I thought maybe if I laid low and acted like I was happy, they'd feel free to leave me by myself again, just once, and I'd have the opportunity to go—no such luck.

Again, my feelings confused me. I liked these guys, so why was I so afraid of them? I didn't trust myself at all and kept trying to shake off my doubts. It was the only way to tolerate the veiled threat without imploding. I'd almost convinced myself to completely relax again. So much so that I fell into a deep sleep that particular night.

I had a lot of happy dreams. None of them made sense, just colors and animals, and Volkswagen bugs, and blue sky, and nice, strong, warm hands massaging my shoulders, arms, fingers, and toes. It felt so good and real. The dream images changed, but the sensation from the hands was constant, now on my face, my neck, lingering over my breasts, my stomach, now back down to my feet, up to my calves, oh, the glory of that. In my dream the hands knew how exhausted and stiff my calves were and worked on them until they were thoroughly relaxed.

Now the knees, now the thighs—front, back, outside—now inside. The thighs—my very favorite place to be touched—so sensitive, so sensual. Now I'm getting turned on. The hands know it and move up, up, up until . . . Ohohoho! Nothing has . . . ever felt so good as this light rubbing on my sex, the hands massaging oh so thoroughly every fold of skin slowly, tenderly, without threat. I, in my dream, totally relax and surrender to these commanding, knowing, gentle hands. This is new. No hands have ever touched me this way before.

All images and colors are gone, and now I just feel and concentrate on the touch. It's so real, I feel as if I am awake. I'm almost sure I am. But the hands are still there. Now one hand is replaced by a slow, warm, wet tongue. Wow! What a delicious feeling. No one has ever done this to me before either. It feels "sooo" good. But I'm sure this is not a dream. I want this touch so badly. It's so soothing, and my body is relaxed, really, for the first time in a long, long time. But "who" is touching me? I'm afraid to open my eyes and see.

This complex feeling of complete satisfaction and the horror of being invaded by someone was something I could not cognize. My body needed this soothing so badly, but no one should be touching me in this manner. After what seemed a lifetime of dilemma over what to do, my need to relax and enjoy won. I decided to keep my eyes closed, pretending to sleep until whoever it was stopped. Maybe they would just go away, and I would never have to face it. Aah, but it felt so nice, nice, warm, easy, loose, released; the tongue was replaced by a hard-gripping violent hand.

Slick's voice sliced through my bliss, low, but clear, cold, and contemptuous, saying, "I know you're awake, Heather."

Aaah! He knew my real name.

"Stop pretending to be asleep, Heather. You've been a bad, little girl, *Heather*. I'm going to tell your mom and sister and *David*"—*he hissed the name*—"what a bad little girl you've been. I'm going to call them in California and tell them what a lazy lying whore you are. Open your eyes."

Slap, slap hard across the face. Two other men came into the room. He turned to them.

"Hey guys, look at these big wet pussy lips." Back to me he said, "How'd you get such fat, juicy pussy lips?"

There was no lust in his voice. He sounded factual, controlled, and livid—hateful. The quality of his voice terrified me.

"Joey, open her eyes so she can see what a whore she's being."

He was on top of me now and Joey was holding my eyes open. The other held my arms.

"Let go of her arms. She can fight and scream as loud as she wants.

Fighting was a non-reality; I was paralyzed with shock.

"Nobody can hear you, Heather. Nobody's going to come and save you, Heather. You're too bad. You're not worth saving. You're just made to be used, like this."

He started f——cking me. His face was the picture of controlled rage, hate, and disgust.

"Are you learning your lesson? This is all you're good for."

The other guys just stood and watched with no expression.

My shock and surprise disappeared. I . . . was . . . numb. I . . . felt . . . nothing.

He climaxed and sat up. Joey let go of my eyes. I closed them.

Slap, slap, slap . . . punch . . . harder, hard. I kept my eyes closed. I only heard the points of contact and noted a gradually increasing warmth taking me over from head to toe. I felt no pain, just *thud* and heat. The hitting stopped . . . more f——cking . . . slaps across the face, breasts . . . Slick's vicious whisper in my ear, "This is all you're good for. I'm going to ruin you. I'm going to make it so no man will ever want you again. I'm going to ruin you. It's all over, little Heather."

After they all f——cked me, they laid back into the beating. They beat me down beyond the ground—beyond numb.

I just lay there when they were done. My hearing seemed abnormally heightened. I heard the scrape of hangers and clothes being taken out of the closet. I heard the rustle of the plastic shopping bag with my little red notebook in it being removed from its hiding place. Then, *click*, the door closed, and they were out of the room.

I heard the TV come on and laughing and talking. I drifted out of consciousness. I don't know how long I lay like that. Hours, days . . . it's a mystery to me.

When I awoke, I had no idea what time it was because there was no window in the room. Not only had they emptied out the closet, *everything* was gone—no clock, no dresser, no radio . . . all gone. Just the bed and a table with a lamp remained. There were no clothes for me to put on, no mirror for me to look in, no phone . . . I wasn't sure what to do.

I didn't feel sore from the beating. I couldn't feel my body at all. This was a momentary distraction for me. I entertained myself by grabbing the carpet with my toes and marveling at the lack of sensation. It was like magic. I saw my toes clutching at the carpet, but I couldn't feel anything. I did it again and again. *Look, Ma! No feeling!* Yes, I had been numbing out at several different points during my journey, but this put that state of nonexistence to shame. It was as if I had no connection whatsoever with the body I was in.

I wasn't hungry. I knew they were in the other room. I didn't experience any fear at that thought. I was more concerned about the fact that I didn't have any clothes to put on. I didn't want to be seen naked. I went and sat on the floor in the corner with my knees up and my head against the wall. This was the only way I felt some sense of modesty, arms wrapped around my knees, head against the wall. The door opened.

"She's up."

"Good, leave the door open."

He left the door open. The light shining in was such a debasing intrusion. But leaving my self-protective position to close the door was not an option.

I sensed a momentary presence. I looked down and saw that someone had brought me a glass of water. I drank it. A little later, I had to pee—the first reentry into the human form known as me. What to do? I didn't want to walk naked past the men to the bathroom. But the urge became unbearable. I walked to the door and peeked around the corner. They were *all* there, all five of them now. Slick saw me. He knew I had to pee.

"Joey, take her to the bathroom. That water went right through her."

He continued to watch TV and eat chips with the aloofness of routine, like everything was normal. That messed with my mind.

Joey came and grabbed me by the arm and walked me to the bathroom. We went in. He didn't close the door. He just stood there with his arms crossed watching. Now I couldn't pee. It was too humiliating, too degrading. I sat there for twenty minutes before anything would come out. He flushed.

"Hey, Joey, I want her to take a shower too."

He pushed me toward the shower. I tripped in, and he turned on the water, keeping the curtain open so he could watch/guard/ shame. I didn't do anything. He moved me under the water and soaped me up. I just stood there with my head turned. He turned off the water and didn't give me a towel. I got out and walked back to the room, back to my corner, wet and . . . I can't even describe the "and."

The door closed. Darkness . . . the floor . . . the wall . . .

I became nothing. The thoughts and feelings trying to creep through were dangerous, degrading, and cheap. I thought I deserved their brutality because I was too stupid not to see it coming. I was worthless.

I couldn't get over the fact that I had no way to hide my nakedness. I couldn't stand being seen like this. It made my skin crawl when they looked at me. I had been a modest girl when it pertained to full nudity, the kind of girl that changed in the bathroom stall in gym class. This was mortifying, this nakedness. I understood that it would give them less power if I could act like it didn't bother me, but that was an impossibility for me. I felt no pain, just embarrassed and truly offended.

The next four days or so deeply intensified these feelings. No one spoke to me or made eye contact. I was always escorted to the bathroom, always washed. I wouldn't eat. The thought of having to sh——t in front of these guys was more than I could bear. They brought me food for two days before they realized I wasn't going to eat.

"Leave the food there, damnit. Let her sit with her own wastefulness."

They followed Slick's orders, and the plates sat there on the floor, the food hard and full of bacteria. I figured out I could have a little privacy if I used my empty water cup to pee in—one less public pee. I would drink my water and pee right back into the empty cup. This was the one thing that made unflappable Slick visibly angry, almost surprising me back into my body. After all hadn't I seen him clean out the perfectly clean ashtrays that fateful day in the car?

"Filthy, nasty little whore. Can you believe this sh——t, Joey? Man, leave those cups in there with her. See how she likes the smell of her own pee after a few days."

I never lay back down in that bed, arms wrapped around my knees, head against the wall. They never tried to touch me sexually or beat me. I basically didn't exist. The only reminders I had that I was alive were drinking water, peeing, me judging myself, and the humiliation of the showers. Otherwise, nothing . . . no kindness, not even from myself. Just stone faces always looking past me—no one acknowledged me at all.

This was punctuated by the fact that I heard them being people to each other. I didn't want to be near *them*, but to hear them laughing and living made me feel invisible.

Hey, what about me? I'm here too . . . I wanted to yell.

This yearning for contact made me kick myself harder. How could I want to talk to them? I *must* be a whore. I *must* be insane. What was *wrong* with me?

I started to lose time. How many days had gone by? Three, four, five? Unacceptable. Not knowing the date threw me into complete and utter panic. I became frantic. *What day is it? What day is it?*

I commenced with counting. From that distraught day on, my job became clear. I had to peek around the corner at least twice a day and see through a window. Daylight, night, one day. Daylight, night, two days. Even though I had lost several days, it didn't matter anymore. Now that I had a starting point, I figured I'd just keep track of the days from this point forward, and when I got out, I would somehow figure out how many days I had lost. Then everything would be fine. Daylight, night, three days . . .

It's okay now. I'm finally not a person anymore . . . at least that's what I'm hoping . . .

CHAPTER 16

And Beyond

I came to. I must've been unconscious, because I came to.

This is a new place. I am lying flat looking up at the ceiling. The lighting is different, bright—clinically bright. And either the lights or my ears are buzzing.

The room feels huge. I can sense the presence of many people bustling about—a normal sound. I want to see, I want to see! My curiosity is all-consuming. Yet, somehow, it seems too much of an effort to turn my head. I don't think to question this because of the persistence of my habitual inquiries: What day is it? Do I have clothes on? How many people are seeing me naked if I don't? I close my eyes—better.

Cool hands on my face. They smell pretty and feel soft. I open my eyes. My view is of an antiseptic-looking blonde with a focused expression on her face. She is sitting next to me. Her fingers move forward and push my eyelids back down. She begins applying makeup. It feels good, that cool wet eyeliner brush running over my lid. My world becomes this feeling. She spends at least thirty minutes working on my face.

"Okay, she's good to go." *Her vocal timbre matches her chilly mien.*

Strong hands are picking me up and moving me. Now whatever I've been set down on is angled so I'm half sitting up. I feel many hands on me, moving my legs and propping them just so with pillows. Careful but uncaring hands are touching me all over, powder on my breasts, on the bottom of my feet, hair primping . . . I want to be embarrassed, but the touch is so detached, I can't. I hang on to the fact that I have some clothes on because I feel the hands adjusting straps and smoothing out wrinkles in the material on my belly.

Slick's voice: "Hey, Tony, let me, okay? I've got some personal stock in this one."

I feel warm, dry fingers pushing my eyes open. There's Slick smiling at me all friendly.

"Hey, kid, you want to see how gorgeous you look?"

He turns toward someone.

"Bring over the mirror."

Someone rolls over a floor-length mirror and places it at the foot of whatever I'm lying on. Slick leans away. I can see my reflection because I'm at an angle. "Oh my God!" I look fully grown in the way that little girls admire—simultaneously sexy and beautiful. I'm decked out in light pink and black lace, all soft and sultry. My hair is greased back and my face flawlessly made up. As soon as my ego absorbs the news that I look great, I'm able to take in more detail. My breasts are pushed up and sticking out for the world to see, and my legs are wide open putting my bare crotch completely out on display.

Of course, my natural reaction is to quickly try to close my legs and fold my arms over my breasts, but I have absolutely no control over my muscles—I mean none. There are at least four strangers in front of me, and who knows how many more are out of my sight line, plus Slick and his four buddies. Complete mortification. They move the mirror out of the way. It is replaced with a video camera aimed directly between my legs and lights are being carefully placed aiming in the same direction. Tony gets behind the camera. A hush falls across the room, accompanied by a tense expectancy.

"Okay, Slick, get her wet. Make that pussy glisten."

He starts licking, purposefully drooling, letting his slobber run all over me. I can feel it running down inside my ass, the wetness under my butt cheeks immediately taking me back to that fateful day on the garage floor, where I had lost my virginity—back to that same bizarre circumstance of surprise and shock and the inability to keep up with the pace of physical and emotional events. Slick steps aside.

"I need a little more shine on the clit."

Slick plunges several fingers in me, and lets spit run off the tip of his tongue onto the designated area. He is uncharacteristically excited. His excitement comes from the fact that he is degrading me in front of all these people, from knowing that I can't move and that he can do whatever he wants to with me. Every reflex in my body wants to kick him, push him away, curl up, cover up, hide . . . I can do nothing, not even twitch. He backs away looking at Tony for approval. Tony is again behind the lens.

"Damn, that looks good, Slick. Mmm. Mmm."

Tony stands up abruptly and claps his hands in a "chop-chop" manner.

"All right, people, set up the next scene."

Everyone goes off in another direction. I can't see them. I can just hear all the activity. I am on such high alert my curiosity is usurping mortification. Confusion beats out fear. The inability to move defies logic and is maddeningly unacceptable. I am a strong, athletic girl, which means I should be able to move. Come on! "Move!"

A short thin white elderly man with nervous, mouselike gestures walks over to me and sticks a needle in my arm. He throws the shot away and starts pinching my breasts and playing with my body like I'm an oversize doll. He never looks at my face, just the grabbing and groping all over. He pulls me down to the edge of the table/bed thing I'm on and starts f——cking me. I scrutinize the top of his head. His skin has a pinkish hue. The short patches of thinning hair are white, while the longer comb-over sections are clearly remnants of a faded blondish dye job. The balding, agitated rodent climaxes and then goes off to help the others.

I never feel any of this groping and f——cking. I can see it, hear it, but absolutely do not feel it.

My eyes start closing . . . with heaviness, not sleep. The muscles can't hold them open anymore. I try to win the eye-open game, but it is impossible.

"They" roll me to another part of the room and push my eyes open. Set two is Victorian: a big antique bed and lace curtains. They keep me in the same outfit and redo my makeup, the same sterile blonde concentrating on her artwork or science project. This time I do not feel the brushes making contact with my skin. I . . . feel . . . nothing. I . . . am . . .

numb. Cameras, lights, lots of men, f——cking, cum on my face, breasts, tummy . . . Slick standing off to the side, watching. I hear the sloppy rhythmic sound of people f——cking me. Smell . . . sweat . . . cum . . . smoke. I . . . feel . . . nothing. I . . . am . . . numb.

Shot in the arm . . . eyes close . . . the buzzing lights. I feel the warmth of the lights and see an uncommitted shade of yellow making its way through my eyelids like the sun does at the beach. I hear the contained moans of men not wanting to shout out when they climax. Women's laughter a little further away. What day is it? What day is it? Needle in arm. I'm getting sleepy.

I wake up someplace else in somebody's house. I can tell by the residual odor of cooked food. I can move a little, although it's awfully hard because I don't have a tactile reference point. I heard Diana Ross's voice, "Tell me mirror, mirror on the wall . . ." With great effort, I turn my head to the left. This is a ladies' room. It smells of perfume, and there are lots of fancy boots and scarves by the vanity. I know this because I can now raise my head high enough to see past the edge of the bed. This gives me great relief, but gravity pulls it quickly back to the pillow.

I hear the woman's voice in the other room. She sounds nice. She must be talking on the phone. It's a mellow, knowing voice, deepened by cigarettes—a voice that likes to laugh, though hints of sorrow are obvious in its tone. I like her. She is soothing me. She's definitely black. I want to see what she looks like, but it's just too hard to move. She hangs up. Click! I hear her leave. The outer door opens and shuts without ceremony. She's gone and then quickly returns. I smell pizza. The TV goes on. It all sounds so normal and friendly. I fall asleep happy.

I wake up. Wow! I can move. I can "feel" myself move. I'm stiff and it hurts, but I can move. I tune out the pain and jump up to look out the window. It's just a hint past sunset. I look at the vanity. There's a clock. It's 6:12 p.m. What day is it? I walk into the other room. All I can feel are my toes and my upper stomach muscles. The first thing I notice is the big fish tank with all the brightly colored varieties. Then "she" moves and I notice her. She's very beautiful in a melancholy way. She reminds me of that actress, Diane Carroll, elegant with good posture even when she's sitting. Her speaking voice remains low and soothing.

"Hey, baby, how're you feeling?"

"Hungry."

"Have at it. Eat whatever you can find in there," she says, tilting her head. "My name's Wanda."

"Hi, Wanda."

I smile and wave as I head toward the "there" she has implied. I am myself in that split second, the "me" that wants to put people at ease and enjoys social graces.

"Look, honey. I've got a play practice to go to. I've got to leave in about ten minutes. Want to come with me?"

"Okay."

"Your clothes are in the bedroom on the chair. We'll get takeout on the way."

I alter my course and head back into the bedroom. There on the chair are my tan corduroys, baby blue V-necked sweater, the silk shirt I'd gotten from Michael in San Diego, and my little red journal. It is a strange feeling to see those things again. They give me hope, which I find somewhat shocking.

I put on my clothes and join Wanda. We walk out into the night. My ears are ringing. I can't feel the breeze, but I know it's there because the leaves are moving on the small well-maintained trees. We take a cab to a little rickety theater that reeks of hipness. There are about ten people inside going over lines and pacing the floor laughing nervously. They steer me toward the phone, and put a takeout menu in my hand. I order chicken and macaroni and cheese from a place next door. Wanda pays when the food arrives and hands it to me. I sit on the worn wooden floor in the corner of the theater, picking at my food like a bird as I watch the rehearsal. The view of ordinary people with dreams and joy is food enough for the moment. Subconsciously and with great trepidation, I begin to reconnect to my body.

Ohhh, I can breathe. I can move. I touch the floor and feel my fingertips as they rasp across splinters. Currently, life is good. I am people watching like back in the day at Ma's house party on Piedmont Avenue.

Wanda is so beautiful in her black sweater and pants with her hair tied up in a colorful silk scarf and her simple yet perfect makeup. I am mesmerized by her elegance. But her face continues to be shrouded with a perpetual sadness. Why? Why can't she be happy? I want to see her relax and be happy so badly. Her sadness begins to gnaw away at some troubled spot in me and slowly steals away my fleeting relief. Her sadness summons fear and disturbance.

We go back to her place, and she tells me a little about herself.

"I can have a place like this because I'm being kept, baby. He's old, white, and wrinkled, but it's not that bad. He comes over maybe once or twice a week. I give him what he wants and he keeps me styling. I don't have to work. I do what I want, when I want. Ain't got no *niggah* beating me or two-timing me. This arrangement here is real cool as far as I'm concerned."

"Where's Slick?"

"Don't think about that. You're safe now. Relax. I'm going to bed. If you get hungry in the night, feel free to help yourself to whatever you find."

I sit on the leather couch and watch TV. I can't concentrate at all. I look at the TV for an hour and don't understand the scenes or the words. I am buried somewhere deep in an undefined darkness. Mercifully, hunger catches my attention.

I go into the kitchen and start with a tuna sandwich. I go off— crackers, cheese, salad, leftover Chinese, pizza, my chicken, and macaroni. I slowly eat bite after bite over a few hours until my tummy can't stretch anymore. This is not a binge. I am hungry. I don't care about my looks now. As a matter of fact, I am thrilled to feel my tummy getting so tight.

I lay down on the bed, too full to move. How wonderful it is to feel this slobby and piggy as I lay prone, breathing a little hard, lips and fingers a little greasy. I am reveling in my sated, slothlike state incredibly aware of every stage of it, and slipping ever so slowly into a deep, deep sleep. This is another one of the sweeter moments in my life.

I sleep on and off through all of the next day. I still don't know what day it is. I know what time it is though, and that seems to satisfy me. 10:00 a.m., sleep; 1:14 p.m., sleep; 6:22 p.m., sleep; 10:03 p.m., the doorbell's ringing.

"Just a minute. I'm in the bathroom."

I hear Wanda running around. I'm groggy and not nearly awake enough to be sure what's real. She comes into the room. Sting—she's shooting something in my arm. She runs out and closes the door. I hear people coming in, their voices low. Wanda smarting off . . .

"She ate every f——cking thing I had, man. Cleaned me out."

I hear someone being slammed up against the wall.

"How could she be in here eating if you kept her drugged down, man? Don't play games with me, bitch. She is not to leave the apartment and not to move. That is your job. Do you understand? It's real simple. You can't afford to f——ck up."

I know that voice too well—Slick's vicious hiss and Wanda making pitiful begging sounds. But I can't pay attention anymore. I'm drifting down somewhere . . .

I come to. It's a new room. I think it's small. I'm with Slick and the original four. I know those voices.

"*Hey,* little Heather. Time to be what you are—a whore. Time to get what you want—all these dicks. You're getting wet just thinking about it."

He starts f——cking me.

"Open your eyes, bitch. Let me see how much you like this."

I open my eyes with quick fire and, therefore, a "how dare you" look. Meanwhile, my body remembers quicker than my brain that the best way to deal is to not be. If you aren't then nobody can do anything to you and you don't feel things. You just hear and see.

"Oh, you're gonna act like you're angry and don't want it? Well, if you want to be stubborn let's see how you like pain."

He pulls out and punches me across the face. My eyes register no pain. He spits on me and hits me again. I give him nothing. He gets off me. Joey gets on. Slick stands smoking. Joey climaxes. As he's getting off me, Slick comes over and touches the lit cigarette to the skin between my breasts watching my face. He keeps touching the cigarette to the same spot. Still, no reaction from me. My brain has caught up.

I was past feeling. I was past numb. I just wasn't around.

Most times, I saw nothing. Sometimes, I saw a bright white light. Occasionally, I would see someone on top of me but just for a minute before my mind and vision would go off into sweet nothing, oblivion, light.

Ah, alas, to my dismay, I'd lost complete sense of time. There were only six periods through the rest of the ordeal when I was present enough to know what was going on.

Once, I woke up at Wanda's again. No more theater outings—she kept me sedated from beginning to end. Every time she stuck the needle in my arm she'd say, "Sorry, baby. It's you or me."

Once, I woke up in a small musty room that was dimly lit. There were two young black men there along with all the regulars. They looked very excited. Slick pointed to one.

"Action, tape is rolling."

He came over and f——cked me. The man was so young, curious, and excited, it made me want to smile—a muscular impossibility. He had no idea what was going on. They told him to wait outside for his friend.

"Action, tape is rolling."

The other young guy got on me. He looked into my eyes. I saw his look of playful curiosity turn to concern and then conviction. He climaxed and stood up.

"What's the matter? You seem nervous."

"A little self-conscious, I guess. I'm not used to f——cking in front of cameras and a room full of strangers. Not my style. Now I know."

He quickly started walking out. Joey followed, gunshots, car speeding off. Did he get away or was that just his buddy? Were those warning shots or more?

Joey comes back and grabs a partner. They go out. I see daylight through the door. Good enough—it's daytime.

Once, I woke up to a very scary-looking white man on me. He was a big person, big like an ex-football player whose muscles have turned to mush. And he didn't look "right" in the eyes. He wore glasses and had a mustache. He wore a white short-sleeved button-down shirt. His hair was light brown in a bad "Peter Brady" cut.

As he methodically pumped away, he had his hands slipped up and around the bottom of my rib cage and was pulling outward as if trying to pull me apart. I couldn't feel it but saw that my body looked like it was going to split.

Slick and some tall skinny white guy named David (yet *another* David) would pull him off.

"You've got to calm down, man. Just straight forward. None of this kinky rib sh——t."

He would nod and just keep staring at me. They'd let go, and he'd come right back at me—pump, pump, pull, pull. This cycle went on three or four times. The last time, he got his hands up under my ribs in a very solid grip as he was pulling me apart. His grip was so tight they couldn't get him off.

Slick got on his back and started choking him. Choked him dead he did. Slick climbed off, looking upset. He had made a mistake and was disturbed because he had failed and created a problem. I recognized his look of self-berating disgust. I knew only too well the merciless dialogue going on inside his head. That was my specialty. He deferred to David, the tall skinny white guy with glasses and curly hair.

David said in a quiet, tempered voice, "You shouldn't have brought that f——cking ape in here."

"I'm sorry I did, man. I'll take care of it."

"You better. You're slipping, Slick. Business, man, business."

They left seeming to have forgotten there was a dead man on me. They were gone for a long time. I knew this because I kept conscious until the door opened. Ah, night. Good enough. I immediately drifted away.

Once, I awoke in an extremely ostentatious condo. It was huge and full of precious things. Plush plum-colored carpeting covered the floor. I was able to move. I got up. There were three other young women there and four bodybuilder types hanging out by the doors.

I cautiously, shyly struck up a conversation with one girl, Raquel. She was pretty and feisty.

Me (*in full voice*), "Hey."

Her (*sotto voce*), "Shh. Just act normal."

Her (*out loud*), "How do you feel?"

Her (*sotto voce*), "I'm trying to figure out how to get out of here."

Her (*to the hard bodies*), "It'd be *nice* if we could get some water around here."

Raquel was a swarthy Italian girl. She wore black velvet and liked the singer Tina Marie and was a Pisces like me. I became very close to her over the following three days. We told each other everything, our favorite colors, our fears, where we were born.

On day four David and Slick showed up with a little old guy. Now that I had my senses, I could see that David carried himself as if he was a very important man. He was gaunt and wore black with a white shirt. He looked like a combination of lawyer, gangster, and Keith Richards. He hardly spoke. When he did, it was usually to issue some kind of order. He *never* acknowledged me with his eyes.

Slick saw me and came toward me. I made a feeble attempt to ward him off. I believe he *let* me get away. I started to run and when he caught up with me, I'd had time to pick up a big granite ashtray, which I sort of tumbled across his face. He laughed and held me still while the little guy stuck me with a shot. Muscle control gone, Slick threw me over his shoulder and dumped me on a bed in the back room. David and the little old guy followed.

They turned on all the lights and the room was blindingly bright. Slick took off my clothes and opened my legs wide. The little guy put some type of salve on the burns between my breasts and some other kind of cream on the burns on my crotch. David was studying every inch of my body. He flipped me over and examined every nook and cranny on that side too.

"You've got to stop burning this girl, Slick. You are ruining her. We won't be able to use her for anything. Wait until we're through with her before you do all this crap. Be a businessman, *goddamnit.* I'm serious."

David walked out. The little guy followed.

Slick's vicious whisper in my ear, "I *told* you I was going to ruin you. No man will ever want to touch you by the time I'm through."

He pulled me to the end of the bed, my legs dangling over the edge.

Raquel came in dressed in a pink negligee, with pink fur covering her breasts, and spiked heels. She went over to Slick and started tongue kissing him, not deep, but little flicking kisses.

"She was easy. She's afraid of drowning in still water, you know, lakes and pools. She wants to be a singer. She hates the fact that everybody is staring at her bare crotch more than anything. What else do you want to know? I'm sure I got it all."

"*Good* girl. You know what I want right now?"

He licked his lips.

"I want to see you suck her titties and look her in the eye while I'm f——cking you from behind."

She proceeded.

"That's it."

He was pretending to be aroused to manipulate her ego. His voice was dripping with anger. Raquel was looking for a reaction of shock from me, which I couldn't begin to give her because of the muscle shot. I shut down the expression in my eyes, which if I had shared it would've been that self-berating look I'd seen in Slick's eyes two awake times ago . . . when he had choked that . . .

I tried to skim over that dead man lying on me, but I really shouldn't have. It's impossible to describe. Have you ever been in a dimly lit room with a dead man lying on top of you? It's so otherworldly, I don't know if I can find a way to sound serious about something so ghoulishly preposterous.

This man had already awakened my fear when he tried to pull my rib cage in half. The fear came from looking into his bleary expressionless eyes. Those eyes showed nothing but robotic determination, no humanity, no lust, no sick and twisted pleasure—just blurred vacancy. If eyes are the window to the soul, he didn't have one.

I watched those soulless eyes bulge and discolor as the life was squeezed out of them—him. And now I was being squeezed by the weight of the dead man's body. The invisible clutch of fear tightened around my throat. I wanted to gasp for breath and tried desperately to push the weight off, but could invoke no movement from my hands or change the slow rhythm of my breathing. The height of incomprehensible absurdity is to be hysterically frightened and have a resting heart rate of less than sixty and a slow, steady breathing pattern. It short-circuits every human system . . .

I sensed myself being flattened by the weight and knew I couldn't exist. I had to go but I couldn't leave. The fear kept me present. I screamed in complete horror, not out loud. No, it was the most chilling scream of all. My body became as cold and rigid as the dead man's and uttered through its every cell this silent scream of terror. It never waned as the hours went by. I wasn't blessed with the relief of falling faint. I felt the thin razor-sharp whistle of the scream, pitched so high it was beyond tone, slashing through my body and soul until the stiffened corpse was wrenched off me and dropped with a thud to the floor. Then, and only then, did I drift happily out of consciousness, the sound of dragging dead feet my lullaby. What a crass Halloween tale. It was so morbid it should be laughable. It should be . . .

Once, I awoke and Slick was aiming a handheld video camera at a little pool.

"Okay, guys."

They picked me up and threw me in the pool. I couldn't move—again terror, fear. I was underwater. I was drowning. I couldn't move. *Yank!* I was pulled out of the water. I couldn't gasp or spit, *nothing.* The panic in my eyes was uncontrollable. Slick was winning.

"Hah! I found your weak spot. Dunk her again."

Terror. *Yank!*

Slick came over with a towel and started drying me off. There were tears in his eyes—tears. He held me and rocked my limp body.

"I'm sorry we've done this to you. I'm so sorry. I won't do anymore. I'll dry you off, and when you can move, I'll let you go."

He looked me in the eyes.

"I'm *really* sorry."

His voice sounded kind and contrite.

Hope . . . oh please . . . thank you . . . you're forgiven, Slick. All this was registering in my eyes as the fear had a moment ago.

Smack!

"You stupid, *stupid* bitch."

His voice was neutral with Spock-like disdain and he was shaking his head incredulously.

"You really *believe* that sh——t?"

Smack, smack!

Once I awoke in the small room. Nobody was paying attention to me. They all had their backs to me and were leaning over a table discussing some kind of paperwork. I became completely conscious and, for just that moment, felt every pain in my body. What woke me so vividly was the certainty that I was going to die. I wanted to stay alive and hoped some avenue of escape would make itself clear.

I don't know how long they had me, or what they did to me when I wasn't conscious. The bottom line is these were some sick motherf——ckers and they wrung me through their wringer with an impressive thoroughness. There was nothing left for me to *do* but die.

I was used up. Their fun was over. Slick had put so many burns on the right side of my crotch that I was no good to them anymore. And the clear cue was them having a meeting in my presence. There was absolutely no reason I should be around them in that circumstance. At that moment, all the survival instincts of the ages kicked in like animals sensing a storm. I *knew* I had very little time left.

And I wanted to live. Why? Because I'm very competitive by nature. They wanted to ruin me, to use me up, and throw me away like a matted old toothbrush. I wanted to live because they expected me to die. I wanted to win because they thought I had lost. It had nothing to do with self-worth or a please-don't-kill-me mentality. It was pure unadulterated teenage stubbornness. It was a control issue. I wanted to pass the test. I wanted an *A+*. Death meant failure. Life meant *they* lost. Death meant they outsmarted me. Life meant at least I could hold my own. Death was bowing to my mother's belief that I was a perverted, spineless whore. Life meant *they* were the motherf——cking perverts.

A shot in the arm . . . I'm out. I wake up in Wanda's bed. This, I know, is my last chance. Wanda likes me. She feels bad about helping them use me. She's really on my side, but the fear of what they would do to her keeps her from letting me go.

Hours go by. What day is it? I hear Wanda fussing about the room. She sits on the edge of the bed with the shot in hand. I'm on the verge of being able to move. I lock eyes with her and silently plead, "No, Wanda, please. I can't die."

"Shut up," she says, quickly breaking her gaze and pushing the needle in my arm.

"Shut up. You know what's up. You or me, babe."

She tries to give me a quick compassionate glance, but our eyes lock once again. My last chance to silently plead, "Then let it be me, Wanda. Please . . ."

I feel the effect of the drugs. My eyes start to close. I fight to keep them open so as not to break communication.

"Girl, you *know* what's up. I'm too old and too tired to fight anyone. I've been through a lot. If I let you go, it's all over. Stop making this hard."

She falls silent. We continue to stare at each other, me using every ounce of concentration I can muster to keep my eyes open.

Time passes. I don't know how much. What day is it? I see the split second Wanda comes to some decision. I can't read her face as to what that decision is. All I know for certain is that she has made up her mind and it isn't going to change. I drift off. My silent pleas won't help now. Whatever she has decided is what will happen. I hope that I wake up again.

CHAPTER 17

Reprieve

I did. I was in complete darkness. The condo was still, just the fish tank bubbling away. The temperature was unusually warm, but every now and then, a cool breeze would gust through. Where was it coming from? The occasional car passing by sounded as if it were driving straight through the living room. I couldn't move but was feeling relatively "clear." I sensed that I was alone.

Where is Wanda? What time is it? What day is it?

It must have been about four in the morning, just late enough for even Vegas to slow down but too early to be light outside.

The sounds start to magnify in my ears: heels clicking off into the distance, the muffled sound of a TV downstairs. I close my eyes.

And as I close them, I can feel my eyelids touching my eyeballs really well for the first time in my life. I spend the next half hour opening, shutting, opening, shutting . . . It feels so good, like waves of Visine. There's the cold breeze again.

I nestle into the covers and curl up. Nestle . . . curl . . . I can move. I can move, and the reality of this is almost too shocking.

The cold breeze is clearing out all the warmth in the room . . . I'm shaking now. I can feel the frigid temperature in my fingers, which seem like icicles ready to snap.

As long as it's dark, I'm frozen with a sweeping terror. As long as it's dark, I can't take a risk. What if it's a trick? What if Slick and David and company are sitting in the room out of my sight line waiting to laugh at

me and smack me, and f——ck me? What if Wanda is setting me up?
What if . . . ? Nope. I cannot get up in the dark. I have to wait.

If this is a trick again, then surely they will win.

The fish tank is bubbling away. I concentrate on that sound as I
persevere the passage of time like wild prey.

My hope is so high now. I feel "this close" to freedom. I'm just wait-
ing for the sun. I can't dwell on freedom because if I am stopped, if I don't
attain freedom, I will die. I won't be able to take it.

Shiver . . . shake . . . hope . . . fear . . . excitement . . . doubt . . .
hope . . .

The light is changing. I can see the outline of the vanity mirror and
the chair. The sun will be here soon. Nothing is more important than the
sun.

Cars driving by more frequently . . . lot of keys jangling . . . doors
opening and closing. I like the vibrating sound that the concrete and
iron make as people go clicking or pounding down the stairs. There is
an electric blue cast of light enveloping the bedroom now. Lighter and
lighter . . . Oh . . . bright light. Sunlight. Golden white rays of sunlight
showing me, beyond a shadow of a doubt, that this is not a trick.

I am alone. All I have to do is throw back the covers and walk over
to the little chair where I can now see my tan corduroys and baby blue
V-necked sweater sitting there folded so neatly, waiting patiently.

The fish tank is bubbling away. I can still feel my fingers, which
continued to freeze.

I push back the covers. I can't feel my arms, but I can certainly see
them moving. I swing my legs around so that I'm sitting and my feet are
touching the floor. I am afraid to stand up. What if I can't? Well, here
goes nothing. I'm up. I'm standing. Numbness persists in my feet—not
even pins and needles. But I'm standing. I walk over to the chair. I feel
light-headed, as if I'm going to faint, but my eyes are very focused. I see
myself picking up the sweater and pulling it over my head.

The warmth and softness of the sweater are a tactile heaven, making
it almost okay to be inside my own skin. I gain a little more momentum.
I walk to the dresser, scrounging around for a pair of underwear. I note
that some of the drawers are half empty and in a state of disorder. Wanda

must've left in a hurry. I throw on the undies and put on my pants. They are practically hanging off me; I've gotten so skinny.

For just a second, I feel glee at the notion of being so skinny. I drop the thought almost faster than it has formed. It brings me too close to remembering what used to be home. And it's not okay to think about that place.

I look in another half-open drawer because an almost impercepti-ble scent, a fruity sweetness, pulls me to it. There's the plastic bag with my silk shirt from San Diego and my little red notebook. I don't want the shirt anymore. It looks too cold. I don't want to be cold anymore. With book in hand and shoes on feet—my favorite old moccasins—it's now time to take the next action: it is now time to walk out of the bedroom into the living room and through the living room, hopefully, out the front door.

What if . . . ? Forget about the what-ifs. I'm too excited to be afraid now. Deep breath—whoops, mistake. I go dizzy and lose my balance. I still can't feel my body with consistency. I slowly get up watching my feet to make certain they are firmly planted, and walk out of the bedroom.

There's the kitchen, the fish tank bubbling away, the living room . . . Everything is quiet and peaceful. The front door is wide open. That explains the breeze, the noisy steps, jangling keys, and loud TV from downstairs. Wanda had left without looking back. I successfully maneu-ver past everything to the front door.

The realization that I am about to be free stands before me a phys-ical presence to be pushed aside. I am paralyzed at the door. This is so anticlimactic, unbelievable even. I'm just walking out into the day like all those people I heard going to work.

The casualness of this is such a surreal juxtaposition on what I have just been through. My mind can't grasp the simple fact. I feel my brain ticking away trying to make sense of the situation just as one calculates a math problem. It's futile. There's no sense to be made. I feel a fog settling in, covering all the latest reality with a dreamlike haze.

I step through the door. I walk toward the stairs. A man in a suit with coffee and a newspaper walks by.

"Good morning, Miss," he said, with a smile.

Foggy haze in my mind, I hear the blaring TV. Aha! A focal point, a moment of clarity as I traverse the stairs. I must pay attention, or I'll be sure to fall. Okay. Made it.

The fog closes in completely. My inner eye can almost see the dark pulsating spots shutting down all the mental areas that store the recent past. Just . . . that . . . fast . . .

Why am I at this place? Am I going up the stairs or down? My hand is still on the railing. Something is wrong with me. I can't think straight. The last thing I remember is David and Rhonda yelling at me because I won't go back to Chauncy's. The red padded bench . . . Money on display at Vegas World. But I know that had happened a long time ago. I'm sure of it. So, how did I end up here?

Something's wrong with me. Bad people, bad people. I have to get off the street. The loud TV cuts through my mental mumbling. I walk zombielike toward the sound.

The condo door isn't quite closed. It's pulled shut, but I can see that the lock isn't engaged. The urge to hide is overwhelming. I find myself looking up at an open condo door on the second floor with much anxiety. Why? I painstakingly inch the door I'm in front of open, and stick my head inside.

The TV is excruciatingly loud. There are beer cans everywhere. Other than that and a box of pizza on the coffee table, the room is meticulously neat—no dust, no signs of daily activity.

I see the back top half of a man's head just above the easy chair. He's alternating between ranting and raving, and snoring. Obviously, he's having a bad dream. I go in and close the door with an ambiguous slowness. I'm fascinated with the scene. This man is not just tossing and turning, he's shouting and ducking and screaming as if for his life, and just when it seems he's about to explode, he starts snoring.

It took me about an hour to work my way fully into the room. I eventually ended up seated in the darkest corner on the floor flush with the TV, looking up at the man in awe. He had a crew cut and a nice square jawline. He wore a white T-shirt and boxers. And he was in perfect physical condition except for the tight, distended beer belly. I felt comfortable around this gruff form of safety (Mr. Alexander, toast and sunny-side up eggs . . . cigarettes).

The man was thoroughly entertaining. Day turned to night as I observed his sporadic violent fits, which were frighteningly funny. He never woke, and I found myself growing quite fond of the sleeping grizzly.

The front door opened. A compact little Italian-looking guy came in. He was around twenty and had an extremely cut physique. Those weren't the domesticated muscles of a gym rat. He was dangerously chiseled under the loose navy blue sweat suit he had on, the angles of fitness coming from some menacing, mysterious activity. I subconsciously tried to become smaller. My movement caught his eye.

"Hey."

"Hey."

He completely sized me up in that short exchange.

"You a friend of the Sarge, here?"

"I just met him today."

"You want a beer?"

"Sh-sure."

He tossed me a *Coors* out of the case he was carrying, went to the kitchen, put it in the fridge, and came back with a couple for him and Sarge. He opened a beer and put it in the dreaming man's hand. The matter-of-factness of his demeanor made everything seem normal.

"Sarge is cool. He's a Vietnam vet. He's shell-shocked."

"What?"

"Shell-shocked." He explained the term to me—how Sarge was reliving the war and all.

"He's f——cked up, man, but don't think he don't know what's going on. Don't eat nothing or take anything. He'll be on you, man."

"Why?"

"Come here. Let me show you something."

We walked back to the bedroom and he slid the closet door open. Wow! It was full of rows and rows of canned food, twine, bottled water, reading materials, sleeping gear, ammunition, and oversize mason jars filled with quarters.

"He's got enough supplies in here to survive for two years. At least that's what he says. He knows every *goddamn* can of tuna, every f——cking piece of dust on the floor, man. Don't touch nothin'."

I was impressed. We went back to the living room. Tony started telling me his story, the only interruptions being trips to the kitchen to get Sarge a beer.

He said he was a strong-arm from Chicago and had killed more people than he could count. He claimed to be in Vegas laying low until he got the word it was okay to go back. I thought he might be exaggerating, but I was enjoying the story so much, I didn't care.

"You don't believe me, do you? You know how many times I shoulda been dead? I got so much metal in my body, it ain't even funny, man."

He took off his shirt. Tony wasn't lying. The perfectly sculpted torso was absolutely riddled with bullet holes, knife wounds, and stiletto gouges. We laughed and talked. The scene was absurdly macabre—the TV blasting, Sarge's Tourette's-like outbursts, and this young warrior telling me the story behind each fresh wound and old scar with childish delight.

"Bullet went in here, came out here."

He twisted and pointed at the entry and exit points.

"Now I've got a little pump in this lung here"—more pointing—"helping me breathe. Feel this plate in my head?"

He took my hand and placed it on his forehead. I nodded, running my fingers over it, my eyebrows raising high in surprise. There really was a piece of metal right under the skin. I was riveted with awe.

"Saved my f——cking life. Took two bullets right in the middle of my forehead and they just stuck in the steel, man. Nurse in the emergency room passed out on the spot when I walked in."

He couldn't stop laughing at the memory. It was contagious, and now we were both laughing almost to the point of tears.

"Bu-hah-ha-ha. But, anyway . . . I love Chicago. Can't keep me away no matter how many people are after me."

We carried on in this manner—my *oohs* and *aahs*, our laughs, the laughter turning to giggles every time the Sarge had a fit.

Then Tony's laugh wanes, and he gives me a longer look.

"Hey, you're all right with me. You're a real cool chick. Guy could fall for you in a hurry. You ain't no whore. I can see that. Maybe you'll come with me when I go back to Chicago. You hungry?"

He stands as he heads out to get some food.

"It might take me a while because people are looking for me, but I'll be back. Just keep Sarge pumped up on the brew."

He left.

I went and got Sarge a beer from the fridge. I was afraid to put it in his hand. Finally I worked up the nerve and shoved the beer in his hairy leathery hand, flinching as I scurried back to my corner on the floor. He drank it and got up wandering into the other room. I heard him pissing. He came back, sat down, opened his eyes, and stared at me really hard. He leaned forward to get a closer look, his face a mask of somber inquisition.

I had nowhere to hide.

"*You!*"

I started.

"Get back in my head, *goddamnit*! Get back in my head!"

His arms were wildly signaling me in the general direction of his cranium.

"Hey."

Poking a finger at his temple.

"*Hey!* Get *in* here!"

Then he was staring past me, through me, at some enemy battleground, running, screaming, frantic! Snore!

I started breathing again. We went through this a couple more times. It got to the point where Sarge would just stare at me with great disappointment and annoyance because I wouldn't listen to him and climb back in his brain. I wish I could. That would solve everything for him *and* me.

Tony was gone for at least two hours. He flew back in all sweaty from running. He had many cartons of delicious-smelling Chinese food with him.

"How're you and Sarge getting along?"

Tony set the food down on the kitchen counter.

"He doesn't think I'm real."

Tony walked over to Sarge and proceeded to smack him about the temples a few times.

"Hey, Sarge. Snap out of it. Come on. I got food, man. Come on."

He went through this for a good ten minutes before any noticeable change took place. Sarge's eyes eventually focused into recognition and his face lit up into a big sh———t-eating grin.

"*Toh-neee!*"

He clamped Tony's head between his rugged paws and rotated it back and forth.

"You been taking good care of me."

His smoky laugh was huge and raucous. It made me jump. Sarge turned his head.

"Hey, man. She's real. You been talking to her like she's some kinda f———cking ghost or guardian angel or something. She didn't come out of your head. She came through the door, man. Now say *hello*."

Sarge couldn't stop laughing. He was rolling, skin reddening, eyes bulging. I had to laugh myself. His big, deep scratchy laugh was commanding me to do so.

The two of them told stupid jokes back and forth. I happily took the fly-on-the-wall position, eating up every last bit of the light-heartedness. Sarge started slipping away into a peaceful, dreamless sleep. Tony guided him into the bedroom and tucked him in. He came back with blankets and pillows and lay down.

"Come lay next to me."

I didn't hesitate. I needed his protection. We were both fully clothed. Tony held me. And the way he held me was remarkable. It was somewhere between comforting me and clinging to me for comfort. It made me want to cry, but no tears came.

"I love you, little chickadee. You're real cool. Just lean on me and sleep. Tomorrow, I want you to tell me who f———cked with you, and I'm gonna go kill him—or them. You just take it easy tonight."

I stiffened. What was he talking about? Um . . .

He sensed my question and mistook my unease.

"Look. In this world people don't just say *I'm sorry* and shake hands. They f——ck with you, they die. If you let 'em live, they're gonna f——ck with you again. End of story. That's just the way it is. You let me take care of this."

I didn't say a word. I just hung on tight to this very real protector.

The next day, Sarge came out, beer in hand, turned on the TV, and got down to it. Tony went out. I relaxed. Now I was used to Sarge and his screaming. I even felt comfortable enough to sit on the couch instead of on the floor. But I wasn't so foolish as to change the channel—no need to poke the bear. I settled in and resigned myself to watching whatever programming came on whether I liked it or not. Boredom quickly set in.

My mind immediately went to the meticulously stocked emergency closet. Sarge was snoring heavily. I tiptoed back and looked in the closet. I just wanted to see. I couldn't decide if this methodical disaster preparation made him crazy or brilliant. I looked at one of the jars of loose quarters. How could he know if one or two quarters were missing? It wasn't about wanting money. I didn't believe that Sarge would empty out those huge jars and count the quarters every day. There had to be more than two hundred dollars' worth in each jar. I opened two jars and took one quarter out of each and screwed the lids back on. I put the quarters in my pocket. He wouldn't notice—no way.

I went back to Sarge and the TV. All was as I had left it, and I wasn't bored anymore. If I were *really* smart, I would've taken the quarters out and added them to another jar to see if he'd notice that. Oh well, I wasn't going to risk that now.

Tony came back late. It was a repeat of the night before, except this time the food was Italian. After lots of laughter and beer, Tony walked Sarge to bed and then held me through the night. Right as I was about to fall asleep he whispered, "What are their names?"

Terror washed over me.

"I don't know."

"What did they do to you?"

"I don't know."

"It's all right. Just sleep. Just sleep. Forget about it."

I relaxed.

We woke up the next morning to Sarge's huge hairy hands yanking us up one at a time and throwing us on the couch.

"Who took my money?!"

Sarge looked ready to kill—red skin, bulging eyes, no laughter.

"One of you took fifty cents out of my closet, and I want to know who."

I was trembling.

"What? Fifty cents? Jesus, Sarge. Relax, man. Here."

Tony flipped him a few quarters. He couldn't keep the laughter out of his voice.

"Here's your f——cking fifty cents. Ain't no thing. I'm sorry. She's sorry. It won't happen again."

"Who took it?"

"Come on, baby. Let's take a walk and let him calm down."

He grabbed my arm and pulled me out the door. We could hear Sarge yelling at us as we were walking away, "You're both going to have to leave by the end of tonight."

Tony was still laughing.

"What'd you take fifty cents for?"

"I didn't. I swear!"

I couldn't admit it.

"You ain't got to lie to me. I love you. Sarge may be crazy, but he don't go off about sh——t unless it really happens."

I shook my head and averted my eyes. Tony saw how panicked and guilty I felt.

"He ain't gonna throw us out. Don't sweat it. Everything'll be cool in about an hour."

He was laughing at me under his breath.

"Let's go grab some breakfast."

We walked over to the strip. It was so weird to be back out there on the strip exposed by the daylight. I was twitching with nervousness and couldn't wait to be in the safety of a restaurant. We ordered. That was better.

My shoulders were up so high it ached to bring them back down. I put my head down and sighed a little sigh of relief.

Tony pulled my face up by the chin with a jerk.

"So, who are they?"

No response.

"All right then, *where* are they?"

Nothing.

"Look, you don't have to be afraid. I'll get rid of 'em so fast they won't know what hit 'em. Tell me!"

I looked away with embarrassment.

I wanted to answer him, but my mind wouldn't work. I couldn't register anything. We ate in silence. He was fuming. I was guilt ridden about the quarters and feeling stupid because I couldn't answer his questions. We walked back in silence. My anxiety magnified with each step. I wasn't looking forward to facing Sarge.

We reached the condo. Tony opened the door and parentally shoved me in. Sarge was out of it. The TV was blaring. Everything was back to normal. Except for me. I downed quite a few beers that day. I wanted to crawl out of my skin. As the beer took effect, I racked my brain trying to dredge up some facts for Tony—nothing, 100 percent blank.

Tony was in the moment. He was back to his animated self.

The phone rang around midnight. It was for Tony. He listened and hung up.

"I gotta leave at 5:00 a.m. for Chicago. Come with me."

I wanted to and didn't want to. He saw my ambiguity but seemed pretty sure he could persuade me to go. I fell asleep in his arms. He was trying to wake me a few hours later.

"Come on, baby. Let's go."

I wanted to respond but just couldn't. He looked so sad and sorry for me. He gently cupped my face in his hands.

"Aw, baby, what did they do to you? You're just lost. I love you, and I'll never forget you."

No response from me. I couldn't take in any emotion. He understood perfectly.

"Stop worrying about the quarters, okay? No biggy. Sarge is over that. Just be safe. Just be safe."

He was smiling tenderly.

"Promise me you won't worry about the quarters anymore. Okay?"

I nodded silently.

And with that, he was gone.

I quickly escaped into a restless sleep.

The following day, I heard Sarge walking around and smelled bacon and eggs. I didn't want to come out from under the covers. I knew I would have to eventually. I heard him picking up the empty beer cans and throwing them away. He didn't turn the TV on. I could tell by the rhythm of his step that he was sober and coherent. He went back into the bedroom. I heard the shower running. He hadn't done that before. I folded up my blankets and picked up the empty food containers. I sat down on the sofa with a timid wait-and-see attitude.

Sarge came out looking completely grounded. He had jeans on and looked like a real stable guy. His face registered shock. It was as if it were the first time he really took me in. I don't know what he and Tony saw in me that made them look at me with a mixture of heartbreak, compassion, and anger.

"Oh, my God. How can I help you, baby?"

"Get me out of this town."

"Okay. You got it."

He looked me in the eye with serious, fatherly concern.

"I thought you and Tony were gonna be together."

I shook my head.

"Sorry you guys didn't work. You were nice together. Hang on just a minute."

He went to his bedroom. I heard him rummaging around. He strode back in with the keys looking small in his impressively large hand.

"Let's go."

Does the child ever die? Ooh, look at all the pretty colors . . .

CHAPTER 18

An Unlikely Tourist

Silence. It wasn't awkward. There was no need to talk. The silence was appropriate.

Sarge drove me through the city, out of the city, into the desert until the flat placid terrain turned to gentle hills. I stared at his profile the entire time, the undulating view beyond functioning as an ever-changing backdrop. He lit a cigarette. The car started to slow.

"See that ahead there?"

He was pointing, and my eyes tracked his arm to the point of his finger. His voice sounded like sand. The car came to a stop.

"That's the Hoover Dam. You walk a little way over that, and you'll be out of Vegas, doll."

He threw the car in park, got out, the engine still running, walked to my side of the car, and opened the door for me. I'm not sure if this was a gentlemanly gesture or if he knew that was the only way I would get out. We walked over to an official-looking man in khakis and waited our turn as he directed a few tourists. Sarge peeled off a few bucks and stuffed them into the man's hand.

"Let her take the elevator ride. I don't think she'll be in these parts again anytime soon, and she's got to see what the dam's all about."

Sarge attempted a polite smile, which amounted to nothing more than a wince. The cigarette looked ideal hanging out of his mouth. He gave me a manly pat on the back. Tenderness was inappropriate in this situation. Walking resolutely to his idling car, Sarge drove off never looking back.

I went on the elevator ride. There was a copper-etched explanatory plaque on the inside panel. One wall of the elevator was glass so I could see the dam, how it was built, and the water it was holding back.

I didn't pay much attention. I was limp as the elevator descended. I leaned my head against the stainless steel interior as I looked at the bubbling water. I exited the elevator and listened to the tour guide tick off dam trivia for a while. His delivery was boring—so boring, the words were lost on me. Well . . . I guess it was time to go. I shrugged my shoulders and walked over the state border. *Bye-bye, Vegas.*

Hello, Arizona. It felt good to be walking again. The air was a little cool but more refreshing than uncomfortable. I liked the smell of the land. It was a kind of musk mixed with eucalyptus or pine. The further I walked, the redder the earth became.

I walked for several hours without complaint. Very few cars passed, maybe one per hour. I started to relax. Once I became habituated to the landscape, I began fantasizing about being an American Indian maneuvering the plains on foot. I was having great fun feeling quite beautiful, regal even. A car broke my spell. Instead of the usual swoosh of a fast-passing vehicle I heard the wheels crunching to a stop.

It was a big old white car spattered with red mud. The back seat was filled to the brim with old junk: hubcaps, toaster ovens, dolls, you name it. The old man driving the car made me smile. He wore a vintage Hawaiian shirt and a big straw hat. His skin had that leathery quality to it of one who smokes too much and is out in the sun a lot. He must've been seventy or eighty.

"You want a ride?"

"No, thank you, sir."

He hesitated and then slowly drove off. As soon as he pulled away, I regretted it. I realized that I was actually exhausted and that the old man would've been harmless. Oh, well. Lost was my royal fantasy. Now I trudged along feeling small and whiny. I walked for another hour. My head was so low, I almost ran into the back of his car. He had pulled to the side of the road.

"I was waiting for you. Why don't you come on and take a ride? I'm going as far as Phoenix."

I hopped in—big internal sigh of relief. The car was roomy enough to let me sit quite a distance from him. And I liked the red vinyl seats. Leatherface was listening to a talk radio station that would play an occasional oldie. It was okay to relax. He was so old, I couldn't imagine him coming on to me or posing a threat. My relaxation morphed into excitement. Phoenix . . . wow! I was getting really far away from California. Motion. It felt proactive.

Leatherface didn't talk much. When he did, his delivery was slow and disconnected—a sentence every seven minutes or so, "I'm a junk man." *Tick, tock, tick, tock* . . . "I sell junk." *Tick, tock, tick, tock* . . . "I'm taking this carload to Phoenix now, to make a little money."

I didn't talk at all. He never asked me questions. How wonderful! My stress level was zero. Being asked questions in my situation was significantly unnerving. Answering them made me feel like crap because everything I said was certain to be a lie. This guy had no curiosity level or societal etiquette. Polite social banter was unnecessary. I could've kissed him.

Because he had such a peculiar personal tempo, I felt emboldened to observe him more directly. He made me want to laugh. He looked like a skinny tan Rodney Dangerfield with his hat, his superbright shirt, his white pants, and white shoes.

Phoenix: One hundred and eighty-three miles . . . we had a long way to go. I leaned back in the seat hunkering down for the ride in complete chill mode. We drove along for about forty more minutes, with nothing but the sound of the engine, the wheels on the road, the mosquito-like voices of the talk radio jocks, and a sporadic croak from the old man.

It was a perfect recipe for sleep. My lids started to flutter. I couldn't keep my eyes open. Aaah, that peaceful feeling of surrender right as you're about to fall asleep when you're more tired than tired. Down, down, down into the depths of . . . a rude awakening.

My skin crawled as his weather-beaten, wrinkled old hand slipped down the front of my pants. I opened my eyes and his face made me ill. Its expression epitomized utter perversion—tongue slightly hanging out, a little sweat on the brow, that I'm-getting-off-because-I'm-living-out-a-sick-fantasy smile splaying across his lips—a very different profile than Sarge's grim nobility.

I yanked his hand out of my pants, grabbed my little red book, and started heading out the door. He sped the car up thinking it would deter me. When he saw that I had already opened the door, he slowed back down a bit. I dived out. Roll, roll, road, gravel, dirt, plants, fence, pole, thud, stop. I crawled under the fence and jogged away from the road.

I wasn't nervous about Leatherface. His car was almost out of sight by the time I stood up. No, my concern was for the other cars that might come along.

I was through, man. Enough is enough! I'd rather starve than take a chance on a helping hand.

I had relaxed so much in that car. My guard had been completely down. As a result, I had felt every move of that old man's scaly, dirty fingers. My body felt polluted to the inside of my bones. I couldn't shake it off. I couldn't run it off. I couldn't get over it. *Jesus!* Even an eighty-year-old man had no integrity. Even *his* dick was more important than treating a young girl like a person—unbelievable. This was the last straw for me. People were inhumane. People were mercilessly self-absorbed. I didn't want to have anything to do with them.

I jog-trotted away from the road until I couldn't see it anymore. This relieved one threat but left me completely open to another. You see, as mentioned before, I am not a nature girl. I find no peace in the fresh air of open, untamed land where silence is broken only by birds calling or leaves rustling in the wind. Daylight in these settings makes me nervous; when night falls, I'm a terrified mess. I was determined, however, to face and fight my fears. I could be brave, I told myself, as long as I didn't run into those motherf——cking *higher forms of life* called people.

Only a few hours of daylight were left. I had to admit that there was an undeniable beauty to the soft rolling landscape. I was surrounded by bright red clay to the left; round soft dunes to the right; and gray-green wispy fields ahead of me.

I decided to sit down and write in my book. I knew what day it was because I had heard it on the radio in the car. I opened my book, and a chill ran down my spine. The last entry had been made just a little after my birthday, almost two months ago. What had happened to the time between now and then? I tried to recollect. Nothing came to mind.

This was the first time I was really scared of *myself*. This was the first time it occurred to me that I might be in big trouble mentally and physically. I couldn't face that possibility. Even a hint of that thought creeping into my mind overwhelmed me and left me feeling fragile, broken, and highly alarmed. Instead of writing, I put the date, three question marks, and snapped the book shut. I got up and started walking with great determination to nowhere. The determination, not the destination, is what mattered. It interrupted my panic.

The sunset was beautiful, and I forgot about everything as I watched it. The intense rose color the open land turned right before the sun disappeared was awe-inspiring. I immersed myself in its natural beauty maximally as I journeyed on.

However, I could no longer ignore my fear of the encroaching night. I was a mess. As each level of darkness set in, the land became more alive with the sounds of the "locals." I could no longer see the ground, and my feet were insensitive and disconnected from the earth. I pathetically stumbled and clawed my way along as fast as I could to nowhere.

The climax of my fear the whole time I was out in the open came when a big owl dive-bombed right into my head. The force with which it struck me and my surprise worked me into a fever pitch surpassing desperation. I started running frantically falling almost every other step, oblivious to the toe-stubbing and gouging rocks. Exhaustion was the only thing that slowed my pace. *Where are you, Nowhere? Can't get there fast enough.*

The night seemed endless. My franticness only showed signs of subsiding when the pitch black started turning to gray black. Day must be coming soon. As I began to concentrate on that fact, my body became aware of the morning cold. I was freezing.

Luckily this was easily remedied. I had refined the art of numbing out. Within three minutes I felt nothing. I was numb. The difference when one is numb is seen in the attitude of one's gait. Instead of walking with purpose and determination, I was truly wandering aimlessly now, just another speck of life blowing around on the plains.

Day . . . night . . . I didn't write anything in my little book except two words: *Another day.* I didn't even date it. I really didn't want to know if I lost time. The night . . . sunshine: *Another day.*

This nature walk was hell, a living nightmare—another silent scream, total desolation. It wasn't like the movies. I never adjusted to my surroundings. My only peace came at sunset.

An occasional house would appear in the distance, or I'd happen onto a small back road. These signs of civilization only served as motivation for me to alter my route to the most unpopulated direction—to nowhere.

Now there were fir trees and little patches of snow on the ground. I knew I had walked pretty far because the terrain had changed so. A town now loomed before me that was too big to avoid. I guess I was still human after all because curiosity got the better of me. Where was I? I went into the bathroom of an isolated gas station. The hot water felt good on my hands. I washed as thoroughly as I could and drank tons of water. I stayed in there for hours undisturbed. I felt refreshed, revitalized, and not cold. Which meant it was time to get going again.

But I still did not know where I was. This nagged at me and caused me to linger. I heard the attendant outside gassing up a car. Aha! I had a short minute to do my sleuth work. I went into the station trying to see something that would tell me where I was. There was some mail behind the counter. I thumbed through a few pieces. Flagstaff, Arizona. Okay, I was in Flagstaff.

I took off. No one disturbed me, and before I knew it, I was back inside the darkness and wind. I was feeling a little better because I'd still looked okay in my reflection in the bathroom mirror. I gleaned a precious fragment of comfort from the fact that I didn't look like a bum or have cuts or bruises on my face. People would still perceive me as normal. I traipsed along without incident.

The next point of civilization I hit was Albuquerque, New Mexico. I passed through uneventfully. It felt a little abandoned there, like a ghost town. The most excitement I had there involved donuts.

Dunkin' Donuts dumped their donuts in the trash every hour on the hour. I knew this because as fate would have it, I walked past the dumpster just as the employees were tossing a batch.

"What a waste, man. Why can't I take these home?"

"Wanna get fired?"

"I don't see what it hurts."

"Don't risk it."

"We do this every hour. Do you know how many donuts we waste?"

I hung around there for about four hours and glutted myself on donuts from the dumpster. I marveled at being so physically depleted that I could *snarf* down two glazed old fashions and one or two cream- or jelly-filled donuts on the hour without throwing up. Jeez, I must've really needed them because I didn't feel them or see any evidence of them in my reflection in the window. Mind-boggling. I considered it quite an accomplishment. Old neuroses die hard.

Another day I found a five-dollar bill. Money always equaled societal ritual. The five bought me a few sodas and a Big Mac, but more importantly, it allowed me to participate in the majority group.

I started feeling less threatened by people. No one even tried to talk to me. I became much more at ease among the buildings and found myself really taking my time about heading back into the desert. It was almost nice being a marginal part of the norm. And . . . I wanted to rest.

After roughly three days in Albuquerque, I left. At last the police cruisers were starting to notice me, marking me as an outsider. I couldn't risk being sent back to Ma—time to vacate.

As soon as the last city lights were left behind me and faded from view, I felt really bad. I just couldn't face the darkness again. I was too tired and weak. I needed to lie down and be warm. I walked for some hours moving forward in silent distressed protest. *Nowhere, where are you?* Then I saw a truck stop with a restaurant.

I went in and ordered a cup of coffee. I only had eighty-nine cents, but I didn't care. If it wasn't enough money, I'd deal with it when I left. I didn't even drink coffee normally, but I needed to sit there for a while and knew that coffee meant free refills. I tried my best to be invisible at the end of the counter. I made each cup the color of lightly toasted marshmallows and just about as sweet. It was fun. I was a kid again enjoying too much sugar and playing with my food.

No one bothered me. The waitresses called me sweetheart and honey. It was deliciously cozy. I never wanted to leave. This was the best I'd felt on my entire adventure so far. This little warm, toasty corner of time was and still is the fondest memory I have of my trek. My cheeks were hot. My fingers wrapped around the coffee cup each time in eager anticipation of its ceramic version of heat and cheer. I literally felt myself thawing out. It seemed if I sat there long enough all my problems would be solved. But all good things come to an end. And so it did.

I could see the manager or owner pushing the waitress to kick me out. His body language was unbiased and matter-of-fact. She walked over.

"It's on me, honey."

She winked and gave me a big knowing smile. I took the cue.

Out I went. *Oh! It's so cold!* I was really not mentally rejuvenated enough to handle this. I walked for an hour and still couldn't shake this whiny indignation. Darn! My distress level had just been waiting for me on ice outside the diner. I thought it had gone away for good.

I quickly realized I was willing to do just about anything to feel warm, rest, and escape my pain. It didn't take long for someone to call my bluff. I noticed another oasis of gas stations and food in the distance and locked in on it.

I passed under a pitch-black viaduct tunnel and was about to step into the light when I saw a bunch of truckers drinking behind a truck. I ducked down. They looked menacing and were talking a lot of sh——t about women. I sensed the danger and stayed submerged in the darkness. A car was leaving the gas station and caught a glimpse of me in its headlights. That was all the encouragement the driver needed to start driving in my direction. It had to be a man the way he was making a beeline toward me. I didn't jump off the road. I'd already made up my mind to get in. I even decided to try to sell myself if he approached me sexually.

"You need a ride?"

"Maybe," I said without looking his way. He cruised alongside me with the passenger window rolled down so he could communicate. I kept walking.

"Well, *maybe* we could work something out. What do you want?"

I stopped and faced him, backing far enough away from the car so I could look straight in the passenger window without bending down. My voice was unnecessarily aggressive, and I was over-enunciating.

"I want a train ticket to the next state and some dinner."

He shook off my harsh delivery and responded.

"Okay. I can do that. Hop in."

I did. *Anything* would be better than my eternal trip to nowhere.

"Chinese food okay?"

I nodded. I didn't look at him. I felt cheap and tawdry, but I was determined to go through with it. After driving in silence for a few minutes, we stopped at a big roadside Chinese place, and he got food to go. Then we drove to the liquor store and he bought some wine. I waited for him in the car and scrutinized him when he got out both times.

Yuck! He had a David Cassidy shag haircut, a walrus mustache, and a polyester button-down shirt, light blue with a dark blue pattern of some kind on it. His dark blue polyester pants were a tad too short and a little too tight. His red skin clashed with his coppery blond hair and gold chain, and he had narrow, sneaky eyes. He would've been more attractive if he hadn't been trying so hard to embody the latest and greatest trends.

We drove down the road another five minutes and checked into a sleazy motel. I didn't say a thing. I went directly to the shower. It was very small and square. The drain was rusted, and the floor surface cracked a little. The water temperature was hard to control. It was too hot no matter how I adjusted it. I got used to it and stayed under the water flow for a long, long . . . long time. Well, at least I was warm. I tried to be pleased with myself but . . .

"Hey, don't wash yourself away now," he chuckled nervously trying to sound playful. "You've been in there a mighty long time."

. . . I couldn't. I turned off the water and the light and dried myself with one of the small threadbare towels.

The moment had come. I left my clothes in a pile on the floor. I opened the door a crack. He had turned the lights out. Good! I made a quick dash to the bed and climbed under the covers. He walked into the bathroom and turned the light back on so we weren't in complete darkness. He came back and poured wine into the Styrofoam motel cups. It was red. I had never tasted red wine before. Yuck! I see why. I drank it anyway. I guess the food was for later because he wasn't paying much attention to it.

He leaned over and started kissing me. I let him. I seemed pretty neutral about it. I didn't feel fear, excitement, disgust, or pleasure. He didn't gross me out. It was just weird to have this stranger touching my body.

I had no response to his touch whatsoever. This was fascinating to me. I saw his hands on me but couldn't feel anything. Where had I learned to zone out this completely? I knew I had been building up the ability to numb out when I was being touched against my will, but it was always in reaction to my initial fear and disgust. This was totally different. I never felt the initial touch. It was like watching a love scene on TV. That sense of foreboding consumed me again for just a second. Something was really wrong with me. I shook it off.

Polyester Man was getting frustrated. He lay back and opened up his pants pulling his underwear down just enough. He pushed my head in the direction of his dick. This was going to be hard—no pun intended. Couldn't he just use me? I was very resistant to actively doing anything to *him*. That was really more than I could stomach, but . . . I closed my eyes and closed my mouth around his dick. My loathing and disgust were temporarily interrupted by surprise.

What was this thing I had in my mouth? I went through the motion of sucking for a maybe a minute. My surprise brought me into the present. I felt the little thing getting harder but not longer. It was like sucking on less than a thumb. A gruesome giggle started bubbling up inside me. Each time I moved my head up and down, I thought it was so funny. Up and down, what, maybe an inch? I couldn't contain my giggle. I really couldn't believe how small his thing was. I just *had* to see. I took my mouth off, looked down, and proceeded to burst out laughing.

He threw me down and started "f———cking" me. I tried (really and truly I did) to hide my laughter in moans but was quite unsuccessful. The funniest moment was when he came. The groan, the clenching of the hands, the wincing face, the little, itty-bitty dick . . . I was just dying. Hysterical laughter wracked my body. He zipped himself up and mumbled something about running out to get some smokes. I was pretty sure he wasn't coming back. Fifteen minutes later, I knew I was right. I wasn't upset.

I was aberrantly, victoriously ecstatic! I had a motel room, TV, and enough Chinese takeout for two or three days. It was a great night. I watched stupid TV and drank the wine like shots, chasing it with Coca-Cola. Soon I was drunk, warm, and happy. The salty, greasy food was a shock to my system, but who cared? Now I was having a good, hearty laugh at myself toasting the thin air at my first and last attempt at hooking. I guess I wasn't cut out for that. Ha! Ma was wrong. No way in *hell* was I a whore! *I love you TV. Entertain me until I fall asleep. What a good friend you are . . .*

Truth? Not sure what that is . . .

CHAPTER 19

Wake Up

Knock, knock, knock!

"For to clean, Señor. You want?"

"No, no. Come back later."

I looked at the clock. Oh, no! One hour after check out. I must've slept or passed out. I'd better get a move on. I quickly threw on my clothes, grabbed my journal and the remaining Chinese take-out, and left.

It was a nice day. I felt a little bit more connected to the world today, a little more with the program. I felt I could brave the elements today. As pathetic as that short human interaction had been with Polyester Man, it had pulled me back into my physical self. Annoyed by the bag of food, I tossed it out—much better. It was too much of a hindrance, and the smell was making me queasy. I felt a little muscle pain today. I felt a twinge in the back of my thighs with each step I took. It was going to be a long day today. The sun was strong. It wouldn't be long before the day's heat matched its brightness. I wasn't afraid of people today.

Nighttime . . . cold . . . muscle cramps . . . hunger . . . day . . . night . . . day . . . night . . . the beginnings of a feeling . . . what is it? Hmmm . . . day . . . night . . . day . . . night . . . day . . . big commercial truck pulling over . . .

I didn't even realize I had stuck my thumb out when I'd heard its engine in the distance. Not looking at the driver when I got in, I slammed the door, crossed my arms, and closed my eyes.

I enjoyed being rattled around by the truck. It was akin to a milder version of surrendering to the surf. The volume of the engine's roar . . . being unceremoniously jolted in various directions. The truck rocked me to sleep. When I awoke (probably because of a particularly jarring jolt) it was nighttime. I studied the driver. He had a nice face—a cute young Mexican face. I inwardly smiled as I closed my eyes and drifted off again. Next time I opened them it was because Muchacho Guapo was gently shaking me awake. The truck was at a standstill. I had to sit fully upright to see out the window.

We were in a motel parking lot. We got out and went into a room. It had two full-size beds. I got in one and immediately pulled the covers over myself including my head. Muchacho Guapo turned the lights out and started trying to touch me through the covers, a hand reaching through here, a face peeking in there (such a cute face). He tried for about fifteen minutes, but I just lay there like a dead fish. Guapo laughed, said something in Spanish, and climbed into his own bed. God bless those Latino men for liking their women to participate.

I slept peacefully that night. He woke me again. I could hear the smile in his voice, and his hands felt kind as they gently shook me to attention. It was just dawn. Through my deep, sleepy fog, it took me a while to understand that he was telling me it was time to go. I got up, and we hit the road. What a nice, dreamy ride! I again fell in and out of sleep almost rhythmically with the truck, further emphasizing the wash of relaxation. It was nice to open my eyes and see Guapo's young gentle face. We reached his/our destination at about sunset: the Nogales Trucking Company.

The place was very utilitarian looking and extremely clean. Waxed white floors, a few shelves of car-repair items for passing motorists to buy—very nondescript. The driver was explaining about me in Spanish to his boss. They both looked my way and smiled a lot, seeming to have come to some kind of agreement. Guapo tipped his hat, gave me one of his winning smiles, and was on his way. My new acquaintance behind the counter pointed to a stool.

"Sit. Sit."

He bought me a thirty-five-cent cup of hot chocolate from the automatic dispenser and gave me one of the company windbreakers to wear. The day was a cheerful one for me. I sat and watched him attend to business. Truckers came and went. He answered the phone and dispatched trucks in Spanish and broken English. He would clean during the lulls.

He had found the perfect balance of ignoring me yet, at the same time, making me feel extremely welcome. We both had a role. He was the busy businessman, and I was the lucky kid who should feel honored and privileged to be at work with "Dad," amazed by his every move. I had no problem with this at all. I sat there for about four hours slurping down as much hot chocolate as the man would give me until it was time to close up shop.

Only then did I notice the actual man and not only his actions. I now saw he had a mustache and very good posture. Suddenly, he had color in his cheeks, warmth in his face, and purpose in his step. The change took place after a phone call home to his wife. Home must be a good place. What a concept!

Parting ways was a little strange. The truck stop was the only building on that stretch of road as far as the eye could see. As we were leaving the shop, I started to give him the jacket back.

"No, no. Keep."

I put it back on. He felt bad about leaving me in the middle of nowhere in the middle of the night, but he was a resolute family man with great self-protective skills. He wouldn't do anything that could possibly jeopardize him or his family. He'd given me all the kindness he could and was pleased with himself. He'd done a good job. God would take care of the rest. He got in his car, almost rubbing his hands together in anticipation of the comforts of home. I walked off into the darkness.

It didn't bother me anymore, the darkness. I thought it was where I belonged now. I had no home. Women wouldn't help me, and men would only help me if I gave them sex and acted like I wanted them. I was still afraid out in nature, but I figured this was just part of the deal. My world had never been secure, so why should I expect it to be now? Who was I to whine about fear and cold and the unknown? As long as I didn't have to deal with Ma's accusing eye and evil mind, as long as I wasn't being raped or molested, I would handle this desert darkness until I couldn't. Night . . . day . . . night . . . day . . .

Two long-distance bicyclists pass by off to my left. Night . . . day . . . two long-distance bicyclists passing by . . . no wait. They're riding back to me. They look harmless: white college boys out on an adventure. *Have fun, kids.*

"Hey, how did you get ahead of us again?"

"I don't understand?"

"We passed you yesterday, and now you're in front of us again."

"I don't know."

"Wow, you just walked through the night? Holy sh——t! Where are you going?"

Stupid keeps asking stupid questions. His friend is a little more perceptive.

To Stupid, "Shut up, man."

To me, "Here, have an orange and take this money."

He handed me a twenty.

"I can't take your money."

"Umm . . . here's my address."

He wrote his address on the back of a store receipt and handed it to me.

"Pay me back someday, okay?"

"All right."

"Good luck. Stay tough."

Off they rode into the distance.

I stuffed the twenty in my pocket. It cheered me up a little even though there was no place to spend it out here in the middle of nowhere.

Something has really changed in me.

I have a kind of death wish mentality. I don't want to do anything to take care of myself. Whenever I pass a homestead, I don't even bother to drink from the hose anymore. I pass a few food stands and don't even think to eat.

The tunnel vision has returned. Something's busted inside of me. The only outward sign of this is the split of emotion playing across my face. The crooked constant smile and the feverish sparkle in the eye denote a certain unsettling unmistakable bliss. If one looks closer, one can observe the clenched jaw and squinting eyes associated with undying determination. Look closer yet, and you can't miss the frozen expression and panting hisses squeezing through the locked jaw—the presence of full-blown panic, pure and all-consuming.

I had crossed over the bridge. I had reached the other side. What's life? What's love? What is? What isn't? What to fear? What not to fear? What is harm? What is safe? Who should I run from? What should I run to?

It didn't matter. Relief. I didn't have to worry about anything anymore. All I had to do was keep my feet moving. If my feet stopped, I would have no purpose. Forward, move forward. No movement, no purpose. No purpose, no life. No life, no worth. No worth, failure, self-hate, death. Night . . . day . . . night . . . day . . .

"Señor! Señor!"

A blue pickup truck stops. I hop in the back and we move along. My feet can stop now because the truck is moving forward. We ride most of the day away. We stop at a gas station. I pretend to be asleep, so I don't have to talk. Off we go again. Night . . . lightning . . . rain . . . the truck stops.

"Señor! Señor!"

I squeeze in the front with three men. I have to take my jacket off because it's soaked. The men are exclaiming to each other in great surprise. I have no idea what's being said.

"Habla Español? You are American?"

"Yes. American. No Spanish."

The driver can speak a little English.

"Ah," he sighed. "We are surprised you are a woman. We thought you were a man because of jacket and hair. Didn't see your face or body. I'm Antonio. Call me Tony."

"Where are we going, Tony?"

"Mexico."

"Okay."

I close my eyes. We ride through the darkness. Tony puts his arm around me. I guess I'm his now. Whatever. We stop at a modest house just this side of the border.

"We'll stay here tonight and cross the border tomorrow. It's easier to deal with the guards."

Two of the men crash on couches. Tony escorts me to his room. Whatever. He shows me the bathroom. I hop in the shower. About five minutes later, I hear the shower door slide back.

"So beautiful . . ."

He slips into Spanish. Hands all over my body.

He was really very sweet. If I were ten years older and healthy, I think I would've thoroughly enjoyed this swarthy young Mexican making love to me with his passionate words and touch. He carried me to his bed and "had his way" with me. It wasn't rape because it wasn't against my will. I had no will. Nothing mattered. I felt as if in a dream. He petted me all night and wrapped his whole body around me in a big hug still whispering sweet Spanish nothings in my ear.

Dawn broke. I woke to the smell of pork, not bacon, cooking. I was in the bed alone. I enjoyed the moment. Not for long though. My usual self-conscious anxiety set in quickly. How could I face those men out there? What must they think of me? Would Tony want more sex?

"Señorita. We have to go soon. Please hurry."

Now I had to face them. How embarrassing. I waited as long as I could. Someone knocked on the door. I came out trying to act cool and sophisticated, hyperventilating all the while. The men were very polite and nice to me. I didn't look Tony's way until he was focused on pouring a cup of coffee. I stole a brief glance. I couldn't believe it. He was blushing!

I instantly relaxed and was truly charmed and amused by his boyish shyness. He was actually *nervous* of me.

For the first time in a long time, I was having fun. The shredded pork concoction I was eating was deliciously new to me as was the peaceful, humble atmosphere this house exuded. And, by gosh, to my timid delight, the precious sparkle of life had returned to me, albeit, faintly. And I savored each priceless second of it with a secret joy dancing way down deep in my eyes. And it was *only* wholesome things that made them shine.

We packed ourselves back into the truck and headed for the border.

I'm a complete failure because I cannot stop feeling or trusting. What is wrong with me . . . ?

CHAPTER 20

South of the Border

"I don't have a passport."

"It's okay. You look Mexican. At checkpoint say, 'A Palomas.' You try."

"A Palohwmas."

"No. A little more like this . . ."

And we drove in this manner with Tony correcting my pronunciation until I had the phrase just right.

"What does that mean, anyway?"

"The town we go to."

We crossed the border without incident. The guard stuck his head in the window pointing at each man.

"You, a donde?"

"A Palomas."

"You?"

"A Palomas."

"You?"

I said the phrase. Tony put the car into gear, and we crossed—no issues, success. A fleeting moment of joyful self-pride washed over my body.

We only had to drive a mile or two before the look of the land changed completely. No more pavement. The highway now consisted of nothing more than tire tracks with grass growing in between. The occasional houses we passed were mere huts. I only saw two finished adobe homes that obviously belonged to the wealthy on our long, meandering drive.

We motored through the afternoon along the roadless way, sometimes seeing signs of humble living, sometimes seeing nothing. Sunset was ravishing. I've never seen sunsets as beautiful as those I saw in Mexico. I don't know if it was the lay of the land or that the sky truly has more magic south of the border, but the colors were more vivid, the reflecting clouds more fantastic, and the light shining down on the hills and huts, more powerful and magnificent—absolutely spectacular.

We hit the town of Palomas just as night had taken over. The center of town was crammed full of people dressed to the nines. The ladies wore midlength black skirts with colorful designs and white cotton blouses, which accented their dark, exotically beautiful faces. The dramatic black and white was further enhanced by big bright jewelry and long manes of shiny flowing hair. The men wore mostly black, looking very dapper and practically bursting with braggadocio. Most people were coupled off and laughing arm in arm as the Mexican music blasted from several different radios. Young and old alike were out for the big party.

"What's the occasion?"

"It's Friday night. Even more out tomorrow. We do every weekend. Nothing else to do in Palomas."

The whole town turned upside down every single weekend? That just wowed me. It seemed like such an extravaganza. We inched the truck through the throngs of people and eventually came out the other side of the crowd continuing to wind our way along the dirt tire tracks. The crowded plaza quickly became a small dot of light in the rearview mirror.

Soon, there weren't even tire tracks. We were simply mowing down the tall grass in search of our destination. It felt like we were driving in circles. Stoplights and street corners were something I took for granted; their absence made the ride feel reckless and fatalistic. It was so unnaturally random, so counterintuitive when, for no apparent reason and with no obvious landmark, Tony would turn left in the middle of open land. But he knew where he was going.

Our final stop was anticlimactic. The car parted the grass until its headlights exposed a tiny one-room hut. The lights were out. It didn't look welcoming. We got out of the truck, leaving the high beams on so we could see. As we neared the front door, the smell of alcohol, sweat, and sh———t were overwhelming. Tony started cursing at the old drunk passed out against the hut, pushing and kicking him, laughing all the while, until the old man woke up enough to crawl off and sleep against the nearest tree.

"That's my uncle," said Tony shaking his head. "Always drunk."

He led me inside. I couldn't see my hand in front of my face. It was so dark.

"Shh . . . Sleep here."

He gently pushed me down, and I found myself kneeling on blankets. I blindly felt my way until I found a pillow and lay down working my way under the covers. I heard Tony walking off.

I was asleep before one could count to five. It was that hard, painful sleep again. I felt like weather-beaten coyote bones embedded and compressed into desert sand. My bones felt brittle, my flesh minimal and taut. I really understood the meaning of the word "wild."

I was pulled slowly, one layer at a time, out of the depths of unconsciousness by the sweet, musical, innocent-sounding voices of children made more charming by the lilt of their native tongue. I didn't want to open my eyes. The moment was so benign and harmless, what with the giggles of the children and the warm orange-black color penetrating my closed eyelids telling me the sun must be shining down on me in all its glory. But youth is impatient, and the childish voices grew little hands that began to gently shake and pinch me awake.

The giggles turned into shrieks of delight as my eyes opened and I turned my head to avoid the light of the sun. There were three of them kneeling and staring at me: beautiful, rosy, golden children with eyes as black as their hair. I couldn't help but smile.

A heavy curtain made of undyed brown cotton was whipped back by a work-worn feminine hand. The shooing sounds of a mother, recognizable in any language, sent the kids scattering off. The curtain fell back into place, and I was alone.

I was disoriented but comfortable. Where was I? The make-shift bed I was in was a little wider than an army cot and a lot more comfortable. Another, just like it, lay next to me unmade. Maybe the children had slept there. What a pleasant thought. I glanced up for a second. The ceiling was nothing more than mosquito netting. I felt the walls: two were solid, the third was makeshift, and the fourth, the curtain. I poked my head out of the curtain. There were five curtains altogether, making an *L* along one half of the hut. The other side of the hut was occupied by one big solid wood table and some contraption resembling a fireplace and stove in one.

A very serious-looking woman dressed in faded black loosely woven cotton was sitting on the floor pounding tortillas. It was impossible to tell her age. She obviously had borne a lot of children, but she wasn't fat. I don't know how better to describe that look. Her hair was pulled back in a tight bun, and one could tell she was no one to mess with, her demeanor as severe as her hairline.

She noticed me and put one of the tortillas she had just made on a plate with some mushy red stuff and tossed it my way. I tried to thank her, but she acted like I wasn't there and went about her work. This put me at ease. I wasn't bothering her with my presence.

The food was delicious, though I had no idea what I was eating. I had barely put the last bite in my mouth when she snatched the plate out of my hand and put it in a bucket with other dirty dishes.

I got up and walked outside. The old man was still leaning against the tree, hopelessly drunk. The kids were laughing at him, and one older one was cleaning him up with some water and towels. He, the drunkard, laughed and sang, his unsteady head continually throwing him off-balance. I didn't see Tony or any of his friends, or brothers, or whoever they were.

No one paid attention to me. I felt free enough to explore. After scoping the place out, I went back in and lay down. This was ideal because I had privacy behind the curtain but could hear the everyday noises of the family. The fact that I was completely ignored was bliss. They noticed me enough to feed me and show me where the well and the outhouse were. If I tried to be helpful, the mother all but bit my head off. This was her turf, and no one but her was allowed to cook or clean.

Life became incredibly simple. Nobody spoke English, and I didn't speak Spanish. Tony didn't come back for three days. I slept most of the time. At first, the food revived me, but then my body started to freak out on this high-starch, high-protein diet. I tried to avoid the meals, but Mama got offended.

When Tony arrived, he had presents for everyone. I was happy to see him though I observed everything from a distance, staying on the periphery of the activity. All the adults surrounded him. After the initial welcome back, the mood turned sober. They were in heavy discussion. Whatever they were talking about was clearly very important. Every now and then Tony would turn and make eye contact with me.

"Hi, Tony!" I felt like a puppy.

He tipped his hat and blushed as I smiled. He was still shy around me. He refocused on the group discussion and then looked my way again.

"The sky is beautiful today, Tony." Wag, wag.

"Si." Blush . . . smile. He turned his attention back to the men.

They stayed up late talking through the night at the large wooden table. I fell asleep to the sound of their voices heavy in the air.

They were gone when I awoke.

I didn't see the men again until next day's sunset. They pulled up in Tony's pickup long enough for him to open the door and tell me to hop in. I did so silently.

We drove around for the next hour making various stops at similar little shacks. At each stop, a man or two would hop into the back of the truck until it was completely jam-packed, the men crushed shoulder to shoulder like so many sardines.

The air was tense; the mood, serious. Whatever we were about to do was a very big deal. I could sense the fear or danger. I knew to do what I was told and not to ask questions. Tony smiled at me with the calm of someone who knew the worst-case scenario and was willing to suffer the consequences should things go sour. He was committed to shouldering the burden. Tony was a person to be admired.

Night was closing in. Tony didn't turn on the truck's headlights. Pitch-black night took over, and still we drove in complete darkness. The lightless ride stressed my senses. The only way to escape was to sleep. I was awakened by the energy rather than the sound of these convicted men.

Whatever we were doing was about to go down. The truck stopped, and everyone got out. We walked about half a mile away from the truck. Then most of the men sat down behind a small dune hiding their presence. Tony, two other men, and I walked in the opposite direction of the dune. We stopped suddenly, and Tony handed me something that felt like a big pair of pliers. "Cut," he said and guided my hand forward until it touched a piece of wire. My eyes focused, and I realized we were standing next to a barbed wire fence, six lines of wire deep. We started cutting. It took a while, but we did it. It was thrilling to feel the last bit of wire give way. Tony told me to stand back, and he and one of the others put on some long heavy stiff gloves and carefully bent the wire aside until they had a big opening about fifteen feet wide.

Tony gave an inhuman-sounding whistle quite natural to the environment, and the men came out from behind the dune and moved toward us. I couldn't see their faces in the dark, but the air was certainly full of sentiment. I imagined there must've been a few wet eyes as each man walked forward shaking Tony's hand as they exited through the fence opening. This was done in silence. Everyone disappeared into the night until Tony and I were left alone. He put an arm around me, and we walked back to the truck and drove off.

I had a big smile on my face. I liked being let in on the deal—not like back in San Diego when I'd been treated like a baby by Michael and Ice Man. We drove back to the hut in complete silence and darkness. The ambiguity of the atmosphere was unacceptable. The only thing that felt sure was Tony. I leaned into him.

The next few days were pretty nondescript. Tony stayed around now and was making obvious calf eyes at me. His mother pointed at the two of us and smiled a lot—a smile made slightly gruesome by the bad teeth and the weathered weariness that veiled her past beauty. She was definitely hearing wedding bells. Tony was my hero. I respected him too much to pretend I could be a wife. It was time for me to move on the first chance I got.

I left unceremoniously in the middle of the next day. Tony had gone out on an errand. I wandered off during his absence so I wouldn't have to say goodbye. It was for the best—superimposed realities and all that.

I walked through Palomas on to another small town and then to another. I walked through several of these mini communities. No one bothered me. In their eyes, I was just another poor tired Mexican trudging along the roadside.

It actually felt good to be walking the sun-beaten land again. I could breathe; my eyes squinted against the sun. There was nothing to lie about or explain to anyone—no one was touching me. I walked through day into the night and landed in the middle of a town in full party mode—must be Friday or Saturday. There was no way to escape the people. I sighed, mostly because I wasn't dressed properly, and dove into the crowd.

I was immediately pulled into a line dance. People were having such a good time. Their joy was so infectious that I quickly forgot I looked a mess and didn't belong. I really got into the spirit of things. All I had to do was stand there. Soon I had a tequila shoved in one hand and a burrito in the other. I whirled the whole night away in a tequila frenzy. I felt hysterical. The joy of the moment mixed with the reality of my situation, and the subconscious, deep-seated sadness I felt was truly a bizarre mental state to be in. What an absurdly weird high—I was flying!

The night went on, and the crowd dwindled as people, pair by pair, went off. One Soave Bolla type had honed in on me. I liked the attention. He was handsome, and by the way other people were treating him, I could tell he was somebody important. I went home with him.

He didn't live in a hut. It was a big beautiful adobe house, very plush inside. The floor was black marble; the furniture, sparse yet expensive. The man had a thing for red, gold, and fur. It was gorgeous—exorbitant but not tacky. It didn't take long to end up in bed.

Ah, the beauty of too much tequila. I was out like a light. Slowly, I came to rather than woke the next day. Fur . . . creating a simultaneous cool and warm sensation—a *real* fur blanket. That is what I was wrapped in. The pure decadence of it was distracting me. I relished the tactile sensation, but my mind was slowly tugging me back into survival mode. I had to get up and be out before Soave awoke. I threw my clothes on and left.

I wasn't doing well. Walking for hours on end in the beating sun was not going to be a good idea. I had a hangover and a badly dehydrated body. Resignedly, I slowly kept putting one foot in front of the other.

As luck would have it, I had ended up in a border town right below El Paso, Texas. I could actually see the signs welcoming me to Texas. Relief and confusion set in. I checked my step and stayed back from the crossing stations, watching. How was I going to cross the border? People were crossing on foot and in cars showing passports to the guards. I didn't have any ID. I wasn't sure what to do.

I hung out for a couple of hours hoping to have an epiphany. No bright ideas came to me, so I headed back to Soave. He was extremely happy to see me. I was goal oriented.

"Border. El Paso."

He understood. We got into his convertible and went back to the border. He drove up to the guard at the crossing station and talked to him for a while. I didn't know what they were saying. Soave was tense, and then I literally saw his whole body sigh with relief. His shoulders relaxed. He turned and gave me a big wet, sloppy kiss.

"Is okay, Señorita. *Thank you.*"

He reached across me and opened the passenger door with a proud smile. I got out and walked over the border.

I immediately switched into the present circumstance. My antenna was up. It was clear that I had to get out of El Paso fast. There were tons of bad news walking around, drunks, thieves. It all equaled danger. Walking incredibly fast, I got the hell out of Dodge.

And here we go again . . . day . . . night . . . day . . . night . . . day . . . night . . . truck stop . . . trouble . . . hunger . . .

Weakness . . . fear . . . numb . . . nothing . . . absolutely nothing . . . and now . . . *loneliness* . . . utter loneliness . . . fatigue in every way . . .

I just can't. I don't know what to do—where, who, how?

Lesson #3: One has to be. There is no alternative short of death, so . . . get over it . . .

CHAPTER 21

The Thaw

So here I am, at that point. Las Cruces . . . the bench. I gratefully, oh so gratefully, was finally drifting back off into sweet nothingness. *Ahhh . . .*

"Hey. Hey, there. It's me, Paul. Don't worry, no more pictures." He laughed nervously as he held his hands up in the air, palms out. "I just wanted to see if you really meant it when you said 'forever.' I had a feeling . . ." He stepped a little closer and crossed his arms. "Do you realize you've been here for about eight hours since the first time I saw you?"

I did not acknowledge his presence outwardly, but inside I was livid. He *again* had yanked me up out of the fog. My anger must've manifested noticeably in the color of my skin or perhaps my breathing pattern. His arms stretched forward suddenly, hands pushing the air in front of him somewhat frantically.

"Don't . . . don't get upset." He started backing up. "I'm leaving. I'm leaving. I've got a plane to catch." He hesitated, not quite sure what to do next—the arms and hands now in a standard shrug. "Look, if you ever get tired of sitting on this bench, call me." He extended his arm while bending toward the bench and quickly turned away all in one motion.

He was gone. I looked down. He had left a business card and a quarter at the far end of the bench. I scooted toward it just far enough so my outstretched hand could grab the items and ball them up.

Night . . . day . . . night . . .

I never did get back to that nothingness. And any state other than that was unbearable. Why did that stupid photographer have to come along and ruin everything? I became fully distraught. The dilemma was truly overwhelming. I didn't want to start walking again, but I could no longer stay on the bench. Every option was wrong.

I eventually concluded that the only viable option was to go down the most uncommon path—uncommon because for the first time in a very long time I felt I had the right to disturb someone else's peace as they had disturbed mine. Paul was to be blamed for my inability to lose myself forever. Since he had *ruined* everything, he would have to pay the price. He'd burdened me by making me stay in the here and now. So, I was going to burden him with my presence seeing as he'd insisted on my continuing to have one.

I opened my hand. The business card and quarter were still there. I got up off the bench. I walked until I found a pay phone. I dialed the number. It was a local answering service. They transferred the call to his Dallas office.

"Hi, this is Paul."

"I got tired of sitting on the bench."

The silent pause was long but not awkward. I had the feeling he was organizing his sentence.

In a very matter-of-fact manner he said, "Okay. Give me the number you're calling from, and stay there until I call you back."

I gave him the number, hung up, and waited. It was a long wait. Well, I didn't have anything better to do. Oddly, I was certain he wouldn't let me down. I knew if I waited he would call. Hours later, the phone rang.

Again, matter-of-factly, "Sorry that took so long. Tell me the crossroads you're at."

I told him. He gave me directions to the local mission.

"Go to the mission, and I'll send you taxi money to the airport and a plane ticket to Dallas. It's going to take a few days, but at least you'll have a place to sleep and some food at the mission." This time the pause was short and awkward—he was leaving room for me to respond. I didn't.

"Um . . . don't feel self-conscious. They are expecting you."

Another painful pause.

"Uh . . . give me your name so I can get this ticket."

"Heather Jacobs."

"See you when you get here. Bye."

Click.

It was as uncomplicated as that. I have to admit, it left me a little breathless. I shook off the simmer of underlying emotions, followed the directions he gave, and found myself at the mission.

Thank goodness for the distraction of judgment. I was disappointed—*very* disappointed. "The mission" did not live up to the romantic fantasy I had constructed in my mind's eye. I'd walked those short few miles anticipating the sight of some stalwart, castle-like religious institution of good will built by early padres and Indians.

Instead, "the mission" was a two-story sorry excuse of a building—a poor imitation that tackily referenced its Spanish predecessors with a few red tiles and swirled black type in its sign. The smell of mildew, dried vomit, and bleach violated my nostrils as I entered the ramshackle structure. And all the surfaces (walls, floors, tables, etc.) were sticky with a mucky residue—a layer of filth left by rags that had been swiped across them only to prove the work had been done, not to clean. My disdain grew.

I was greeted neutrally by a thirtyish-looking woman with bent shoulders and an air of weary suspicion. She did not smile or make eye contact. She talked past me like there was someone standing behind me and slightly to my left. I found this insulting. She handed me a set of threadbare sheets and pointed toward a cot. My manners flickered on automatically for a millisecond in the form of a thankful nod as my hands came in contact with the worn cotton sheets.

The place was set up dorm style—men on one side, women on the other. The only coed moments were spent in the cafeteria where we ungratefully swallowed the barely passable watered-down food.

And I acted like *such* a snob. My graceless, haughty, holier-than-thou attitude was embarrassingly out of hand. In my eyes all the women looked scrawny, trashy, and drugged out reeking of cigarette smoke and aged, infected urine. I saw the men with the same narrow vision and wondered what I could possibly be doing here with these . . . with *them*. I needed to be away from this place. It was bringing out the worst in me.

And the mindless chatter! All the women did was talk about sex and blow smoke. Where did they get all those cigarettes anyway? And the men would laugh arrogantly about how some yuppie had given them a ten or twenty.

"I put on my pity face, man, and guilted the dough out of the stupid motherf——cker."

That particular comment hardened me against beggars for years.

Sleep would not come for me at "the mission." I couldn't stand the smell of these poor white trash women. I didn't even want to lie on the sheets that had maybe been touched by their weary bodies. I cringe now at how poisonous my attitude was.

The money and ticket came on the third morning. If I was a snob before, I was a raging bitch now. I announced my good fortune to everyone within earshot.

Out loud with preppy enthusiasm: "A perfect stranger sent me an airplane ticket. His name is Paul. I need to call a taxi. I'm going to *Dallas!*"

In my head, with the self-absorption of the shallowest of popular girls: *I'm so cool and you're so not. Goodbye and good riddance, you lowlifes.*

I strutted out to the taxi, my nose high in the air, feeling like Cinderella going to the ball.

"Airport, please."

I felt so official, so authoritative, so much like I was somebody—like one of the angels (Charlie's, that is) undercover. You can imagine the thrill when I handed the driver the money and said, "Keep the change." It was my fee, granting me full-fledged membership back into the human race.

As I checked in at the boarding gate and handed my ticket over, I was a superstar, the most beautiful woman on the planet. The entire flight was a game of child's play—a tea party.

"Yes, some more 7-Up, please. Thank you. What a lovely day."

Only when the plane landed did my discomfort resume.

What would happen now? I didn't want to deal with anybody. As I walked down the ramp, I forgot my nervousness for just a moment because of all the distracting cowboy hats. Everyone was wearing them. I liked the way they looked. They balanced out the formality of the business suits and the cityscape. I thought of JR and Bobby and Pamela and Lucy. I was happy.

Then I saw him—Paul. He was easy to spot. His head in a quirky tilt and that crooked smile of uncertainty undulating across his face. He wasn't wearing a cowboy hat.

Hostility consumed me. I didn't want to deal with any man again. Why did I ever get up off that bench?

He walked up, a greeting smile now firmly in place. If I had feathers, they would've been ruffled. If I were a cat, my tail would be bushy and every hair on my back would've been standing straight up. My body was frozen with tension.

"Look, I'm not going to say 'thank you,' 'cause you didn't do me any favors. I just got tired of sitting on the bench. *Okay?* That's why I'm here. It doesn't matter whether you're nice to me or mean, because I don't care. I just got tired of . . . sitting on the bench."

He kept smiling.

"Let's go."

We drove to Dallas with him pointing out the sights the entire way, completely ignoring my fear-based hostility. We went past all the bad neighborhoods, all the medium neighborhoods, and pulled down Greencove Lane, a very nice street in a very, very nice neighborhood.

I was temporarily distracted again. Goodness gracious, the guy was loaded. We pulled into an alley and up behind a garage with a fourteen-foot newly waxed yellow-and-white motor home parked next to it. He led me inside the main house.

"Hey, Blaine. Mom. This is Heather."

I was dizzied by the wealth on display and the big friendly smile from his fourteen-year-old son. I don't even know how I responded to the socially required introductions. His mother was a little stuffy old blue blood with blue hair from the East Coast. Gawky teenage Blaine showed me around the house flipping his uncontainable blond locks from side to side every few steps so he could see.

We sat around the dining room table—Blaine, Blue Blood, and I—while Paul dug up blankets, etc., for me. He quickly joined us.

Everyone was talking. I couldn't hear them. The light seemed amazingly bright. I noticed every groove and reflection on the big wooden table. I was overheated.

A vibrant-looking fortyish lady walked in the back door and went over to Paul and kissed him. She reminded me of Jane Fonda and Sally Fields kind of morphed into one person.

"This is Sally. Sally, Heather."

She smiled looking less than pleased with my being there. Is it possible to simultaneously smile and frown? I heard somebody coughing in the front room.

"That's Father. He's a little tired. Come on. Let's go." He signaled for me to follow him.

We walked out back. Paul was gleeful. There was a jaunt in his step as he walked ahead of me, almost skipping. He would turn his head sporadically and talk to me over his shoulder.

"I figure the motor home will give you the privacy you need."

Walk, walk, walk, head over shoulder . . .

"I stocked it with food. Just relax and rest."

Walk, walk, walk, head over shoulder . . .

"It's all heated and everything. Make yourself at home."

He opened the door, helped me up the two steps, and waved goodbye.

Suddenly, abruptly, I was alone. The feeling I experienced in reaction to that was unexpected. I felt broken, like a very heavy glass paperweight that has been dropped on a concrete floor and split in two. My feelings and my physicality scraped against each other like someone was trying to piece back together the thick broken glass but couldn't. I hurt. No position that I sat in made me comfortable. Thinking was not possible in my state. All I could do was be broken.

Night . . . day . . .

Knock, knock, knock.

"Good *morning*. How are you doing in there?"

"Fine," I said through the door.

"It's beautiful out today. You might like to walk around the neighborhood and get familiar with the place."

I didn't respond. I didn't know what to say to this man. I just couldn't function and couldn't be witnessed. Silence. A hesitant knock.

"Okay, well—have a nice day."

I heard the rev of an engine and peeked out the window in time to see him drive off, this time on a BMW motorcycle.

For those of you who don't know this, let me tell you; when people aren't functioning, it's because they can't. I was hungry but couldn't make myself eat anything. Any action on my part to take care of myself and keep myself alive was truly beyond me.

Ever since I sat down on that bench in Las Cruces, I had committed to checking out. I couldn't seem to check back in.

The only thing that was alive in me was my vanity. What stamina that fault has! I was still consumed with what I looked like. All I *could* do was admire myself in the mirror and be happy that I looked so good. My hair was messed up again though; it was broken off and very dry.

I mildly gawked at an incongruence on display in my physical self. My body looked healthy and strong; however, I was having no functions. I didn't sweat, pee, sh——t—nothing. I didn't smell. I didn't ache. I hadn't had my menstrual cycle since that first day I had walked out the door back in California. It was as if I was a three-dimensional photo. I had no personality about me at all—broken.

A skein of pink yarn on the magazine rack by the couch caught my eye—soft pink yarn just a little too dark to be called baby pink. There was a crochet needle in a clear plastic bag with a yellow skein of yarn sitting next to it. I knew two different types of stitches. My grandma had shown them to me one of the two times I had met her.

I went to work immediately. I loved crocheting, and the two stitches came back more easily than I thought they would.

Now I was in bliss. Nothing was more important than making these stitches. It was going to be a blanket. Not one of those tiny little Afghans too small to do any good, but a real blanket that I could wrap around my feet and over my head at the same time. I worked the yarn through the night in eager anticipation of the cocoon I would soon spin. The pink ran out and I attached the yellow. Oh, I was so happy, so peaceful!

I ran out of yarn. This was motivation. I needed more yarn. I looked through every cupboard and found one more skein of yarn—blue.

I got to work, and without thinking, opened a can of soda I found in one of the cupboards. It was a natural motion done without drama. I forgot that I hadn't been eating or drinking. It didn't take long for me to go through the yarn. I had satiated myself temporarily. I knew I would finish my blanket and would get more yarn fairly soon.

It was late afternoon. I looked out the window, and there was Blaine kicking a soccer ball around in the backyard, his unruly blondness making him look like a Muppet. He saw me and waved, giving me one of his toothy smiles. I waved back. Night came and he went in.

I was uncomfortable again.

Food was still a big problem. I didn't want any. The soda had activated my body enough to make me realize I needed something. Digging through the cupboards, I bypassed everything and went straight to the cake mix because I knew it would make me sick. I mixed it up, ate the raw batter, and, without even trying, threw it all up. Well . . . it made me feel better. It was nice to taste and swallow; it was nicer to heave. I felt a little lighter, a little happier.

I'm not talking about physical lightness. Throwing up the cake mix was like exorcising certain demons from my body. I became a little less tense—a little less frightened, angry, and sad. I had rid myself of some of the dead weight burying my spirit. Hence, I could sleep and, when I awoke, glory of glories, I could eat!

The next day was stressful. I was aware of a kaleidoscope of emotions twisting and turning inside me. They were clearly dangerous. The lid had to stay on. I wrestled with them until I saw Blaine playing in the yard again. He was such a toothy goof! I couldn't help but be charmed. On day four I actually went out and joined him in his fun. Paul rode up on his motorcycle while we were playing. I was so caught up in trying to be good at kicking the ball I didn't shut down. I just waved and kept playing.

"So what else do you like?" he said grinning like a Cheshire cat.

"Music."

Hearing my own voice made me self-conscious. I bolted back into the motor home.

Paul knocked on my door at eight that night.

"Come on. I'm taking you somewhere."

"No thanks."

He opened the door and said, "I'm not asking. Come on."

He grabbed my hand and yanked me into the car.

We drove downtown. I was going numb. What was he going to do with me? Where were we going? We stopped outside of a nightclub. He got out and talked to the doorman for a while and then came back to get me. He walked me through the doors upstairs to a table, ordered me a Coke, and patted me on the back.

"I'll be back in three hours. Enjoy the music."

A flash of pure joy: I am in a nightclub all by myself . . . He's treating me like a grown-up!

The club floor was black and shiny. There was a lot of brass and frosted glass. The stage spotlights were pink and blue. Everyone was conservatively dressed up to the point of perfect anonymity.

The instrumental band filled the air with dulcet tones. The smooth saxophone washed over my soul. I felt like I was dreaming. I was there but didn't seem a part of it all—my spirit was not a natural part of the scene. It was very nice though. I felt relaxed. The doorman came up and checked on me occasionally bringing me Shirley Temples. The musicians looked like protectors to me—quiet, focused, serious, and confident. I felt them more than I heard them.

The time just was—it didn't fly by or stand still. Then Paul was back to get me. We drove in silence for a while.

"How was the music?"

"I liked it."

"Well, good."

We got out in the driveway; he looked at me hard for a while and then grabbed my head and planted a big hard kiss on me. It was a strange kiss. Not sexual, not caring, just . . . like how a night is supposed to end. It gave me something to think about, though I wasn't sure of the thought. I slept well that night.

I call this period the thaw. I stayed in that trailer for almost two months, and reentered humanity a little bit more with each day. Nothing eventful happened in this time. That was probably the most exciting thing of all.

I eventually started feeling grateful and would go in the house and bake banana bread while no one was home, leaving the loaves as small tokens of appreciation. I started assisting a little in the house. I even went so far as to ask if there was any way I could help out.

"Well . . . yeah. It would be great if you could drive my mother on errands a couple of days a week."

"No problem," I said, failing to mention that I didn't know how to drive.

I'm surprised his mother didn't die of a heart attack. Paul rented a beautiful forest green Mercury Cougar. His mother could barely see over the dashboard—she was so small. I swerved my way around Dallas proper, turning the wheel when I turned my head to talk, and terrorizing this poor little old East Coast blue blood with my over-zealous attempts at braking. She never said a word to me as I almost ran over a gas pump or locked bumpers with another car while trying to park.

After a few days of this, Paul came out to the trailer as if to say hi.

"Oh, by the way, I was wondering if you would take me for a little drive around the neighborhood. She's probably exaggerating, but my mother seems a bit nervous about your driving."

"I don't blame her. I'm driving terrible. I'm not used to big cars. I had a VW rabbit and a bug before that."

Lies, all lies. Those were the cars my mother had driven.

"Oh! That big green boat must be terrible for you. You should have told me. Don't worry about it."

He left. I sighed with relief. I was off the hook. Or so I thought.

He showed up the next day with more car keys.

"Here you go. This should be much better. I borrowed Sally's Subaru. Try it out when you get a chance."

I waited until midnight, figuring I could practice all night and be a better driver. I unlocked the little car and got in. Oh, boy. It was a five-speed. I was really in trouble now. Well, here goes nothing.

The first two hours were a complete disaster. I got the hang of it a little bit and learned not to turn the wheel in synchronization with my head. By morning I was driving at least as well as I had been in the Cougar.

I spent my days in these quiet ways with lots of average catastrophes around me. Unfortunately, the better I felt, the more I thawed out, and the more guilt I experienced when my thoughts turned to Ma.

My mother had no idea where I was. When *my* days had been traumatic, I didn't think about her at all. The logic—if I was suffering, then any anxiety I might be causing her was excusable. Now that I was experiencing normalcy and at times even having fun, I felt I was betraying her in some way. My loyalty to Ma wouldn't let me enjoy the finer points of life. I knew she was worried and probably working herself into a paranoid reality shift. She did that well enough on her own without the added stimulation of her whorish daughter running away. What could she be thinking and how was she taking it out on Sis? It was time to make contact.

I sent her a picture of me and a one-sentence note: I am fine. I didn't talk to her on the phone. I couldn't. She sent me some of my clothes and a nice letter. There were no words of anger or any acknowledgment that anything was out of the ordinary in her communication. If there's such a thing as monotone writing, this was it.

"Dear, Hedy . . . Glad all is well . . . We've got new pink *moo-moos* for uniforms at the Holiday Inn . . ."

I responded in kind, "Dear, Ma . . . I'm fine . . . Finally lost those ten pounds . . . I don't like the humidity here, but the cowboy hats are cool . . ."

Having my clothes made me feel great. I had lost so much weight it was exhilarating to have everything not fit. I wish my confidence had had the lasting power of my warped vanity; no one could've messed with me *ever* if that were the case.

I started braving civilization a bit on my own. I drove out to Fort Worth late at night because I wanted to see *Billy Bob's*. I remember the nightclub from the Travolta movie *Urban Cowboy*. It looked exactly the same. I took a deep breath and walked up to the entrance. The doorman whisked me inside, no questions asked, and I two-stepped the night away. Willie Nelson was singing live, and I could hear his voice floating around me even though I couldn't see him. I decided I really liked cowboys. They seemed very polite and like a lot of fun. They danced well enough and even took me on a cattle feed at the end of the night.

What a blast! The only form of helplessness I had enjoyed in my life thus far, other than my ocean surrenders, was being in the back of that pickup truck in the wee hours of the morning watching the cows come in. Their large slow presence was frightening yet calming. The smell of the sweet alfalfa and the not-so-gentle tug as the cows fed off the alfalfa squares we held out for them charmed me. And the one moment when it seemed that they were going to overturn the truck in their hunger and then the strange communication between the cattle, cowboys, and their dogs that suddenly left us room to drive off inspired a giggling glee in me. Yee haw! Well, I'll be!

I remember going over to Momar's house. He wasn't a cowboy. He was from Iran. I met him while running errands with Blue Blood Granny. She liked tea, and we would have it regularly midday at a fancy downtown hotel. Momar worked there. He was very polite and would try to talk to me when I went to get the car. I eventually listened to him and said yes to his dinner proposal. He took me out on a few dates, and spending time with him was easy over a candlelit table. I really didn't have to say anything. He would talk about himself and compliment me. The third time, he made dinner for me at his apartment. He gave me my first taste of jasmine rice with saffron seeds, which made a lasting and delicious impression.

After dinner he tried to be sexual with me. He kissed me a few times and then grabbed my hand, guiding it toward him. I'd tense up, and he'd back off and then try again a few minutes later. I froze at every initiation, leaving him puzzled. Poor Momar was frustrated to no end. He couldn't understand why the mere idea of grabbing his dick sent me into revulsion and panic.

"It won't bite, for God's sake! What's *wrong* with you?"

He went limp.

"Get out! Get out!"

I can still see his hurt look and shooing hands playing against the romantic candlelit background.

That was the end of that.

It was nice to be able to actually laugh at those scenarios as I drove back to the motor home. I found most things amusing these days.

How are you doing, Ma? Are you finding things amusing?

It was time to go deal with my mother. My guilt was slowly eating away at my false sense of norm—my guilt and the smoldering volcano that lay beneath. This was not life. I was on some alternate plane where everything was everybody else's reality. I didn't have my own yet. In order to get that, I had to go back to California and at least make an attempt at dealing with my mother's whack world . . .

A rude awakening is better than none; however, it makes me crabby. I've gotten up on the wrong side of the bed. I need to hit snooze two more times . . .

CHAPTER 22

The Door

Paul set it up. He drove me to the airport and walked me to the gate. It was time to say goodbye.

"Well . . . I never thought I'd say this, but thanks—thanks a lot. How can I ever repay you?"

"Never contact me, and never remind me of what I did."

He wasn't smiling. I was thoroughly confused, shocked by his response.

"Okay. Bye."

What else could I say? My offended surprise registered in one extra blink and a slight accent of the word *bye*. I turned and got on the plane without looking back.

Huh . . . I really hadn't expected that. I wanted to feel angry. I wanted Paul's last words of rejection to cancel out all his acts of kindness—but they couldn't.

I sat in my assigned seat holding my breath. Hmm . . . I wanted to categorize him as a motherf——cking asshole—but I couldn't.

The plane engines revved up, rattling me into the present.

My mind was one big zero during the flight. No thought registered as the plane landed. Little sounds became magnified, the click of the seat belts, luggage thumping as people eagerly pushed toward the exit doors. I walked down the accordion airplane ramp with measured steps, my eyes methodically scanning the LAX crowd. There was Ma—a vision in lavender. She was still beautiful. She still had a bulldozer of a personality. I loved her. I was afraid of her.

The up close reunion was anticlimactic. I was glad she looked well. She smiled, but I could see the tension and anger hiding behind it. I looked expressionless and powerless—no hugs, no gushing.

We rode in silence, everything on pause but the car.

It was a long way back to the dank little adobe house on Anacapa Street in Ventura—"back" being the operative word. By the time I walked through the front door I knew I had made a crucial mistake in returning. Talk about surreal. Talk about the twilight zone.

Poison. Nothing had grown or changed while I'd been gone other than the determination with which my mother kept me on lockdown and the height of her fears about what I would do if she didn't. Her thesis statement regarding our relationship was now a more emphatic version of the original point she'd always been trying to prove. I was a whore not to be trusted and she was ashamed to be my mother.

Me, myself? I didn't say much. I had gone through some serious changes. But be they for better or worse, the changes were real and permanent. How on earth could I relate to this woman? My view of reality and perspective of space and time made walking back into that atmosphere seem as if I were marching over centuries.

Well, we had to start somewhere. At least there was one point on which we both agreed: I was guilty.

My running away put the seal of approval on all of Ma's previous accusations. In both our eyes I had wronged her through my actions, removing all my rights to privacy. At last she had the self-righteous authority she'd always dreamed of. Consequently, she was almost easy to deal with. She felt so validated in and called to her conviction. There was an aura of relief about her. She was victorious. The magnifying glass was out, and the chains wrapped tightly around the double-bolted door. I felt no need to protest.

If I ventured out of my room and even close to the front or back door, it was, "You are *not* going out of this house! I can't trust you. I won't put myself through that worry. You brought this on yourself, and that's the end of it! Not a word."

"Okay."

I wasn't going to argue with her. Even when she went back to work, I didn't peek my nose out the door. She called every fifteen minutes, and I certainly wasn't willing to chance the barrage of anger and paranoia I would get if I missed even one of those phone calls.

I tried to be oblivious to the guaranteed failure and misery this situation would bring; however, the time bomb was too obvious not to notice. Ma was not passive, and it wasn't in her makeup to be satisfied no matter how much control she had.

All one could do was look the other way. To be there, I had to not be. And that was fine by me; I was master at that. I had great confidence in my newfound ability to reach a state of total physical and emotional numbness. Bring it on, lady. This is a cinch for me.

Not so. Ma's mere presence could cut through it all and bring my soul to its very knees, begging desperately for peace. Maybe it's because I was born of her body. Maybe it was the familiar smells of the house. I'm not sure, but try as I might, I could not completely shut her out.

My head began to spin with this nasty reality. I didn't have the luxury of predicting my *own* behavior now. I was off-balance, unsettled, and unpleasantly surprised to discover I had to be on my toes in constant relevé to maneuver her anger and fear. I was clearly not up to the challenge.

There was no way the days could pass in this manner for long. It was too uncomfortable for all involved. If only she realized how little the door symbolized freedom for me, she would relax. I knew for a fact what awaited me on the other side. That was no longer an option.

Dave called.

"Glad you're okay. It really pissed me off when you ran away. I thought you were trying to make me feel guilty. Good luck in life."

My friend Kelly called.

"You lied to me! You told me you were out of state, but you called me from San Diego! Why did you do that? I don't think I can trust you. I'm glad you're all right, though."

I just couldn't relate or respond, defend or explain; hence, I . . . was . . . *almost* . . . numb . . .

Time passed in this manner. I'm not sure how much. One day Ma came home early.

"I'm taking you to see a psychiatrist."

"No way!" I shouted, suddenly clear and very present for the first time in a long time.

"You don't have a choice. There's something very wrong with you, and I can't have you worrying me so much."

"Something wrong with *me*!"

I was seething, and then, suddenly, very flat. *No need to get excited*, I told myself. Why? Because I knew I wouldn't cooperate with this psychiatrist person. My anger was just the trigger I had needed to activate. I felt capable of murder.

"Fine. Take me."

We got in the car and drove a short distance to a generic-looking practice (a beige stucco building, gravel, shrubbery . . .). We situated ourselves in the waiting room, looking like the typically concerned parent with a defiant teenager in tow.

I sat there with my arms folded, passing judgment on the brown carpet and the white bucket chairs with silver legs. The lack of life in the sterile, clinical air nauseated me. And my undying vanity just *knew* I must look my worst under the office fluorescence.

"Heather . . . ?"

My Pavlovian response to hearing my name called in an office manifested in a raised head and a polite, slightly nervous smile. I was led alone into an inner office that looked even more sterile than the waiting area. Time passed slowly, giving my already bad attitude time to settle in and take hold.

How could a man help me with an office this cold looking? How could a *man* help me? My mother was the crazy one, not me. If he took her seriously, I wouldn't give him the time of day. If he didn't take her seriously, I would at least be polite.

The name placard said "Dr. Howard B. Worthing." The shiny gold doorknob turned. A tall, somewhat athletic-looking man walked in. He was a balding but otherwise youthful forty-some-thing—looked like he played tennis or swam. His square jaw and droopy eyelids framed in crow's feet told me by nature he was a man who laughed a lot. But now, his face was disciplined into neutrality.

"Welcome. Your mother is concerned."

Bad opening line. He kept talking. I sat there with my arms folded, my legs crossed, and my heart pounding with fury and embarrassment.

"You seem to be very hostile."

Brilliant observation.

"I can't help you if you don't tell me what's going on."

Awkward silence.

"Your mother let me help her while you were gone."

That caught my attention in the worst way possible.

"I don't want to be here. I have nothing to say."

"Why are you so angry?"

End of conversation.

This guy was an idiot and, as far as I was concerned, working with my mother against me. We spent the last forty minutes of the session in silence broken occasionally with some feeble attempt on his part to get me to *open up*.

I left with my mother in continued silence. I'd had it with her. The fact that *she* was trying to get *me* straightened out was just too much. She seemed pleased with my refusal to speak. When we got home, I went to my room and closed the door.

And that's where I stayed for the next two months except for meals, the bathroom, and my weekly fifty minutes of silence with Dr. Howard B. Worthing.

The first two weeks of my solitude were strangely beautiful. I sat in the comfy armchair, the reflection from the peach-colored carpet creating a warm, insular atmosphere. I was pleased with the orange felt flower I'd pasted on cream-colored satin and framed, oh, so long ago. I enjoyed recalling the pure satisfaction I'd gotten when I'd picked and bought the now faded "field theme" bedspread and what a score the thirties-style vanity had been at the thrift store for only twenty bucks.

Yes, I sat there and wrote song after song in the peachy room. The oddity is that all of them were happy, joyous, sexy songs full of hope, wonder, and belief in love. It made me shake my head more than once. But they kept pouring out of the pen at a rate I could barely keep up with. I say pouring out of the pen because I wrote these tunes effortlessly without a conscious thought. They just seemed to come from some place, and I happened to be the one holding the pen. This process distracted me greatly. I felt my tensions start to ease. I immediately put the book aside and didn't touch it or look at it again for months.

I couldn't afford to relax. It hurt too much—literally. As tensions eased, I was suddenly aware of and surprised at the state my body was in. My ribs felt like they'd been stretched apart with a vice and ached like swollen bruises at the slightest touch. I was obviously riddled with some sexual disease and took to taping medical gauze between my legs so everything was separated and wouldn't rub together and burn. The ordeal and discomfort of this was easier to put up with than my mother's reaction if she found out. The muscles in my legs felt as if they were in a constant state of flex. The feeling was frightening, like I was on the verge of having a major muscle cramp at all times. I had tiny little points of pain in my breast and ass that hurt a lot when touched with pressure. I had some on my crotch too. *What the hell were they?* But the burning between my legs overrode all the other aches and pains. I was messed up. Yeah, there was something wrong with me all right. Something Dr. Worthing couldn't fix.

During one of our sessions, he had me take a written test—a what-would-you-do-if quiz of sorts. I liked tests and took it with enthusiasm.

"Based on your hostility and the results of your test, I've come to the conclusion that you are manic-depressive."

My eyes bugged out in reaction to his diagnosis. Then, for a moment, I was consumed by a sweeping sense of sadness. From my point of view, running away had been the only sane reaction to home life with Ma. And my numb state now was the only way I could deal with what I had gone through in my months on the streets. Was he a complete moron? If I didn't keep my cool, he would probably rationalize putting me in a crazy house. It was so obvious to me what was wrong. How had my mother fooled this man? Unbelievable.

He prescribed lithium. Ma watched me to make sure I took the pills and checked my mouth to make sure I hadn't hid them in my cheeks or under my tongue. I did take them the first few times, but they felt dangerous. What little grip I had on reality was quickly swept away. I couldn't feel joy at eating one of my favorite meals or the flash of anger you get when you stub your toe. These little commonplace sensations had become absolutely crucial to my existence. Those small emotional reactions were the only feelings that were safe to have. They were my security blanket, and the lithium was killing them. I promptly flushed the rest of the prescription down the toilet. Ma got more. More went down the toilet. We were in full battle now. She marched me in to Doc Idiot.

"Why don't you take your pills?"

"Because I can't feel anything at all."

"Oh. That must be terrible for you."

He prescribed antidepressants to counterbalance the lithium. I now felt I was dealing with someone as irrational as my mother. What on earth was *he* thinking? I needed to do something drastic, or I was going to be in deep sh——t. I was truly alarmed. I felt the Ma/Doc team could actually kill me.

We got the new pills, little red ones this time. As soon as we got home, I flushed them all down the toilet and calmly watched Ma rant, rave, and tirade all around until she wore herself out with her antics.

My wheels were turning. I needed to strategize.

"Look. I need to get out of this house. I want to go back to school. That'll help me a lot more than any drugs."

She called Doc Idiot and checked with him. He seemed to think it was a good idea and "an excellent sign of improvement." At least we were all in agreement. Who cared why?

I was so excited about my small victory that I almost bought my own story. I even exuded something that looked an awful lot like eager anticipation as I stepped out of the car in front of Nordhoff Senior High back in Ojai.

That first day was a shock for me. Not sure why I hadn't seen that coming. I watched all the students zooming around and felt like

I weighed two hundred pounds. It was as if I were wading through quicksand. I kept looking in the mirror to make sure I wasn't fat. No, it was the weight of my emotional and spiritual pain.

People that knew me from before were very curious.

"So what was the commune like?"

"Commune?"

"Yeah. We heard that you had joined some commune that was . . ."

The rumors were rampant—anything from my having moved in with a thirty-year-old man to joining an underground political party. I didn't know what to make of it. All I could think to do was laugh it off and walk away.

Nope. I couldn't come back to this school, to this world. It was a whole lifetime away. These kids were light and normal and trying to relate to me like that. I felt as out of place as Bette Davis looked in her portrayal of Baby Jane Hudson trying to frolic on the beach with the regular folk. And the haze between me and the here and now grew that much thicker with each naïve inquiry.

So, if I couldn't do school and needed desperately to be away from my mother, what was I going to do? How could I get it together? The situation was taking on life-and-death proportions. The theme of mortality was magnifying at an alarming rate. Then *click*, and calm. Survival mode took over with a laser focus. In runaway terms, it was time to move on but, this time, with a *plan*.

ABOUT THE AUTHOR

J.J. Maze is a singer, composer, and educator in Chicago. She was a runaway and high school dropout at age fifteen. After surviving some harrowing experiences on the streets, she toured internationally as singer/songwriter for over a decade then got her GED and went back to college as a performance major. She received her MM in classical vocal performance in 2008 from Northwestern University. J.J. Maze is on the voice faculty at Merit School of Music, which serves talented Chicago youth. She is also a teaching artist for Ravinia's Reach-Teach-Play program, which reaches out to youth in underserved communities all throughout Chicagoland. Ms. Maze remains an active part of the Chicago music scene. She received the 2016 Clementine Skinner award for her contributions as a singer and educator to the black music culture in Chicago. In her downtime, she likes nothing more than laughing with good friends and walking her two dogs, Bella and Lenny.

CPSIA information can be obtained
at www.ICGtesting.com
Printed in the USA
LVHW112137100119
603534LV00001B/114/P